OFF LIMITS

NASHVILLE FURY
BOOK 4

CHELLE SLOAN

Cover Design: Jessica Lynn Draws

Content editing: Amy Maranville, Kraken Communications

Line editing: Kiezha Smith Ferrell, Librum Artis Editorial Services

Proofreading: Michele Ficht

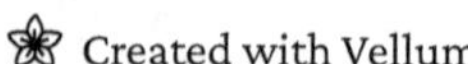 Created with Vellum

To Claire...
Thanks for keeping me organized. And sane. And being on Zoom
with me when I needed a dedication.

PROLOGUE
COLE

SENIOR YEAR OF COLLEGE

MOST COLLEGE GUYS would give up a kidney to be where I'm at tonight.

Then again, I'm not most college guys.

I'm two short months from graduating from Clemson with honors. The professional football draft is in a few weeks, and despite battling through a knee injury this past season, I'm still projected to go in the second round. I can see the light at the end of the tunnel. I've worked my ass off these past four years; I've studied hard, never missed a class or a practice. I kept my nose to the ground, didn't get in trouble, and kept the partying to a minimum.

Don't get me wrong, I had my fun. But I was smart about it. Small gatherings. Safe places. Drinking with trusted people I knew wouldn't plaster my face on social media. I stayed far away from the party scene that usually included frat bros, bad music, and drinks made in plastic tubs.

Until tonight.

Because for the life of me, I can't say no to Brenna Donald. Even when she asks me to take her to a fraternity party.

"I don't wanna leave!" Brenna yells as she stumbles out of the fraternity house. I'm pretty sure she'd be eating pavement right now if I wasn't holding her up.

"Considering you can't stand up right now, I feel like it's time for us to go."

"You're no fun." Her slurred words shouldn't make me laugh, but they do. "Why aren't you fun, Cole?"

"I'm fun."

"Then why did you make me leave? I was 'bout to dance. Didn't you want to dance? Do you like to dance? I bet you're a good dancer."

I am, though she doesn't need to know that. Then again, she's so drunk right now I could bust out the Worm right here and she wouldn't remember a thing.

"We left because you're drunk. And despite what you might think, that's not my idea of a good time."

I don't know why I'm saying all of this like she can have a conversation right now. The girl is shitfaced, and I'm still not sure how it happened. I tried to watch her. Hell, at one point I tried to figure out a way to attach myself to her. She doesn't go to school here. She doesn't know who to trust—or who to avoid. She's my best friend's twin sister, for fuck's sake. Infuriating, yes, but I sure as shit wasn't about to let someone take advantage of her.

But then I got stopped by a group of guys who wanted to talk to me about my standing in the draft, and she snuck off. Next thing I knew, she was on the dance floor, a guy standing on a chair pouring a bottle of something down her throat.

I should have known that you can only keep Brenna Donald on a leash so long. The girl has a wild streak a mile long.

"What's a time good?"

I stop and look at Brenna, because in no way was that English.

"Are you asking me what's a good time?"

She nods. "Yup. What's a good time according to Cole Campbell? Let me guess. Football. It's always football with you guys."

She's not completely wrong. Football has consumed my life since I was six years old. But I'm more than the game. Just not many people know that.

"I like to do more than just play football."

I shake my head because again, why am I having this conversation? Besides the fact that Brenna is so drunk I can't believe she's only mixed up a handful of words, why do I care that she knows that I'm more than just a meathead football player? It's Brenna. The girl I've known since childhood. The girl I nicknamed "Trouble," because she was. And still is.

In third grade, I was upset that Bryce and I weren't in the same class. But Brenna was there and sat by me all year. She said if I couldn't sit by one Donald, might as well sit by the other. When we were in high school, I remember her mouthing "good luck" before every game. And after we won, she'd always give me a thumbs up from the crowd. I looked for that thumbs up every time. She never forgot.

And she was always the cheerleader who made me treat bags or painted a sign for me.

Bryce might be my best friend, but Brenna is right up there. She has always been a part of my life, and always will be.

It's kind of comical, considering I'm the always-serious football player, and she's the popular wild child. We have very little in common. Yet, every time she's around, she has a way of putting a smile on my face.

Even right now, when she's three sheets to the wind.

"I like to draw."

My words stop both of us: Me because I can't believe I said them. Her because when I stopped walking, so did she. At this point I'm basically carrying her.

"You do?" Her big blue eyes look up at me, and for just a second, I get lost in them. Have I ever noticed how beautiful they are? They're the color of the sky on a perfect summer morning at the lake?

"I mean, I dabble," I say, all of a sudden feeling self-conscious.

"What do you draw?"

"Mostly landscapes. Nature. That kind of stuff."

I want to smack my mouth shut. Did I really just admit that to her? No one knows that. Hell, Bryce knows everything about me, but he doesn't know that. What kind of voodoo magic does this woman possess?

Granted, I've probably asked myself that question at least twenty times since she showed up on our doorstep yesterday —unannounced—looking for a couch to crash on for the weekend. What were Bryce and I supposed to do? Tell her she couldn't stay with us after driving from our small town in Southwest Ohio all the way to South Carolina?

Then today she begged Bryce and me to go with her to this party. How she got invited I still don't know. Then again, Brenna makes herself known wherever she goes. I'd guess she was getting coffee this morning, and before she knew it, she had an invitation to every party on campus this weekend.

"I bet they are beau—"

I don't know what startles me the most, Brenna not finishing her sentence or how she's pushing me off her with a force that rivaled a defensive lineman. For someone who is barely five-foot-four, the girl has some strength behind her.

"Brenna! What are you doing?"

She doesn't answer me as she staggers toward someone's

shrubs. I hear the sound of retching as Brenna hunches over in some poor person's yard.

"Brenna!" I run over to her and quickly pull her hair back off her neck. "Hey...it's okay. Get it out."

I try to comfort her the best I can over the next ten minutes. Every time she thinks she's done, another wave hits. Eventually, she stands up, and I don't know whether to have pity on her or crack up laughing.

Her makeup is all over her face, and she has a little bit of puke on her shirt. Her hair looks like it's been styled by a tornado. Yet somehow, she's still fucking beautiful. I don't know if I realized how gorgeous she was before tonight.

"Fuck!" Brenna yells, as she slaps my hands away from her.

"What's the matter?"

"I puked on my shirt!"

"It's okay," I say. "We're just a few blocks from the apartment. We'll get you cleaned up."

"No!" she yells. "It smells."

Before I know it, Brenna is pulling up her shirt and tossing it over her head.

And she isn't wearing a bra.

"Brenna!" I tear my eyes away from her chest and run over to her, wrapping her in my arms. I ignore how soft her skin feels—and how I just got an eyeful of the most perfect set of tits I have ever seen.

She wiggles away from me and holds her hands up in the air. "I'm free! Come on! Let's race home!"

She starts running...well, her idea of running after just puking for ten minutes and still not being able to walk in a straight line. "Brenna! Stop! You have to put on a shirt."

"Says who? Are you the shirt police?"

Before I can respond, the worst sound I could ever hear stops me in my tracks—the whoop-whoop of the actual police, flashing their red and blue lights as Brenna faces them, topless and doing the Running Man.

"What is going on here?" the officer asks as he gets out of his car. "Ma'am, can you please put on a shirt?"

Brenna shakes her head. "I don't have one. It has puke on it."

The officer takes a few more steps toward her. I do as well.

"Ma'am, are you drunk?"

She looks at the cop, then at me, then back to the cop. "I am. I am drunk. But it's fine. Don't need to worry about me, occifer. This guy isn't fun, but he's taking care of me."

The cop doesn't look amused. "Ma'am, if you don't put a shirt on right now, I will be forced to take you in for indecent exposure."

"That won't be necessary," I say, hurrying and pulling my T-shirt off. It might look like a nightgown on her, but at least she'll be covered. "Here, Brenna, put this on."

She takes the shirt from me, but instead of putting it on and shutting up, she acts like it's a rope, lassos it over her head, and chucks it back to me.

"No!" she yells. "How come when I'm topless it's indecent exposure and when he is it's just hot? This is sexist! So fuck this! Fuck you! And fuck the patriarchy!"

Oh. My. God.

"Ma'am, put your hands behind your back. I'm taking you in."

Like hell he is. Before I know it, I'm in front of the cop, blocking him from Brenna. "Look, man, she's just drunk. I live a block away. Let me take her home."

"Sir, please move out of the way, or I'll have to arrest you as well."

"For what?" I demand, my anger spiking.

"I'll figure it out later. Both of you, in the car."

Before I know it, he has both of us handcuffed and sitting in the back of his cruiser. Neither of us have a shirt on, though he did pull out a blanket from his trunk to cover Brenna.

And for the millionth time tonight all I can think of is *how the fuck did I end up here?*

"Hey," Brenna says. When I look over at her, she looks more sober than she has all night. But she doesn't look worried. In fact, it looks like she's about to start cracking up at any second.

"This isn't funny," I say. "I'm two weeks from the draft. I can't get arrested now."

"You aren't going to get arrested," she says with confidence. "All Officer Prude is going to do is give us a warning. Maybe I'll get a ticket for the boobs. Relax, Campbell, everything is going to be fine."

Our eyes stay locked as we sit in the back of the cop car. And for maybe the first time in my life, I don't look at her like she's my best friend's sister. Or like the Brenna I knew in high school.

No, this is a woman whose brown hair and blue eyes are making me forget how to breathe. Whose boldness makes me crazy. Who I want to protect more than anything at this moment. She's bold. Beautiful. A little crazy. And apparently, quite the feminist.

How have I never noticed these things about her? How have I never thought of her as anything more than Bryce's sister?

I let my head hit the back of the seat as one thought runs over and over through my head. It's not concern that I might get arrested. Or that some website could pick this up and my draft stock could tank.

No, right now I'm having an epiphany in the back of a cop car: I'm in love with my best friend's sister.

So, no, Brenna, everything is not going to be okay.

CHAPTER 1
BRENNA

"NOPE. TOO SLUTTY."

I turn to look at Lucy with a questioning eye. "What do you mean *too slutty*? We're going to dinner then dancing. Of course it's going to be a little slutty."

My best friend, who is also my soon-to-be sister-in-law, sits up from her space on my bed, tilting her head as if she's analyzing every inch of fabric of my dress. Of which, I'll admit, there aren't really that many.

"I don't know. I know you want to be sexy, but I think it's the whole no-back thing for me. It just puts it over the top. Plus, this is a first date, Brenna; don't you want to leave him wanting more?"

I let out a defeated sigh. "Yeah, you're right. But then what do you suggest?" I walk back into my closet, examining every piece of clothing I have, including the eight other dresses I've tried on, which are now beginning to make a pile on my floor. "Dexter is going to be here in a half hour, and I'm running out of dresses."

I don't know why I'm freaking out over what to wear. Yes,

it's a first date. But I'm a first date professional at this point. Maybe it's because Dexter is football famous? I know people are going to recognize him. He's one of the more social members of the Nashville Fury, so his picture is always on social media at some club or bar. Maybe it's that? I don't know...but I do know if I don't find a dress in a few minutes I'm either canceling or going nude. In which case, I might as well wear the slutty dress.

"What about the blue one? With the one sleeve?" Lucy says. "You look great in blue."

I sift through my clothes, wishing that I had used some sort of system when I moved in here. Then again, I was just so happy to have found a place I could afford—and out of my brother's apartment—I wasn't thinking about closet organization. I was just thinking of a good night's sleep without having to hear my brother make my best friend pray to gods I didn't know she believed in.

I find the blue dress and slip off the slutty one. I don't even have to look in the mirror to know this one is going to be the winner. It's a tight one-sleeved royal blue dress just a few shades darker than my eyes. The fabric has some shiny thread weaved through it that makes it jazzy without being over the top.

I love it.

I reach up and grab my nude heels as I make my way back to my bedroom, where I take a seat on my bed next to Lucy. "I should let you make all the decisions in my life. You're usually right. It would save me a whole lot of trouble."

"If I made all your decisions for you, you wouldn't be needing this dress tonight, because you wouldn't be going out with Dexter."

My brow creases as I look over to Lucy. She won't meet my

gaze. Apparently something on my pillow is far more interesting.

"Is this because of the whole birthday clusterfuck?" I ask as I get up and sit at my vanity to finish my makeup. "You know that it wasn't Dexter's fault."

"I know, and it's not that," Lucy says. "That was all your brother being an idiot. But I choose not to think about that day."

I lean in closer to the mirror because somehow that will make my mascara go on cleaner. "Then what's the problem?"

"He's a manwhore and a player, and you deserve better than that."

I switch eyes and try to conceal the fact that I know Lucy is right. I've been choosing to ignore the gossip, but yes, I know Dexter's reputation as the team playboy. Still, I'm of the belief that you have to see something with your own eyes to truly draw a conclusion.

"Maybe the rumors are just that," I say. "Who am I to judge someone before they've had a chance to defend themselves?"

"You realize I've seen him in action, right? This isn't some tabloid rumor. This is me, your best friend, telling you that he's not for you."

I shrug Lucy off as I apply my lipstick. I know she's not a fan of Dexter, but this is the first guy who has asked me out since I moved to Nashville. So what if he has a few red flags? Who doesn't these days? Plus, this can't be any worse than any of the dates I would have had back when I lived in Ohio. I mean, that bar is set so low that if he came in under that he'd have to dig a tunnel.

"And I appreciate your warning, but I'm a big girl. Plus, Dexter passed the arm test. You know I have to go out with him just on that alone."

It's almost as if I can hear Lucy's eyes rolling. She hates the arm test. She thinks it's one of the most ridiculous ways that I judge if I want to go out with a man.

I think it's science. And if there is one thing I know, it's science.

Some women have a thing for asses.

Some women get their hearts and lady parts all tingly from the sight of a good smile.

Me? It's all in the arms. As in, I want to be able to look at them and know for a fact the man could pick me up and pin me against a wall without breaking a sweat.

Needless to say, Dexter passed the test with flying colors.

"You know who else passes the arm test?"

I turn to look at her and send her a glare. "Don't even say it."

"What?" she says with mock innocence. "I'm just saying, Cole's arms are quite...large."

"How many times do I have to tell you? Cole is Cole. He's basically my brother. His arms don't count."

"But he's not your brother," Lucy says. "Are you telling me you've *never* checked his arms out? If you can honestly say you haven't, then I'll never bring him up again."

I don't make eye contact with Lucy as I get up and walk to my closet to locate the clutch purse I want to take tonight. Because she's right. I have.

Not recently. It was years ago. In college. In the back of a cop car. And yes, for a second I had the flash of a fantasy where Cole lifted me up with ease. As if I weighed no more than a feather as he pressed me against the wall and kissed me.

But then the cop slammed the car door shut, and I came to my senses. Well, almost to my senses. I was pretty out of it at the time.

"Why aren't you looking at me?" Lucy says as I emerge

from the closet. "Is it because you *have* fantasized about Cole and you can't lie to me?"

I sit back down on the bed. "Fine. I have. Once. Years ago. But it doesn't matter. His arms don't count."

Lucy raises an eyebrow. "What's that supposed to mean?"

"It means that even if he passed the arm test and every other one I could think of, it's Cole. My brother's best friend. I've known him since we were kids. It would just be weird. Plus, you also fail to consider that it needs to be a two-way street, and Cole Campbell absolutely would never go out with me."

Lucy just shrugs. "You never know."

"Oh, I know. I've been the annoying sister since we were six. Something like that doesn't change." I say as my phone vibrates with a text message. "That's Dexter. He's downstairs."

Lucy starts to make her way off my bed. "He's not coming up to get you? We will file that in the red flag column."

"He probably couldn't find parking," I say as I grab a jacket and my clutch. "Thank you for coming over and helping me."

We walk downstairs together. "I hope it goes well. I hope I'm wrong about him. But please be careful. I don't want you to get hurt."

We exit my ground-floor apartment, careful to walk around the huge puddle that has been growing since this rain started last week. No one tells you how much it rains in Nashville in the spring. I stop for a moment to give Lucy a hug. "I'm a big girl. I can take care of myself. But I appreciate you."

We turn toward the parking lot, and right in front of me, in all of his flashy glory, is Dexter. He's standing next to some sports car that I'm sure is worth double my teaching salary. He's wearing all black and more gold jewelry than I own. And then there are the jeweled sunglasses, which I don't get. It's dark out.

"Hey sweet stuff. You ready to kick it?"

I have a very bad feeling about this...

"Please call me every hour for a status update," Lucy whispers. "Or if you need a ride home. Or anything."

I nod and give her another hug before I make my way to the car.

"You look good enough to eat," he says, opening the door for me. Well, at least he did that. "I have a whole night ready for us. Just wait until the crew at the club gets a load of you."

The crew? The club? What the hell have I got myself into?

I should run. Run back up the stairs right now, and put on my sweats, and catch up on the latest Turkish soap opera I'm binging. Those fuckers are addicting.

But instead, I take a deep breath, get into his car, and try to breathe through the smell of his cologne.

It's one of those that should smell good because it costs a fortune but actually smells like three-day-old takeout food.

"You ready?"

I nod as Dexter puts the car in gear. I wish I could recapture my earlier optimism, but it's too late to back out. Plus, it's just one date. How bad can it be?

I NEVER UNDERSTOOD why anyone would mock people who play video games.

I can't speak for everyone, but for me, it's a way of detaching from reality. It gives me something to concentrate on and lets the things rolling around in my head go away, even if it's just for a few hours. Some people read. Some do crafts or projects. I used to draw, but I never have the time to do it anymore. So now, I choose to blow people up in virtual worlds.

And lately, I'd much rather be in a virtual world than the real one.

"And that's how we do it!" Bryce yells, ceremoniously flipping his controller onto the couch as we successfully get through another level. He even adds a little victory dance for good measure. It's as bad as his touchdown dance.

"If this is how you celebrate moving to the next level on a video game, then I don't want to see you if we ever win the league championship."

"Not 'if,' my friend," Bryce says as he tips his can of Dr Pepper toward me. "When. *When* we win the title."

I tip my can to him and sit back on my couch as Bryce navigates to the next level of our game.

"Thanks for letting me hang out tonight," Bryce says.

I set down my drink and grab my controller. "I didn't have much of a choice when you showed up at my door, barged in, and grabbed the second controller before saying hello."

"Yes, you did," Bryce says before taking another drink of sugary goodness. Yes, we both know these are all sugar and crap for us. But Bryce is going on five months sober, and it's the offseason. The occasional Dr Pepper won't kill us. "You could have kicked me out at any time. But you didn't. Because that's what best friends do."

"True," I say as we start the next level. "By the way, why are you here tonight? Lucy already tired of you? She hasn't been living with you that long. I figured it would be at least a year before she had her fill."

"Not even a little bit," Bryce says with a smile. "Things couldn't be going better."

"Then why, my friend, did you take the elevator down three floors to come hang out with the likes of me tonight?"

"Can't a guy want to hang out and play video games with his best friend?"

I shoot him a look that clearly says I see through his bull-shit. "He can. But since his fiancée moved in with him, he doesn't anymore. So spill."

"She's at Brenna's," Bryce says as we start fighting our opponent. "She had a date tonight. Lucy went over for moral support."

It takes every ounce of self-control in my body to not crush the can in my hand, but I manage not to. It takes an equal amount of strength to keep my face even. Actually, that's a lie. I'm so practiced at not having a reaction to hearing about Brenna's dating escapades, I could win the World Series of Poker.

I wish I wasn't.

It used to be easier. Before Brenna moved to Nashville, I only occasionally had to hear about Brenna and her quest for Mr. Right. But now that she lives in Nashville? It's constant. I thought it would get better after she moved out of Bryce's place and into her own. It hasn't. If anything, it's worse.

It's one of the reasons why virtual worlds are much better than the real world these days.

So here I am, pretending not to give a shit she is out with some loser while also beating myself up about the fact that I even give a fuck at all what she's doing.

I fucking hate being in love with my best friend's sister.

"So who's the guy?" I ask. I hate that I need to know, but if I don't ask my imagination will run wild.

"That's the thing," Bryce says. "Neither she nor Lucy would tell me."

That's interesting. But I can't tell him it is. "Probably not worth the mention."

I go back to playing, hoping that's the end of this conversation. Then the game suddenly pauses, and I realize it's not.

Lucky me.

"I mean why wouldn't they tell me? What's the big secret?"

"Maybe, and hear me on this one, it's none of your business?"

Bryce shoots a look at me like I've grown a second head. "What do you mean none of my business? She's my twin sister! Of course it's my business. Don't you care who your sister dates?"

I put down my controller and turn to Bryce, who clearly can't see beyond his ego right now. "For one: My sister is eight years older than me and married with three kids. I think she's fine. And second, did you care this much about who she dated when she was back living in Laurel Heights? Why do you suddenly give a shit? It's Brenna's life. Let her be."

Those last two sentences are part of my mantra when it comes to Brenna Donald. Every time I hear about her and another failed date, or about how she just wishes she could find a love like Bryce and Lucy's, I tell myself that I need to let her be. That I need to not let it concern me.

Because it can't. I can't be in love with my best friend's sister. I've been trying to fall out of love with her every day since I realized it three years ago. I've tried everything. I've tried going celibate. I've tried to fuck her out of my system with random women. I even tried seriously dating one. I've tried punishing myself by snapping a rubber band on my wrist every time I thought of her—that just left me with a really red wrist.

I've even sometimes wondered what it would be like if we were together. If she felt the same way about me. That train of thought leads me down a road where I imagine holding her during quiet nights in; her running up to me after a game and jumping into my arms; and of course, imagining what it would be like if she were to be in my bed.

But that train of thought only ends in disaster. Because I don't see a world where Bryce would be okay with me dating his sister. Especially after this past year, when he has made it his mission to be the involved and protective brother he never was before.

And if that wasn't enough, there's the unwritten and unspoken rule of professional football: Don't fuck your teammates' sister. Or the coach's daughter. Or pretty much anyone related to anyone who steps foot in the locker room with you.

No matter how I examine this, I'm fucked. And not in a good way.

"I just want her to be happy," Bryce says, pulling me from the Brenna rabbit hole I just went down. "Plus, I'm trying to be a better brother. For so many years—"

"You were a selfish asshole?"

Bryce pretends to throw his controller at me. I don't even flinch.

"I was going to say that I was preoccupied with football and life. I'm just trying to make up for it now."

He's not completely wrong. Though I would say the way I described Bryce would be more accurate.

"I'm sure they didn't tell you for a good reason. Maybe it's someone you know? Maybe he's a teammate?"

I don't know why I brought that up, but I guess since we're already on the topic, this isn't the worst way to gauge his reaction. Better than me randomly bringing it up. Plus, this is as close as I'm ever going to get to asking him what he would think if I asked Brenna out.

"A teammate?" he yells. "Which teammate?"

I hold up my hands in defense. "I was just giving a hypothetical."

"Well then, I hypothetically would kick any of their asses if they took Brenna out. Who would even think of doing that? Don't they know the rules?"

I shrug. "Some of the guys might not care about the rules."

"Well then, if they don't care about the rules, then they won't care about me making their lives hell. There is not one single team member who is good enough for Brenna."

Ouch, that kind of stings. "Not even me?"

This makes him laugh. "You? You and Brenna? Cole, seriously. I know you're trying to distract me from whoever the hell she's out with, but you don't need to go that far. You and Brenna! Ha! She's like your sister. That's fucking hilarious."

I guess I have my answer.

"But, speaking of you and Brenna," Bryce says. "I did want to talk to you about something."

"What's up?"

I can't even begin to imagine where this might be going. Besides the fact that we are best friends and play on the same football team, we live in the same building. We see each other literally every day. We text or talk multiple times a day. What on earth could he want to talk about that we haven't talked about already?

"I wanted to talk to you about the wedding."

Now it's my turn to pause the game. "If this is your grand way of asking me to be your best man, I kind of assumed I already was so you can save the mushy stuff."

Bryce shakes his head. "It's not, but what if it was? Were you going to rob me of that moment? That moment that two best friends only share once in a lifetime?"

Now it's my turn to pretend to throw a controller at him. "Don't make it weird."

"Anyway," Bryce says. "Yes, you are my best man. And now that it's official, I wanted to tell you that Lucy and I set a date."

"Great. When should I plan on showing up in the tux?"

"April sixth."

I have to blink a few times, because no way did he just say the date I thought he did. "April sixth? As in the April that's a month away?"

Bryce nods. "That is correct."

"Okay, and I ask this in a completely supportive way, is Lucy pregnant?"

He shakes his head. "No she's not pregnant. If that were the case I don't think I'd be here because I'm pretty sure her parents would have killed me already."

That's true. Lucy's family is a bit scary. "Then what's the rush?"

Bryce sits back, turning the game and the television off. "Because we're ready to start our life together. We've waited so long for this. Seven years, dude. Do you know how long that is to wait to be with the woman you love?"

Maybe not seven years, but I know better than he thinks.

"All right then," I say. "One month. I'm guessing that means you're going to need some help getting this shindig off the ground?"

Bryce nods. "I've told Lucy to hire a wedding planner, but she refuses. She thinks that between the four of us we can get this all done. And whatever my future wife wants, I'm bound and determined to give her. So, wedding mode activated. Also, get ready to spend a lot of time with Brenna. I have a feeling Lucy is about to put you two to work."

I pick up my can of Dr Pepper and chug the remnants. This time I do crush it in my hand. Thankfully, Bryce doesn't seem to think anything of it.

Me and Brenna. Together. Doing wedding things.

Me and Brenna. Walking down an aisle together. Dancing in front of friends and family.

Fuck. Maybe I need to start wearing the rubber band again.

CHAPTER 3
BRENNA

I HAVE BEEN out on a lot of bad dates. In fact, I could probably write a book. It would for sure be a best seller and likely optioned for a movie. And a real one; not one of those crappy ones starring a former child star no one remembers.

What makes my bad dates different from those of others? I give nicknames.

There's Mr. Forgetful. Not only did he claim to forget what restaurant we were meeting at for dinner, he also conveniently forgot his wallet after running up a two-hundred dollar bar tab.

Then there was The Magician. He thought he was the next Criss Angel and wanted to test some tricks out on me over drinks. I kept wishing he would make me disappear, but no luck.

The best worst date was by far The Italian Stallion. I really thought that guy had potential. He was a resident at a hospital in Cincinnati. He was smart, good looking, and super close with his family. And he had the cutest little dog.

Who he talked to. In Italian. While we were having sex.

The list goes on, and tonight, we have a new entry.

"So you know I'm the highest paid wide receiver in the league?" Dexter says as he casually sips on a glass of champagne poured from the chilled bottle that he insisted on ordering despite me telling him I don't drink champagne. Guess he's not driving me home, then.

"Good for you," I say, not knowing how else to respond. Though the smart ass in me wants to say, *"Well that's great. You still make a million less a year than my brother."*

"That's how I can afford fancy restaurants like this."

I don't know what I'm supposed to say. Thanks? I mean, yeah, it's a nice restaurant, and the steak I ate was great, but I would have been just as happy at a restaurant where I didn't think I'd need to sell a kidney just to afford a side salad.

"So, Dexter, you're from Indiana, right? How have you made the transition to the South? I can't speak for Bryce, but for me it's been quite the culture shock."

He sets down his glass of champagne and leans back on his chair like he owns the place. "Baby, I didn't need to get adjusted. I owned this town the second I was drafted."

It takes everything in me not roll my eyes as Dexter goes on to tell me about how many places he can get into and all of the perks he has around Nashville. It makes me want to vomit.

I take the opportunity to think about what I will name Dexter in the *Brenna Donald's Failed Dating Chronicles*. The obvious choice is The Football Player since that is his profession. And, even though I've grown up around football players, he's the first one I've ever gone out with. A few asked me out over the years, but it felt weird going out with one of my brother's teammates. I didn't want it to cause friction when the relationship inevitably failed.

But for some reason, I gave Dexter a chance. Maybe it's because I'm still getting used to Nashville. Maybe it's because

I've been feeling a little lonely. Maybe it's because I was blinded by his good looks and those very nice arms. He seemed like a nice enough guy.

Then he showed up spewing the doucheness, and I honestly have to wonder if this is the same guy who asked me out.

Oh. Maybe I could name him The Douche. Though to be fair, I could have named many men that over the years. I'll just stick with The Football Player.

I slyly check my phone to see what time it is and notice I also have a text from Lucy. Though I don't know why I'm trying to be stealth about it. For one, Dexter has checked his phone multiple times tonight. Second, I doubt he would notice. I've just finished listening to a list of all the country music stars he's met so far, and now he's counting all the restaurants or clubs he can get into with just one phone call.

Lucy: Regretting it yet?

I put my phone back down because I don't want to admit she was right. Though the playboy aspect hasn't come out yet, he said something about wanting to go to a club after this. I'm guessing it's only a matter of time before his female entourage shows up.

I look back up at Dexter, and he's staring at me like he's waiting for something. Shit, how much of his long-winded answer did I miss?

"I'm sorry. What was that you said?"

He signals for the waitress to come over and hands her his credit card. At least I didn't have to pay.

Is it bad when that is the highlight of the date?

"I was just asking you if you were ready to head to the club.

I know it's early, but I like to make sure my VIP area is set up before my crew comes through."

I pick up my phone and notice that it's already ten-thirty.

"This is early?"

My question was sincere, but apparently to Dexter, this is hilarious. "Baby Girl! You got jokes. Yes, it's early. Are you telling me you're one of those old people who go to bed at eleven? You're young! Live it up!"

"I'm not in bed by eleven," I say defiantly. Though I don't go on to tell him that by eleven I'm on the couch. In my pajamas. With my latest binge on the television and my latest knitting project on my lap.

As we both stand from our table, I notice that most of the champagne is still in the bottle, thank God. The last thing I want is an awkward interaction about drunk driving with this guy.

"So answer me this," Dexter says. "When was the last time you seriously went out and partied? Like had a night out where the drinks kept coming and the night never seemed to end?"

"I..." I trail off because I don't know how to answer that question.

Shit... Am I the oldest twenty-five-year-old on the planet? When did this happen? I'm Brenna freaking Donald. I was the cheerleader who shotgunned beer in her uniform after football games. I'm the one who has almost been arrested more times than I'll ever admit. I'm the one who once organized a senior prank so legendary that the cops in Laurel Heights have to sit with the senior class each year and explain to them why it's not a good idea to allow livestock inside a high school.

When did I become this old lady? I'm the girl who drove to Clemson on a whim just because I heard about a few good parties. When was the last time I even went out, let alone got drunk?

Well, that ends tonight. This might be one of the worst dates I've ever been on, but I'm going to get something good out of it.

I'm going to get my groove back. Or something like that.

"All right, Dexter," I say as I stand up, grabbing my purse and righting my shoulders. "Let's do this."

CHAPTER 4
COLE

SIX MISSED CALLS. Three text messages.

All from Brenna.

I shoot up out of my bed and throw on my glasses to see what the fuck is going on. It's only then I notice that it's just after one-thirty in the morning. What the fuck is Brenna doing calling me this late?

> Brenna: Are you up?

> Brenna: I'm stuck. No one is answering.

> Brenna: I don't like champagne. Shouldn't I like champagne? All girls like champagne, don't they?

I hurry and pull up her number, ignoring whatever the hell that last text was. Shit, she was on a date tonight. Is she with him? And who is him? Are they both drunk? The more the phone rings, the angrier I get.

"Cole!"

I can barely hear her. She must be at some club because all I hear is shitty bass and a lot of people yelling.

"Brenna, go to a place where I can hear you."

"Cole!"

"Yes, Brenna. Can you walk outside or to a patio so it's a little quieter?"

"Cole, did you know that there are different kinds of champagne?"

I get out of bed because I have a feeling I know what I'm about to do. "I did know that."

"Well, I didn't. Turns out, I don't like any of them. And, they don't get better the more you drink. Dexter told me it did. But he lied. He's a liar."

I stop mid-step. "Dexter? Is that who you're out with?"

The background finally gets a little quieter. It's still loud, but at least I can hear her now.

"Yeah. He asked me out a few weeks ago."

And that is the answer to the million-dollar question of why Brenna and Lucy wouldn't tell Bryce or me who her date was. And when Bryce finds out, he's going to fucking kill him.

"Where are you? What did you mean when you said you were stuck?"

"Oh, that."

I wait for a few seconds for her to continue, but she doesn't. My guess is she's either so drunk she doesn't know how to speak or she's the kind of drunk where she has the attention span of a gnat.

My guess is the latter.

"Brenna? Where are you?"

"I'm at Fire Lights. It's Dustin Wild's new place. It's sooooo cool. The bathrooms have women in them who will fix your makeup! Mabel did such a good job on mine."

I hurry up and throw on a pair of joggers and a T-shirt. "Brenna, were you trying to leave? Is that why you called me?"

"Yeah," she says, and if I can hear her right, she's a little defeated by that. "I thought I could be the fun Brenna, like I used to be. But I'm not. I'm not fun Brenna. I'm boring Brenna. I'm tired. I want to go home. Dexter won't take me home."

I'm grabbing my keys and out the door before she finishes that last sentence. "Meet me outside in ten minutes. I'm coming to get you."

She doesn't say anything for a second, and all I can think is the worst. Did she pass out? How much did she have to drink? Did someone spike her drink with anything? God help the motherfucker if that happened. He'd be dead, and I wouldn't even care.

"Cole?"

I let out a sigh of relief as I turn on the ignition to my Jeep. "Yeah, Brenna?"

"You're the best friend ever."

I let out another breath as I pull out of the parking garage of my building and head down Broadway.

Best friend. Yup. That's me.

———

I'm an idiot for thinking that she was actually going to be outside when I arrived. Or that she would answer her phone again. Granted, it took me more than the ten minutes I told her to get down here. But I'm willing to bet she wasn't here then, either.

Luckily for me, there's a spot on the side of the building for me to park, and I happen to know Sid, the bouncer working the door — he also does security for the Fury. Thank fuck, because I don't have the patience tonight for dealing with some 'roided up clown who thinks his dick is big because he's a bouncer in Nashville.

"Where is Dexter's table?" I ask, pushing past the people in line.

Sid must see the panic in my eyes as he points to the elevator. "Third floor. Use the staff elevator. Stairs have been packed all night."

I give him a quick nod as I hop into the elevator. Though I know this is the fastest way up, and I'm grateful to avoid dealing with drunks, it feels like I'm waiting forever for the doors to open.

Now that I'm not moving, I have five seconds to process what is going on. Fucking Dexter. Out of all the guys on the Fury, *he's* who she had to pick to go out with? He is all kinds of wrong for her. And I'm not just saying that because the girl drives me crazy seven ways from Sunday.

But Dexter is the actual worst. She had to know Bryce and I would forbid her from seeing him; that's why she was so secretive about tonight. Yes, Dexter is my teammate. Yes, I put my body on the line for him every week. But that doesn't mean I like the guy. He's a pompous asshat manwhore who likes to show off his money and toys. He prides himself on how many women he's slept with. If I had a nickel for every time he came into the locker room and talked about his "pussy-filled" night, I'd be able to buy my mom another new car.

I've tried on more than a few occasions to get to know him. I thought maybe it was just a front he was putting on. You know, trying to show off in front of his teammates. It's not a front. It's not a facade. That's him. I have to fight back the urge to punch him every time his mouth opens.

Tonight will be another night of exercising restraint. Apparently, he doesn't care about the bro code of football. Bold move, considering just a few months ago Bryce hated him. And now he's out with Brenna?

That boy must have a fucking death wish.

The doors to the elevator open, and my eyes quickly do a scan of the room. This must be the non-country music floor, judging by the music the DJ is blaring. There's a bar to the left, dance floor straight ahead, and as I look to my right, a section with a bunch of roped-off couches.

I don't have to see anyone to know that's where Dexter is at. I make a beeline that way, looking for anyone I might know. It doesn't take me long to see Dexter, flanked on either side by women who are definitely not Brenna. As I get a few steps closer to the roped-off area, I see her. *Passed out on a couch.*

"Brenna!" I shout as I step over the ropes to get to her. I have one foot over when someone who must feel like getting in a fight tonight puts his hand on my arm.

"You aren't on the list."

I turn to look at the guy, who's wearing a shirt that says "Security." He's big. Not as big as my six-foot-four, three hundred and fifteen pounds, but to most people, he would come off as intimidating.

I'm not most people.

"I'm here to get my friend. She's the one passed out on the couch that no one seems to give a fuck about," I say, pointing to Brenna.

"Hey! Cole!" Dexter says as he slides up next to the security guard. "What you doing here, man? Come on in. He's good."

I shrug off the security guard as I take the five short steps it takes to get me to Brenna.

"Oh shit! She passed out?" Dexter says, standing over my shoulder as I lean down to make sure she's okay. "I didn't even realize she was still here."

I shoot a look up to Dexter that is meant to kill. "How do you not fucking know if she's here or not? Didn't you bring her?"

He just shrugs. Asshole. "Yeah, but I hadn't seen her in a minute so I figured she dipped out. I had...other things to attend to."

He looks back at two women, who are subtly waving to him.

"You're fucking something else," I say as I kneel down to try and wake Brenna up.

"What's that supposed to mean?"

I turn back to look at him. This guy really doesn't get it. "You were here with Brenna. You were on a date with her. I'm guessing by the text she managed to make to me that you got her stupid drunk and what—you just left her cause she wasn't going to fuck you? What kind of fucking man does that?"

The man rolls his eyes at me. Fuck, I want to punch him so bad. "Don't be so fucking dramatic, Campbell. Not my fault she can't handle her booze. She's fine."

I want to fire back at him, but out of the corner of my eye I see Brenna start to stir.

"Cole?"

I turn my attention back to her, brushing the hair off her forehead. "Hey, Trouble. It's me."

She tries to sit up, but immediately groans and falls back down. I quickly reach for her, catching her just in time.

"Watch it there," I say, adjusting my hold on her so I can pick her up. "How about we get you out of here?"

She nods...or at least she tries to. It looks a little like her head is going to fall off every time it goes back. "That sounds good. Can we go get pizza?"

I laugh. "Sure, we can get pizza."

I put her arms around my neck and pick her up off the couch. As we begin to walk out of the VIP area, I see Dexter, looking bored since everyone else is watching me and Brenna. I stop in front of him because he needs to hear one more thing.

"If I find out there is anything in her system other than alcohol, you better fucking run. Or demand a trade. Either way,

I will make your life a living hell, and that's if I choose to let you live."

He does his best to hide any fear, but the swallow he just took makes me know he heard me loud and clear.

"Dexter!"

I almost drop Brenna because I thought she was asleep. Apparently not. One arm is still behind my neck but the other arm is pointing toward Dexter.

"Yeah?" he says, trying to seem bored.

"You are a really shitty date. And your contract isn't even that big. I bet your dick isn't either. Let's get pizza!"

All I hear are "oohs" and "oh shits!" from the crowd that has gathered as I step back over the rope and head back to the elevator.

I might not be happy about having to come here, but at least the night ended on a high note.

And the assurance I never need to worry about Brenna going out with Dexter again.

CHAPTER 5
BRENNA

I HATE EVERYTHING AND EVERYONE.

I take that back—I hate the sunlight hitting my face right now. I hate Dexter. I hate champagne. I hate whoever invented hangovers. I hate the thunderstorm that just woke me up.

I probably hate more things, but those are the top three—shit, four—things right now. Stupid hangover.

What I don't hate is this pillow. Or these sheets. Why do they feel so soft? How have I never realized my sheets are this soft before?

And why do they smell like the best cologne I have ever inhaled in my whole life?

I slowly open my eyes and quickly realize that I'm not in my apartment. Then I remember: I called Cole last night. And not only am I in his room and sleeping in his bed, but by the looks of the T-shirt that I'm currently swimming in, I somehow ended up in his clothes.

What the fuck happened last night?

"Good morning, Trouble," Cole says as I pull the sheets up, trying to hide whatever I can from him.

"I'm going to need you to take that volume down to like a three," I say, rubbing the sleep away from my eyes.

"I figured by now you'd be immune to hangovers," Cole says as he takes a seat on the edge of the bed. "But I got you water and aspirin just in case."

"I'm not as young as I once was," I grumble, holding out my hands for the cure. "Which is what got me in this mess in the first place."

Cole lifts an eyebrow. "Dexter wasn't the one who got you in this mess?"

I swallow the aspirin and take another pull of the water because damn is my mouth dry. "He wasn't exactly part of the solution. But you of all people should have realized last night had Brenna Donald written all over it."

"Well there was no sign of police presence nor was there a riot started, so I wasn't sure."

I shoot a glare Cole's way. "If I had the strength, I'd throw a pillow at you."

This only makes him laugh. "And I'm sure it would do damage."

I shift a little, sitting against his headboard. "Anyway. I was out with Dexter. It was horrible. I hated every second of it, and I was counting down the seconds until we were done with dinner so I could go home."

I can't help but notice that Cole smiles a little bit. I'm glad he finds such pleasure in my bad dating luck.

"Quit smiling."

That only makes it grow bigger. "I'm not."

Cole lays down on the bed, propping his head up with his rather large, rather girthy arm.

Don't look at his arms, Brenna. Those are off-limit arms. Even though they are sexy as hell.

"Anyway," I say, giving myself a shake to clear any dangerous thoughts from my brain. "Dexter made some sort of comment about me being the oldest twenty-five-year-old in

Nashville. And for some reason, it rubbed me the wrong way. I don't want to be old! I want to be young and fun and go dancing until the sun comes up."

"But do you, though? Is that what you really want?"

I hesitate for a moment. "I thought I did. When I moved to Nashville, I had these grand ideas. There's so much more to do here than in Laurel Heights, and I wanted to do it all. I wanted to learn to line dance. I wanted to go to a different honky-tonk and hear live music every night. Try new restaurants. I've heard all about this hot chicken, but I've never had it. I want to meet interesting people from all over. Date men who didn't already know I was Bryce Donald's sister. I wanted to do everything I couldn't do in Laurel Heights."

"But?"

I slump down a little further into the bed. "But now I'm not sure."

"You know," Cole says in his wise-beyond-his-years tone. At least that's what Bryce calls it when Cole's about to give one of his speeches on life. "People can change. And that's okay. Look at your brother. He changed. It took work, but he's a better person. Maybe your change just came more naturally. But just because you want to be in bed before midnight doesn't mean you're boring."

Now it's my turn to give him the questioning brow. "Really? You think a night of takeout pizza, a glass of wine, me knitting while watching a foreign soap opera is exciting?"

"I think it sounds like a perfect night."

I don't know if it's from the hangover or not, but all of a sudden I feel a shiver run down my back. Has he always smoldered before? It's...intense. I've never been looked at like that before. By anyone. It's...I don't know how to describe it, but I'm pretty sure I need to put on a thicker shirt because it is doing something to my body.

"Can I ask you something?" I say, needing to change this conversation.

"Anything."

I look down then back up at Cole. "How did I end up in one of your shirts? I remember calling you to come get me, but frankly, after that everything is blank."

The question seems to snap Cole out of the intense reverie, thank goodness. I don't know how much longer I could take that.

"Well, after I picked you up—literally—I didn't want to take you back to your place and leave you alone. You were passed out, and while I didn't think anyone slipped you anything, I wanted to be sure. So I brought you back here. As for the shirt, you announced you couldn't sleep in your dress because it would get wrinkled, and took it upon yourself to take it off."

My eyes grow about three sizes. "I did what? Oh my God, I'm so embarrassed. Then again, it wouldn't be the first time I've done that in front of you."

He shakes his head. "Don't be. I quickly turned away, found you a T-shirt and left the room. I didn't see anything Bryce would kick my ass for."

"I'm sorry. And thank you. For everything. Last night was definitely not one of my finer showings."

"I'm not sure about that," he says. "Before we left the club you did tell Dexter that he had a small dick. That was entertaining."

"I did not," I moaned, burying my head into the comforter. "That's it. I'm never drinking again."

"Sure..." Cole says, though his tone clearly doesn't buy it. "Now, my turn. Why did you go out with Dexter in the first place? You had to know his reputation."

I let out a long sigh. This might be more painful to admit

than anything else we've talked about this morning. "Because he's the only one who's asked since I moved here. And he seemed like a nice guy when we first met. And while it might not have gone great, I did get to cross 'go on a date with a football player' off my dating Bingo card."

This gets me a laugh. "You know not all football players are like that."

"Well I don't plan on finding out," I say. "No more football players. Or celebrities, for that matter. No one who has an income that is newsworthy. From now on, just normal guys with normal jobs who want to do normal things at normal times of the night."

Cole doesn't respond—not that I expected him to—and it stuns me a bit when he just suddenly pops up off the bed and heads to his dresser. He pulls out a pair of shorts and tosses them to me on the bed.

"You should get dressed. I'll take you home."

I blink a few times, thrown from the sudden shift in mood. I want to ask if I said something or did something, but I don't have the chance. Before I can even get a word out, Cole slams the bedroom door so hard I feel an air gust when it closes.

What the hell was that?

"NO, no, Lucia. Too much skin. You need something more traditional."

I can't help but laugh as Mrs. Valenti tells her daughter what she thinks of the wedding dress she just came out to show us. Like mother, like daughter.

I think it's gorgeous. A little revealing? Sure. But compared to some of the dresses I've seen in this shop, Lucy looks like a nun right now.

"Mom, it's not bad," Lucy says, turning right and then to the left to see all angles of the dress. "What do you guys think?"

I look at the rest of the entourage gathered today at the wedding boutique in Nashville. Everyone is wrinkling their noses.

"It's just not you," I say honestly. "I thought you wanted something more on the traditional end of modern?"

She nods then looks back at the room. "I do, but my consultant insisted I try this on. I didn't have the heart to tell her no."

I signal for her to go back to the room. "Tell her to go back to the stockroom, and if she brings you another dress you didn't pick, come get me. I'll make sure she knows who's in charge."

Lucy smiles and walks back to the dressing room. I love my best friend, and when it comes to certain things, she can push back her shoulders and take control. Then there are the times when she wants to please everyone and doesn't stand up for herself. That's when I come in and remind her that shit won't fly.

"This champagne is delicious," Mrs. Valenti says. "Brenna, why don't you have a glass?"

I shake my head. "No thank you, Mrs. Valenti. I'm not a champagne kind of girl."

Celine, Lucy's other bridesmaid and wife of her former fiancée, takes a sip of hers, which quickly becomes a full-on gulp. "How can you not be a champagne girl? It's so delicious. Even this cheaper kind."

"That's because you were born in France. Don't they feed that to babies in the hospital?"

She laughs at my joke. "No, silly. They waited until we were at least three."

We all laugh and sit back as we wait for Lucy to come out in her next dress. As I look around at the women gathered, I can't help but smile at everyone who traveled here from Laurel Heights. And it wasn't just a simple drive a few hours down the highway. Storms have been nearly flooding Nashville for the past week. But that didn't stop her mom, Celine, and her mom's best friend, Guiliana —who is also her ex-fiancée's mother—from driving down here.

It could definitely be awkward, especially if you knew the history between these women. And the fights. And the name calling.

But everyone has aired out their laundry, and even if they hadn't, I'd make sure they were on their best behavior. I know

Lucy has been looking forward to this day since Bryce asked her to marry him. She hasn't said much about the wedding, but I saw the bridal magazines when I was living with them, and I'm on Pinterest enough to know that she has been pinning dress after dress on her board.

My best friend is in full bride mode, and I couldn't be happier for her.

"So, Brenna," Mrs. Valenti says. "Will we be seeing you with a special someone at the wedding?"

I nearly choke on the sip of water I was taking. "Unfortunately, no. I think I'll be at the singles' table."

"Oh we can't have that!" Celine says, putting down her flute of champagne. "The wedding is still a few weeks away. That's still plenty of time to find you a date."

"She could have a date, but she doesn't want to look and see what's right in front of her," Lucy says as she walks out of the fitting room. "What do we think of this one?"

We all fall silent in awe of the beauty in front of us. *This.* This is the dress for Lucy. The long, lace sleeves don't look conservative on her at all. Maybe it's because they are stemming from a sweeping low neckline that almost gives it an off-the-shoulder look. And the rest of the dress? The lace fits her like a glove.

She looks like a princess. And Bryce is going to lose his mind when he sees her in this.

"That's it," I say, standing up to get a closer look. "This is your dress."

"Oh, Lucia," Mrs. Valenti says with a sniffle. When I glance back, she's dabbing at her eyes, Guiliana hugging her close with one arm. The two women are looking at Lucy just like mother figures should at this moment. Then there is Celine, who's crying harder than any of us.

"It's just so beautiful," Celine says. "You're going to be the most gorgeous of brides."

"Is this really it?" Lucy says, examining the dress again. "I mean, I think it is?"

I give a nod to the consultant, who must be reading my mind as she heads over to the veils. She brings back the one I had my eye on the whole time. It has a subtle tiara that spills into a beautiful lace that looks like it was cut from the same material as her dress.

"Oh my," Lucy says, holding back tears as the consultant places it on her head. As she turns to look at herself in the mirror, everyone is a crying mess.

Our girl looks perfect.

"This is it," Lucy says, a smile coming across her face that I have only seen a few times in her life, and all of those moments have been because of my brother. "This is my wedding dress."

Everyone jumps up and starts clapping, including the consultant, who realizes she's about to get a hell of a commission on this dress. We cause such a commotion that another sales woman peeks out from the dressing room next to us. I might not have noticed her except for her fire-red hair. She shoots us a look like we're out of line. *Whatever, lady.*

No one is going to put a damper on this day. Lucy said yes to the dress!

After the commotion dies down, Lucy goes back with the consultant to pay for a dress I'll never be able to afford in my life as the rest of us sit back down.

"So what was Lucy saying about how you could have a date to the wedding?" Celine asks. "Are you playing...what's the phrase...hard to get?"

I shoot Celine a look, but apparently it must get lost in translation because she's looking at me like she didn't just open a can of worms I'm not interested in eating. "Lucy is insistent that our friend Cole has a thing for me. She's been not-so-subtly trying to push me toward him since I moved here."

"Cole is such a nice young man," Mrs. Valenti says. "You could do worse, Brenna."

I know that's the truth, but I don't admit that out loud. Instead, I don't say anything, choosing at that moment to get up and pretend to peruse the bridesmaids' dresses, even though Celine and I already picked ours out.

Cole is a nice guy. I mean, would most men leave their house in the middle of the night to pick up a drunk friend who couldn't figure out how to order an Uber? Not many I know. And he could have taken me home that night and left me to fend for myself. But he didn't. He took me back to his place to make sure I was okay. And I would assume most guys were lying about not looking while I changed clothes, but somehow I know he's not. He's seen them before; he could have seen them again.

I hate how much I've thought about him and that night since it happened last week. I haven't told Lucy about it. If I did, she would only ramp up her push on getting us together. I definitely haven't told her that I've slept in his T-shirt every night since, either.

For comfort. It's comfortable. That's it.

"Will this Cole be bringing a date to the wedding?" Celine asks.

"No, he isn't," Lucy announces. How has she timed her entrances so well today? "Which is why he and Brenna should go together. I mean, it only makes sense for the best man and the maid of honor to go together."

I shoot her a look. "It's not going to happen."

"Why?" Lucy asks as we all stand to start making our exit, dress in hand. "Tell me one good reason why."

"Because, I'm done dating."

This makes everyone stop in their tracks. "You're done dating?" Lucy echoes.

"Yes," I reply. "After my last bad date, I've decided I need a break. No more dates. No more setups. I'm deleting the dating apps. I'd rather sit at home on a Friday than go on another horrible date with a guy who isn't worth my time."

Now, this is something I had been thinking about all week, but until this moment, I hadn't made the actual decision to quit dating. But as these words come out of my mouth, I regret none of them.

I'm done. For now, at least. I'm going to focus on me. I'm going to explore Nashville how I want to. I'm going to be the best maid of honor I can for Lucy and Bryce. I'm going to be the best seventh grade science teacher I can be. Yes. That's it. This is my time. And I'm not going to let some random guy I meet on an app, who only says the right things for five seconds, ruin this part of my life. Even if all of these beautiful dresses surrounding me are making me ache for the time that it's finally my turn.

My turn will come. It's just not my time yet. And I'm okay with that.

"Whatever you say," Lucy says as we walk out of the door. "But if I catch you checking out Cole's arms tomorrow while we're at the cake tasting, you owe me twenty dollars."

I reach out my hand. It's going to be like taking candy from a baby. "You've got yourself a deal."

CHAPTER 7
COLE

WHEN I AGREED to be Bryce's best man, I thought I knew what I was getting into. Throw a bachelor party. Keep him alive during it. Make sure he gets down the aisle, and don't lose the rings. That was all I signed up for.

I did not sign up for this.

With her.

"Err my God, they have to put this on the menu," Brenna says, despite her mouth being half-filled with whatever flavor cake she is trying now. "Cole, you have to try this."

I want to say that I don't *have* to do anything. Then again, if I was really standing by that mantra, I wouldn't be here.

"Sure," I say, trying not to come off as grumpy as I'm feeling. I try to take the fork from Brenna, but instead she holds it up for me as if she's going to feed me.

God, I hate everything.

Except this cake. I can't deny that this is really fucking good.

"Definitely a winner," I say as I turn away from Brenna to wipe my mouth.

"I'll add it to the yes list." Brenna writes down the flavor on her notepad. "Ready for the next one?"

I nod and Brenna grabs the next piece of cake, which looks like some sort of all-chocolate concoction. I'm guessing it's going to go on the list, too, if the last five flavors are any indication. By the count of the samples still in front of me, I imagine we'll be adding at least ten more flavors to that list before we're done.

I sigh inwardly. When Lucy and Bryce invited us to the cake tasting, I just thought we'd be another vote if they didn't know what they liked. What I didn't realize was that the wedding venue provides all of the services in-house. So while Lucy and Bryce are in the back with the chef talking about the menu, Brenna and I are on solo duty to pick the five flavors needed for the cake.

Normally this wouldn't bother me too much. I've become quite the pro at being in the same room with Brenna and keeping my cool. But after the drunken club night...I don't know. Something shifted in me. Maybe it was when she said she wouldn't date an athlete. Or the fact that I can still smell her perfume on my pillow, no matter how many times I wash the damn thing. Either way, I'm in a piss-poor mood, and it looks like this is going to take all day.

"So what have you been doing since it's the off season?" she asks before taking a bite of the chocolate cake.

I shrug my shoulders. "Not much."

"Don't go into too much detail there. It might lead to conversation."

"What do you want me to do? Name all the video games I'm playing or walk you through my daily workouts?"

"Geez," she says, passing me the cake. "What's up your ass today?"

"Nothing. I just don't feel like talking."

We sit in silence through the next three pieces of cake. I

don't even tell her audibly if I like it or not. I just give a thumbs up or thumbs down.

Fuck, I really am an asshole. I don't want to be an asshole to her, but apparently that's my default setting when I'm trying to hide the fact that I want to kiss away the little dab of icing on her mouth. I mean, how do you act around someone you can't stop thinking about when you know the feelings aren't reciprocated? And who do I talk to about it? I wish I knew. But since I don't have any of those answers or people, I'll just be an asshole.

"What do you think of that one?" Brenna asks of the cake she just passed over to me.

I barely look at the piece as I cut off a piece and stuff it in my mouth, chewing mechanically. "It's fine."

"Okay, what the hell gives?" Brenna asks loudly. It nearly makes me jump out of my seat. "No way did you like that piece."

I give her a scowl. "How do you know what I like or dislike?"

"Because—" She leans over the table and grabs the plate, holding it up to my face. "This has coconut on top. You hate coconut. So that means you're so out of it you didn't taste it, or you've had a stroke you didn't tell me about."

I look down at the cake. Yup, sure as shit, there are coconut shavings on top of the frosting. And unless I took the world's smallest bite, I would have had to have tasted a few. And she's right. I despise coconut. It tastes like tanning lotion. Fuck, I really am out of it.

"Okay, Campbell, what's the deal?" Brenna puts her fork down and leans on the table. "Talk to me. Are you okay? I'm used to you being a bit surly, but this is a lot, even for you. What's going on?"

"It's nothing," I lie, because no way can I tell her the truth. "Just didn't sleep very well."

Actually, that's not far off base. The thought of her has kept me up every night since she stayed at my place. Hell, if I'm honest, she's kept me up most nights for the past three years.

"Bullshit," she says.

"It's not."

"It is," she says with confidence. "Only one thing can make a person this angry and out of it at the same time. So, who is she?"

This takes me off guard. "What do you mean, 'who is she?'"

"I mean that only a woman—or a man, if I were the one acting like a mega bitch today— can cause this kind of grumpy mood. So tell me. Who is this woman who is making you all angry-bear, and what can I do to help?"

It would help if you weren't my best friend's sister so I could shoot my shot. It would also be great if you quit wearing leggings that hug every inch of your curves.

"Nothing," I lie again. "Don't worry about it."

"So it is a girl!" she says excitedly as she stands up and walks around the table to sit beside me. "Tell me who she is."

Fuck. Fuck. Fuck. I'm not a good liar. I never have been. It's why I keep saying the word "nothing." It's the only thing I can safely pull off. Plus, the truth is always the best.

Except for now. The truth is definitely not the way to go here.

"Fine. Her name is Jessica."

Shit. What the hell did I just do? I should have come up with a random name. Instead, I dropped the name of the last girl I dated. Though I don't take complete blame for it being on my mind. She texted me out of the blue earlier today, wanting to get coffee.

I haven't replied yet.

I also don't know if "dated" is the best term. I took her out three times and slept with her once in one of my many failed attempts to get Brenna out of my head. I never told anyone about her, though I almost had to when Bryce found her underwear in a couch cushion last year.

She's a nice girl. She has a good job, and if I brought her back to Laurel Heights, my mom would be over the moon about her.

Unfortunately, she's not Brenna. And while my head knows I should have tried harder to make it work with Jessica, my heart wouldn't let me. When I broke it off, she didn't take it very well. She kept calling and texting me, asking me to reconsider. Eventually she gave up. Needless to say, I was shocked when I saw her number on my phone this morning.

Brenna moves a little closer. "There. Was that so hard? Now, tell me what's the problem? Let's fix this. We have a lot more cake to try, and I'm not about to do it with you being all grumpy pants."

I take a drink of the water while deciding what I want to disclose. "We went out a few times last year."

"Oh! So an ex?"

"In a way," I say. "She texted me to get coffee this morning. That's it."

"That's not all of it," Brenna says. "I can tell. Do you want to call her again? Is she seeing someone? Did it end badly? I need details if I'm going to help you here."

Ugh, why won't she drop it?

"Things just kind of fizzled," I say.

"Well then you should definitely call her."

"And why would you say that?"

Brenna shrugs. "Because, I can read between the girl lines,

and she's still totally into you. Maybe you two just weren't in the right space the last time. I mean, what could a dinner hurt?"

I try to say something, but nothing comes out. Because... maybe I should. I mean, it has been a while since I've been out. And it's not like Brenna is going to come flying into my arms anytime soon.

I need to get over her. I need to actually try to move on because just waiting for these feelings to pass isn't working. They aren't going to go away if I'm sitting alone every night on my couch playing Halo.

"Fine, I'll give her a call."

"Great!" Brenna says loudly. Does she not have an internal volume control today?

"Yeah, great," I repeat, trying to make myself believe it.

Brenna passes me another piece of cake. "Oh! I meant to ask you. Are you free to help me move a few boxes next week?"

I give her a confused look. "Didn't we just move you to your apartment? Why are we moving stuff again?"

"Bryce didn't tell you?" Brenna shakes her head as she passes me a piece of what looks like carrot cake. "My apartment and the complex had massive water damage from the storm last week. We've been told to find alternate living arrangements for at least the next month. So I'm staying with Bryce and Lucy. I should be there at least through the wedding. So get ready to see my smiling face every day! I have a feeling that every minute we're not doing something, Lucy will be putting us to work."

Fucking lovely.

Last time Brenna lived with Bryce and Lucy, it was during the season, so I wasn't around much. Now? I have a feeling I'm never going to be able to shake her.

Brenna goes back to trying cake while I try to decide whether texting Jessica back is something I really want to do.

Maybe Brenna is right. Maybe this time will be different. Maybe this time we'll hit it off, and I'll look back to this phase of my life as just that: the Brenna phase.

I guess there's only one way to find out.

CHAPTER 8
BRENNA

"OH, BRYCE! YES…YES! RIGHT THERE!"

"Fuck, Lucy! You feel so fucking good."

"I'm going to…ahhh!"

I take the pillow and bring it back over my head. At the minimum, it will muffle the sounds of my best friend and *my brother* having sex. At the worst it will suffocate me. I don't hate that option right now.

It has been four nights of this. I didn't know people did it *every* night. I mean, I knew they were very active…and loud. But this has been on a whole new level. This morning, after Lucy's screams woke me up in the middle of the night from a melatonin-driven slumber, I asked her, as nonchalantly as I could, generally how active she and my brother are. Because I don't remember it being this bad when I lived with them a few months back.

The difference? Bryce was in the middle of the season. Many nights, he was either tired or on the road.

But now that we're in the middle of the off season, and the two love birds are in pre-wedding bliss? It's like living with humping bunnies.

I've tried everything. Headphones worked, but they were

so uncomfortable I couldn't sleep. I tried drugs, hoping they would knock me out. They did, but not enough. I even tried moving from the bedroom I was staying in that shared a wall with them to the living room, hoping a little distance would help. It didn't. My future sister-in-law is quite the screamer.

It has gotten so bad that I fell asleep during my planning period today at school. And worse? The kids didn't wake me up when they came into the room. I slept for the first twenty minutes of class before someone dropped a book that shot me straight up out of my chair. The kids thought it was hilarious. When I asked them to be cool about it, somehow they conned me into bringing them pizza on Friday for their silence.

Middle schoolers are ruthless.

"Bryce! Again? Oh! *Oh!!!*"

I sit straight up on the couch once I realize that tonight is going to be a multi-round performance.

"I can't do this anymore," I say to myself, gathering my phone, pillow, and blanket. "Nope. Fuck this shit. I'm out."

Without a second thought, I leave Bryce's penthouse condo and take the elevator down three floors. It might be one-thirty in the morning, and it might be bold to think that Cole won't have company over, or if he's even home or awake, but I don't care. I can't. I'm at my wits' end, and if I have to hear one more Lucy orgasm, I might rip my ears off.

I pound on the door, which I know is rude for the middle of the night. Luckily, he answers it rather quickly.

"Brenna? What are you doing here?"

Cole barely has the door open as I push my way inside. "I'm getting away from the sex noises. My brother is a moaner. Lucy is a screamer. I can't unhear that. I'm sleeping on your couch."

"Wait. You're what?"

I drop my things on his sectional and turn to look at him, something I neglected to do when I barged in here. He was clearly in bed. If his gravelly voice and confusion didn't give that away, the fact that he's only in a pair of boxer briefs right now confirms it.

Holy hell. Cole is big...everywhere. I mean, I've known the man my whole life, and he's always been the biggest person I know. You knew the kid was going to be a professional offensive lineman when he was five-foot-five and a hundred and twenty pounds at ten years old.

But seeing Cole like this? I have to force a swallow and make myself not look at his arms. Or his chest that begs to be used for a pillow. Or any other part of him that is more on display than normal. I believe I read last year that he's over six foot and three hundred pounds. The man is big, burly, and towers over me and my five-foot-four self. Add in the adorable glasses that I didn't know he wore and his look of confusion, and I kind of want to wrap my arms around him and give him a big hug. And if I get lost in those big arms as they are holding me, then so be it.

Shit. Where did that come from? Lack of sleep. Has to be the lack of sleep.

"Hello? Earth to Brenna? Want to explain again what you're doing here?"

I shake my head; I hope I wasn't staring with my mouth open. "You know that I've been staying at Bryce's."

He huffs. "Yeah, I vaguely remember something about that."

I don't know why he said it like that, but I'm too tired to care. "Well, apparently my brother's off season cardio workout is the *horizontal* kind. I can't take it anymore. I haven't slept all week. Can I please stay here tonight?"

I know I barged in here without warning, but Cole isn't saying anything. I really didn't think it was that big of a request. He has a couch that isn't being used. I'd like to use it.

But he isn't saying anything. Instead, he's just staring at me. And not because he's confused at my request. It's like he can't take his eyes off me.

"Cole? Can I stay?"

"Is that my shirt?"

I look down, a little thrown by his question. "Yeah, I guess it is."

"You're wearing my shirt?"

I suddenly feel very...conspicuous. I'm also now realizing that I don't have a bra on. And Cole's shirt is white. And very comfortable. Which is why I'm wearing it. No other reason. Not that it still vaguely smells like him. Just the comfort.

"Yeah," I say, quickly crossing my arms over my chest. "It's comfortable."

"That's... I'm glad," he says. "That it's comfortable, I mean."

Neither of us say anything for I don't know how long. Which is bad, because that gives me a chance to look at Cole again. Why does he look so good right now? It's not like I ever thought Cole was ugly; I guess I just haven't really looked at him in a long time. He has a strong jawline, but because of his size, there's a little roundness to it. His blue eyes are behind glasses, but for some reason, I'm seeing them as clear as ever. Then there is his body, which is just big. *Everywhere.*

Shit. Stop, stop, stop. This is a consequence of my lack of sleep. That's it. I've never been this sleep deprived, and that's the only sensible answer. The only one I can accept.

I also need to get this conversation back on track, or I'm going to start picturing him without the boxer briefs.

"So is it okay?" I ask.

"Okay what?"

"Okay if I sleep here?"

He gives his head a shake. "Yeah. Of course."

I turn to make my way to his couch, which right now looks like the best bed I've ever slept on. I lean down to situate my blanket and pillow, only to realize Cole has moved right next to me.

"You can go back to bed," I say. "I'm sorry I woke you, but thank you. Thank you so much. You're a lifesaver."

"Are you sure you're okay?" he asks. "Why don't you take my bed? I can sleep out here."

"No," I say, even though memories of his soft sheets and fluffy blankets start dancing in my head. "This is plenty. I don't want to put you out any more than I already am."

"Are you sure? I don't mind. It might make up for the nights of sleeplessness."

This man... God, how is he still single? Here I am, barging into his place in the middle of the night, and not only does he let me in, but he's willing to give up his bed? Guys like this don't exist anymore. At least, I didn't think they did. Especially ones who look like him.

Stop it. Stop it right now.

I shake my head and reach for his hand. I don't know why I do, but it feels right at this moment. And I'm going to blame my exhaustion for the zing I feel when I give his hand a squeeze. "I'll be just fine out here. But how about this? You let me keep the shirt, and you keep your bed?"

This gets me a smile, one that relaxes me from my head to my toes. "Sounds good. Night, Trouble."

Now it's my turn to smile. "Good night, Cole."

CHAPTER 9
COLE

GOOD NEWS: Brenna looks like she finally got a good night's sleep.

Bad news: She was the only one in this apartment who did.

I tried. God, I tried. I tossed and turned all night. But every time I closed my eyes, all I saw was Brenna in my shirt. Then I thought what it would be like if she was sitting on me, straddling my legs as I slowly took said shirt off her.

There is something about seeing a woman in your clothes that is the biggest turn on. Add to it her crazy, messy hair and her sleepy blue eyes, and there was no way I was going to be sleeping a wink.

"Good morning," she says over her shoulder as I make my way to the kitchen. She's still in my shirt, which I was prepared for, considering I didn't see her bring a bag last night. What I wasn't prepared for was to see it slowly riding up her legs as she tries, but fails, to reach for something in my cupboards.

"Do you need help?" I ask as I walk into the kitchen.

She doesn't look back at me. Instead, she continues to try to extend her reach because she's a hard-headed woman who has always refused to ask for help. "No. I almost...got it..."

I laugh as I walk behind her, easily grabbing the to-go

mug she was reaching for. I really must be tired, because I do this without thinking about the fact that she is trapped between me and the counter. The remnants of her perfume hit my senses and nearly knock me on my ass. I know I've been close to her more than a few times recently, but this feels different. I'm so close that all I'd need to do is lower my head ever so slightly, and I'd be able to place a kiss on her shoulder. So close that if I don't step away soon, she's going to feel every inch of how happy I am to have her here.

"Here you go," I say, handing her the travel mug before taking a step back. "Did you get some sleep?"

"Thankfully, yes," she says. "Do you mind if I get some juice for the road?"

"Not at all," I say as she makes her way to the refrigerator. "You still don't drink coffee?"

She shakes her head. "If there was a week that was going to change that, it would have been this one. But I held out. And I'm going to continue to be strong. Because that's where you come in."

I was about to start making myself some coffee, but I have a feeling I better sit down for this. "What do you mean, this is where I come in?"

Brenna takes a seat next to me at my kitchen island. Her eyes are already pleading. I know that look. The last time she gave it to me was in college when she asked me to go with her to that party and we ended up in a squad car together.

"So, I had an idea. And you absolutely can tell me no."

I don't have a good feeling about this. "Why do I already want to say no?"

"Well, you can. But let me at least ask first," she begins, then pauses to take a deep breath. "My apartment manager called me yesterday. The damage is worse than they thought.

They originally said four weeks, but now it's going to be closer to six to eight."

"Okay..."

"And, well, I love my brother and Lucy. You know that. But if I have to listen to them bang one more time it's going to drive me to join a convent."

Oh hell, I think I know where this is going.

"What are you asking, Brenna?"

"I mean, you have a spare bedroom. I know there's not a bed in it, but there could be. Or you have a couch. A really nice couch that's actually bigger than my bed. And I'll pay for groceries. And cook meals. And anything else. Just please, let me stay here so I don't have to go back to the sex den."

I was afraid that was what she was going to ask.

I want to say no. I should say no. I need to say no. No matter how many ways I look at this, saying no is the best thing to do for everyone involved. I told myself I was going to do everything I could to get over these fucking feelings I've had for her. Hell, I even took Brenna's advice and called Jessica. I made a commitment to myself that I was going to get over her. How can I do that if we're living together?

"I don't know, Brenna," I begin, trying to figure out the nicest way to say no without letting her know the real reason she can't stay here. "I just don't think—"

"Please, Cole," she says as she stands and wraps her arms around me. "Please, Cole, I'm begging you. Please let me stay with you."

Ah, fuck me.

————

"Hey hey, roomie!"

Brenna sets her purse and bag down, only to go back into

the hallway. This time when she comes back, she's rolling in two huge suitcases and another bag over her shoulder.

"How long are you staying for again?" I ask, setting down my game controller.

"Don't judge me. Then again, you should see how much I left behind," she says, dropping her bag before falling down on the couch. "So what did you do today?"

"You're looking at it," I say, nodding to the controller. Wow, I'm getting really good at this lying thing. "Welcome to the off season."

"You don't just play video games all day, do you?"

I shake my head. "No. I work out. Sometimes I have appearances. Sunday is grocery day. But today was an off day, so I took full advantage. How was your day?"

Brenna tells me about her day, and the pizza she had to buy as hush money for one of her classes. I hate how normal this feels. How we can just slide into conversation like this. I don't want to slide into conversation with her. I want it to be awkward and forced so my brain can rationalize not talking to her. And not doing other things with her.

But no, it has to be smooth. It has to feel as natural as breathing.

This is going to be the worst six to eight weeks of my life.

"So, is it time to figure how all of this is going to work out?" I ask.

Brenna nods. "Yes. If we're going to live together, then we need to be on the same page. And I'm going to say this now, do not go out of your way for me. I'm already so grateful that you said yes."

Everything happened so fast this morning that Brenna and I really didn't get a chance to go over how this is going to work logistically before she had to go to school. In fact, she left so quickly that I almost convinced myself that I had imagined the whole thing.

It wasn't a dream. It was real.

Brenna Donald is moving in with me.

When that hit me earlier today, I knew what I needed to do.

"I can sleep on the couch," she says. "I was more than comfortable last night, and that way you don't have to get a bed for your spare room."

"Well, I wish you would have said something earlier," I say, a smile I can't control growing on my face.

"What did you do?" she says, looking around like something is going to pop out and scare her.

I nod back to the guest room. "Go take a look."

She pops off the couch and nearly sprints back to the bedroom. I'm a few steps behind her when she stops and stares at the guest room, which is now furnished with a brand new bed and dressers.

"Cole..." Her voice is nearly a whisper. "You didn't. No. This is too much."

I shrug. "I needed to furnish it anyway. Now my parents have a place to sleep when they come to visit. It's no big deal."

She turns to look at me, and I think if I look hard enough, I can see tears forming. "It's a huge deal."

She takes two steps before wrapping me in her arms, hugging me with all of her petite might. I smile, hugging her back.

"I'm glad you like it," I say.

"I love it," she says as she slowly pulls away. "Thank you."

We step in the room so she can get a closer look. "Dressers are all yours. And the closet. I only have a few things in there, so consider this your space."

"I don't know what to say," she says, looking around in awe.

"You don't need to say anything. Though, speaking of saying things, have you told Bryce and Lucy?"

She nods. "I did when I went to grab my suitcases. Lucy felt bad. Bryce seemed a little *too* happy. I have a feeling he was putting on a show to make me as uncomfortable as possible."

"Sounds about right."

"Yeah, well, what are brothers for? And speaking of, he did say that if I were staying with anyone, he's glad it's you. Something about protecting family or something."

Well, that makes me feel like a piece of shit. If he only knew what I really thought about Brenna. Or what I was thinking about today when I was buying this bed.

Stop. Stop it now. No more. You're done.

"I'm glad to help," I say, turning to leave the room.

"Cole, wait, there's one more thing."

I turn back to her, noticing that she looks nervous.

"Everything okay?"

"Yeah," she says as she starts twiddling her fingers. "It's just this isn't an easy conversation, but I want to make sure you know that I'm totally cool with it."

I tilt my head, not sure what she's talking about. "What's that?"

"Your dating and sex life. What should I be prepared for?"

If I had a drink, I would have spit it out. Instead, I start choking on saliva because *wow*. I was not expecting that. "Excuse me?"

Brenna shrugs. "You're a grown man. I don't know what kind of life you lead. And I'm just saying that if something happens, just let me know, and I can make myself scarce. I know no girl wants to come home and see another girl on the couch. Or across the hall."

I don't even know what to say. "Don't worry. Nothing like that will happen."

Brenna quirks a brow. "Didn't you set up a date with Jessica?"

Shit, she's right. How did I almost forget about that? Clearly, this is a sign I do need to start getting over Brenna if I forgot about a date I made literally days ago.

"Yeah, that's not until next week," I say. "But don't worry. I won't bring her back here. We're just going to get dinner and drinks."

Brenna wags her eyebrows. "That's how it always starts."

"Are you trying to insinuate that I put out on the first date?"

"Why, Cole Campbell! I was insinuating nothing of the sort," Brenna says with a thick— and fake—Southern accent. "I've heard you are a perfect gentleman when it comes to courtin' the ladies."

"Courtin' the ladies?"

Brenna shrugs. "It just felt right."

"You're crazy, you know that?"

"So I've been told," Brenna says, jumping onto the bed. "But seriously, just give me a heads up if things escalate, and I'll make myself scarce. I'd hate to put a damper on your personal life."

Oh, Brenna.... if you only knew.

CHAPTER 10
BRENNA

"LOOK AT YOU, SNAZZY PANTS!"

Cole gives me a confused look as he clasps his watch. "Snazzy pants?"

Yup. Snazzy pants. That's what I said. Did I mean to say it? Nope. Have I suddenly become oddly nervous around Cole? Have random things started spewing out of my mouth? Yup.

It started the day after I moved in when he asked me if Italian was okay for dinner. I responded with a five-minute speech about the proper rankings of pasta noodles and why angel hair is supreme.

I don't know why I reacted like that. It was a simple question. Then again, he was in gym shorts, without a shirt, and sweaty from a workout. That sight alone would be enough to make any woman's brain go to mush. Hence, the pasta rant.

Now tonight with *snazzy pants*? That's completely different. He's completely clothed. But he looks just as good as he did the other day. What is it about a man in a dress shirt with the cuffs rolled up that makes a woman want to pull her panties down?

"Well, if you were Lucy, I'd be calling you a 'hot mama' or 'hot piece of ass.'"

Why am I still talking? I just need to stop talking.

He laughs as he sprays on a bit of cologne. Thank goodness he's not asking me to speak right now because I don't know if I could. I'm currently wondering how you feel a smell in your lady parts, because I definitely am.

And it's freaking me out.

I've always had a love-hate relationship with cologne. I'm of the firm belief that you can tell a lot about a man by whatever he wears. One of my first boyfriends, back in high school, used to drown himself in some sort of knock-off of a name brand. I'm sure it would shock no one to learn that he became a fraternity president.

Dexter's might have been the worst I have ever smelled. I want to vomit just thinking about that scent.

Then there's Cole. It's woodsy, but with a sweetness. Kind of like him. He's this big, bad offensive lineman who gets paid millions of dollars to mow down men just as big as he is. But when you get to know him, he's a sweetheart.

A sweetheart who bought me a bed when I asked to move in. Who covered me up with a blanket the other night when I fell asleep on the couch.

Who gets my juice ready in a to-go cup and puts it in the refrigerator the night before so all I need to do is grab it and go in the morning.

I inhale the addicting scent, which takes me back to the morning I woke up in his bed. I might not remember much about that drunken night, but I'll never forget his smell. I was sad when it finally faded from his shirt.

Maybe I can sneak back in here later and give it a little spray. That wouldn't be creepy, right?

"So do you need something or are you just going to stand here and stare at me?" Cole asks.

"I wasn't staring," I say quickly, even though I absolutely

was. "I was just wondering if you needed any help for your date tonight. Need any pointers? Where are you taking her?"

Again, why am I still talking? I had an out. I should have taken it. Now I get to hear about Cole's date.

Which I'm not in the least bit jealous about *at all*.

"And why would I ask you?" Cole says, walking past me toward the living room. "Aren't you the same person who just a few short weeks ago declared from the rooftops that you were done dating? Doesn't exactly strike me as a person I'd want to take dating advice from."

Well, I guess I'm in it now. Might as well go with it.

"See! That's where you're wrong," I say as I follow him out to the living room.

Cole sits down and gives me a questioning look as he slips on one of his shoes. "Okay, now I'm intrigued."

I take a seat on the part of the sectional that I quickly claimed as mine. "I have been on so many bad dates that I can identify a good date in the blink of an eye. Also, I know all the red flags, so I can spot those a mile away."

He thinks about that, slipping on his other shoe. "Somehow, that actually makes sense."

"I'm not just a pretty face," I say, sitting back. "So, tell me, what's on the agenda tonight?"

"We're going to go to dinner at the new sushi place in The Gulch. Then I thought maybe we'd get a few drinks."

I nod. "Sounds safe enough. Cool area to spend an evening. Appropriate first date protocol. Or, I guess this would be a second first date?"

He shrugs, standing up from the chair. "I remember she said before that she liked sushi, so I thought she'd enjoy that."

Of course Cole would remember a detail like that. "Bonus points, Campbell."

"Thanks. I forgot my wallet in my room. I'm going to go grab that and then head out."

I wave him away. "You do you! I'm just going to sit here and boot up my binge for the night while I wait on the pizza to be delivered."

"Are you watching another one of those crazy-ass Turkish soap operas?"

"Don't hate!" I yell. "And don't think I didn't notice that you were trying to sneak peeks of it last night…"

"I plead the fifth."

I laugh as I fire up the show and get situated for a night of leisure on the couch. Usually I don't think to do that, but I'm not going to have Cole here to bring me my knitting when I forget it in my room and don't feel like getting up.

He's really too sweet.

I knew living with Cole would be a breeze, but I didn't realize how quickly we'd fall into a routine. I know I told him I'd do the cooking, but he hasn't held me to it. Sometimes I'll make dinner, sometimes he does. After we eat, I sit on the couch and grade papers while he plays his video games or watches TV. Occasionally we've done wedding projects while talking about anything and everything. And despite his denial, he has watched my Turkish soap operas. In return, I've watched more hours of ESPN than I can count. He hasn't asked me how to knit yet, but I'm waiting for the day. Each night when I break out my yarn, I feel him taking more and more of an interest.

If I could just control my spewing of random words or rankings of pasta, I'd say this setup was pretty much perfect.

The apartment buzzer alerting us that someone is downstairs scares me for a second, but then I remember I ordered a pizza. I spring from my spot on the couch and hit the enter button without even asking who it is. I open the door before walking over to the table to grab my tip money for the delivery person. When I come back, I don't see anyone with a pizza. Instead, I'm staring at a redhead who looks quite confused.

"Can I help you?" I ask.

"Is Cole here?"

"Jessica?" Cole says from a few feet behind me. "What are you doing here?"

I look back and forth a few times before stepping out of the way so *Jessica* can enter the apartment, which she does without a formal invitation.

Red flag number one.

Also, why does she look familiar?

"I know we said we would meet at the restaurant, but I figured since I had to drive past your building to get there, I'd just come here first. Though I didn't know you had...company."

And this is why I said I would make myself scarce if Cole was dating. I know how this has to look to her. Then again, he would have had to know said company was coming.

Red flag number two.

"Hi, I'm Brenna," I say, extending my hand for a shake. She just stands there so I quickly pull my hand away. "I'm staying here with Cole for a few weeks. In the spare bedroom. My brother is one of his teammates. He lives upstairs. He and his fiancée have a lot of sex, so I'm staying here. But don't worry, there is no sex happening here. Because Cole and I have known each other for years. Since we were kids. Nothing but friend-ship in this apartment!"

I really just need to not talk. At least this time it wasn't Cole who threw me for a loop.

No, it was Jessica, who is stunningly gorgeous. She has long, red hair that flows over her toned shoulders in perfect waves. She's wearing a fitted red dress that shows every one of her perfect curves. And *wow*. I usually don't look straight at a woman's breasts, but it's kind of hard not to with Jessica. Especially in that dress. I almost want to ask if they are going to pop out, but even I know better.

To take my eyes away from the girls, I quickly look to her shoes. If I put those on, I'd probably fall over like a baby giraffe. But on her? She looks like a runway model. She's giving me vibes of that hot secretary from "Mad Men" who made every straight woman in the world question their sexuality.

Judging by the look she's giving me, pin-up model Jessica isn't a fan of my ramble. Or me. Maybe both. Without saying another word to me, she takes another step into the apartment, reaching out her hand for Cole.

"Can we go? I can't wait to try that new place. Should we just take one car since I'm here?"

Oh, I know this trick. Usually it's the guy trying to pull it so that way he can be in control of when the date stops and starts. Ballsy move for Jessica. But hey, men these days like a strong woman who knows what she wants. And clearly Jessica knows what she wants.

Maybe Cole is into that? I honestly have no clue what he's into. But the longer she's here, the more I hope he isn't it.

"See you later," Cole says as he leads her out the door.

"Have a nice time!"

I tried to genuinely mean that one. It's the polite thing to say. And I'm not a mean person. I do hope they have a nice time.

Even if the thought of them kissing is making my skin crawl.

———

"Brenna? What are you—?"

I don't wait for an invitation. Just call me Jessica. I barge right into her and Bryce's penthouse apartment.

Because I can. I'm the sister. And the best friend. And the woman who is currently experiencing a *very* unexpected emotion.

"Just seeing what my bestie and my brother are doing. No plans? It's Friday night!" I take a seat on the couch as Bryce appears in the living room. "Want to watch a movie? I have pizza downstairs. I can bring it up."

"I think that is my cue to head out," Bryce says, placing a kiss on Lucy's forehead. "You two girls have a fun night. Or whatever."

Bryce exits the penthouse, and Lucy takes a seat next to me.

"Where's Bryce going?"

"The rings are ready, and he is insisting on picking them up to make sure they are exactly what he asked for," Lucy says. "If there is one aspect of the wedding he has taken an interest in, it's the rings. So I've let him have it. It's one less thing for me to worry about, and I'm sure if I saw the price tag, I'd panic. It's better this way."

"Well, good for Bryce. And good for me that you could use some company!"

Lucy quirks a brow at me. "What's the deal? You haven't been up here since you moved in with Cole. What gives?"

I pick up the remote, suddenly very focused on finding something to watch. "He has a date tonight."

Lucy rips the controller out of my hand and turns the television off. "He has a what? With who? How can you be okay with this? I'm not okay with this!"

Not the reaction I was expecting. "Her name is Jessica. They apparently dated last year. She texted him a few weeks ago, and he agreed to give it another shot. And what do you mean *how could I let this happen?* I encouraged it. I told him it would be good for him. You know, get out of the house and all that."

"I can't believe it," Lucy says, standing up and starting to pace.

"What can't you believe? He's a good guy. A great guy, actually. If there is anyone in this world who shouldn't be single, it's Cole. He's made of boyfriend material. This is a good thing. And! And, she looks like Jessica Rabbit's twin. Well, her name is Jessica. Her twin probably wouldn't be named Jessica. So I guess she looks like Jessica Rabbit. I mean, good for Cole, am I right? Did I just say a lot of words?"

Lucy just stares at me.

"What?" I mean for it to sound normal, but for some reason it reaches a high pitch I'm not familiar with. "I'm happy for him. He's been grumpy lately. Nothing gets a man out of a grump funk than some good ol' fashioned hanky panky. And if her actions so far are saying anything, Cole can have as much of the hanky and the panky as he wants tonight."

I want to mean the words I just said, but the more I talk, the more I taste the bile in my mouth. And why is my stomach all twisty? Probably because the thought of Cole having sex is gross. You know, since he's basically my brother.

My hot brother with big arms who smells like sex. Okay, maybe I should stop thinking of him as my brother...

Lucy is now sitting back with her arms crossed. She gives me the exact look my mother used to give me when I did or said something stupid. "Seriously?"

"What? Just what? I know you want to say something, so say it."

"Ok, I'll say it. I think you came up here to vent about Cole being out on a date because it bothers you more than you want to admit."

"Pshh," I say, waving my hand in the air as my stomach simultaneously drops from her words. "I'm fine with Cole on a date. Didn't you hear the part where I pushed him to do this? Why would I do that if I cared if he was out with another woman?"

Wow, if I really listened, that almost sounded believable.

"Because," Lucy says. "You haven't realized you like him. Or you're just realizing it, and it's hitting you like a ton of bricks."

I forgot how smart my future sister-in-law is. And how she knows me better than anyone.

Because she's right: I'm crazy jealous because I think I like him, but I'm not sure if I like him, but I'm pretty sure I like him... but I can't like him.

"What makes you say that?" I say unconvincingly.

"Because every time I bring Cole and you up in the sense of a relationship, you get super defensive. Perhaps a little *too* defensive."

Ugh, I need another friend who knows me less. I also need to make her believe I'm fine with this. Because if I can convince her, then maybe these pesky feelings will go away.

Because I can't like Cole. I really, really can't.

"Okay Miss I Know Brenna So Well," I begin. "What can I do to make you believe that I'm completely fine with Cole being on a date?"

Lucy gets a devilish smile on her face. "Okay, I'm going to ask you a series of Cole-related questions, and if you say no to all, I will drop this forever. Hell, I'll go out with whoever this chick is and invite her to my wedding."

"You have yourself a deal."

"Okay, question number one—and remember, you have to be honest," Lucy says, taking a second to ponder whatever bullshit question she's going to throw at me. "Have you given Cole the arm test in the last three months?"

Maybe this quiz isn't as easy as I thought. "Yes, but in my defense, every guy I meet gets that test."

"Fine, but did he pass?"

I shake my head. "Again, not fair. You've seen his arms. They are tree trunks. Next."

Okay. I'm fine. If that's the only question she forces a yes out of me for, then I'm fine.

"Question number two: At any point tonight when thinking of Cole out with Jessica, did you feel the urge to punch a wall?"

"No," I say with certainty. I didn't want to punch a wall. I wanted to puke and scream into a pillow. Totally different.

Lucy eyes me like she's trying to tell if I'm bullshitting or not. "Okay, question three: Pretending he's not where he is at this physical moment, if Cole asked you out on an official date, would you say yes?"

I shake my head, take a big swallow, and say the biggest lie of my life.

"No."

Fuck, that physically hurt to say. Because if Cole were not who he was, I'd go out with him in a heartbeat. I think we would have a nice time. We'd laugh over dinner. Maybe people-watch at the bar, which always provides good entertainment, especially in Nashville. Or maybe the date would be a little simpler. Maybe we'd go mini-golfing and get ice cream. Maybe he'd come up behind me and pretend to show me how to putt. Maybe we'd hold hands as we walked, just talking about whatever comes up.

Now I really want to puke, because all of those sound amazing. And not just the activities; also the man I pictured doing them with.

My roommate. My brother's best friend.

"You said no, so I'm going to keep my word," Lucy says. "But I'm going to protest that I don't think you meant that last one."

I don't say anything, opting instead to just lie down with my head in her lap. "Do you mind if I stay here tonight? I don't want to be there, you know, just in case."

"Of course." Lucy gives me a little squeeze before putting a blanket over me. "And just because I know you're a liar and you're finally starting to realize that you're actually crazy about the guy, I'll make sure Bryce and I don't have sex tonight."

At some point I fell asleep, but I woke up at least three times in the night. No, not because of Bryce and Lucy. She kept her word. No, I couldn't sleep because of the mental movie playing in my mind. It was of me the next morning, making my way back downstairs, only to open the door and see Jessica in one of Cole's shirts. She's making him breakfast and wearing a smile a woman only wears after the best sex of her life.

Fuck...this is bad. So bad. Because Lucy is one-thousand-percent right— I'm up to my eyeballs crazy about Cole. And I have no idea what I'm going to do about it.

GROWING UP, Bryce and I always had this dream that one day we were going to live next door to each other. We'd build houses on a big piece of property, our wives would be best friends, and our kids would grow up closer than family. Yes, I know it sounds like a weird thing for boys to even talk about, but that was our dream. It still is. One of the first things we did when we both got drafted by Nashville was figure out where we would eventually build our houses.

But in all those years, we've never been out on a double date together. Why tonight is the first, I'm not sure, but Lucy was insistent on meeting Jessica. I couldn't tell her no even though I was ninety-nine-percent sure this second attempt with Jessica wasn't going to work out. We've been out nearly every night since our first date, and with each date, I become more and more sure she's not it for me.

She's...a lot. I don't mind a woman being what society would call high maintenance, but Jessica takes it to another level. I asked her the other night if she wanted to grab a late-night bite, and she said yes, but she needed two hours to get ready. It was already nine o'clock, so I told her we'd take a raincheck. I mean, we were going to a diner, not the Four Seasons.

Then there is her Instagram. She's obsessed with it. If she's not posting on it, she's talking about it. On our first date, she made me take no less than a hundred pictures of her standing outside the restaurant.

She called me an Instagram Boyfriend in Training.

I didn't like the sound of that whatsoever.

But I'm trying to keep an open mind. Maybe this is just how women are, and I'm being too harsh. So I agreed to the double date, hoping it would help me see if this was a me thing or not.

But now we're sitting across the table from Bryce and Lucy, and the more Jessica talks, the more sure I am that this isn't a me thing. At all.

"So Jessica, how did you and our boy meet?" Bryce asks. "If it's an embarrassing story, I won't hold it against you. Him? Probably."

"Oh it's nothing like that," she says, flipping her red hair over her shoulder. Something I found sexy at first, but now that I know she does it incessantly, the act has lost its luster. "We actually met at the grocery store. I don't know if you knew this, but Cole goes to the grocery store at the same time every week. And, crazy enough, so do I! I kept seeing him over and over at the deli, and one day I just pulled up my big girl pants and went over and said hi. The rest is history. This is, of course, after I drooled over him for months during football season. I had a bit of a crush."

She leans into me, wrapping her arms around my bicep as she leans her head on my shoulder. She's acting like she just retold the plot to the greatest love story ever told. What she doesn't know is that after I broke up with her last year, I had to change grocery stores. Which sucked. I failed to remember that when I gave this a second chance.

"That's so nice," Lucy says. "It's crazy where people meet each other nowadays."

"Tell me about it," Jessica says. "I hear about different places all the time. I'm the general manager at Eva's Bridal. You should just hear the stories we learn about how couples meet."

Lucy's eyes go wide. "You work at Eva's? That's where I got my dress!"

"What a small world!" Jessica says, giving the table a slap for extra measure.

"It is," Lucy says. "I was just in there a few weeks ago. I can't believe I found my dress on the first shopping trip. And thank goodness, because the wedding is next week and I needed a miracle."

"And it is beautiful on you," Jessica says. "That lace! My gosh, it's going to be gorgeous. Bryce, just wait until you see her. She's going to blow your socks off."

This all gets three very confused looks shot her way.

"How would you know that?" Lucy asks. And good, because I was wondering that too.

"Oh...well...I was at the salon during your appointment, actually. I was with another client. I happened to sneak a peek. I mean, how could I forget a bride as beautiful as you?"

We let it go, because it does make sense. I look across the table and can tell that Lucy's brain is working overtime. Something isn't sitting right. Bryce teases her that he can sometimes see the hamster wheel spinning in her brain. I now know what he means.

"I can't wait to see it," Bryce says, cutting the awkward silence. "But no more wedding talk. It's been a crazy month getting ready, and tonight is the first night we've taken a break from it."

"Well, anything I can do to be of help, please let me know," Jessica says. "I mean, it *is* kind of my thing. So anything I can do, even the day of, I'd be happy to help. I mean, since I'll be there anyway, I might as well make myself useful!"

The awkward silence returns as her last words hang in the air. Now I'm the one with the hamster wheel going. Did I invite her to the wedding? I don't think I did. I have a pretty good memory, and I feel like I would remember that. And if I did, then I didn't tell Lucy, because that's the look she's giving me right now.

"Who needs refills? Everyone? Great!" Lucy says, standing up from her stool at our high-top table. "Cole, how about you help me carry?"

Lucy gives me a look that screams "follow me now" so I do as I'm nonverbally told. But not before Jessica looks up at me, silently asking me to give her a kiss.

I do, but only because I'm scared that if I don't, I'll accidentally forget I proposed to her.

"So, Jessica," Lucy begins as we wait for a bartender. "She's…"

"A lot?"

"That's one way of putting it." Lucy sits on the barstool, so I do the same. Though she has always been Bryce's girl, I've always felt a connection with her. Maybe because we are the only two people in the world who get the fucked-up mind and world that is Bryce Donald, we share some sort of connection ourselves. "Now, I'm going to say this, and I'm being completely honest. If you want to bring her as your date, that's fine. I'm not mad. You can bring whoever you want and I'll completely support you, but—"

I cut her off. "Lucy, I didn't invite her. In fact, I never even mentioned when it was. And she never told me that she saw you in the store. All I said was that my best friends were getting married, and I was the best man. I don't even think I mentioned your names."

"Oh," Lucy says as she puts back on her thinking face. "Well, I mean, the engagement has been on social media. She seems like an Instagram type of girl."

"Oh she is." I look back at the table, and she's proving my point for me, turning her phone six different ways as she takes a selfie. Bryce is watching with a look of incredulity. I might laugh if I didn't have to go back to the table and sit with her.

"Well maybe she saw it there?" Lucy says. "And if she did see us at the bridal store, then she might have put everything together."

"Isn't that kind of..." I trail off, knowing what word I want to use but I'm not sure if it's the right context, or a bit too harsh.

"Stalkerish? Yes. It's screaming stalker vibes."

"That's what I thought."

"Actually," I say as the lightbulb all of a sudden turns on in my brain. "She texted me the day after the dress fitting."

"She did?" Lucy asks. "How do you remember that?"

"Because I was telling Brenna about her the day of the cake testing, which was the day after you guys went dress shopping. Do you think she messaged me out of the blue because she saw you at the store?"

"Would she know who I am?"

I nod. "Oh yeah. She's a huge Fury fan. Between that and her Instagram obsession, she would absolutely recognize you if she saw you in public."

"Do you think she messaged you because she saw me and was like, 'Hey, I miss that guy?'"

I shrug. "I have no idea. I'm starting to think there's a lot about Jessica that I don't know, and I'm not sure if I want to."

"Well then you have a choice to make," Lucy says. "She

obviously thinks she's coming to the wedding. You have to either suck it up and bring her, or somehow tell her that she's not coming."

I let out a groan because both of those options sound horrible. Then I look back to the table where she is still in selfie mode. I can only imagine how many pictures she'd make me take at the wedding.

I look back to Lucy, who has just put in our drink orders. "Can we try and not bring it up when we go back to the table? I'll talk to her about it in private tonight."

Lucy nods. "I can do that."

"Thanks," I say. "Also, can I ask you something?"

"Of course," she says, turning more to face me. "I know you're technically Bryce's friend. Bros before hoes and all that stuff. But I want you to know that I consider you one of my best friends, and if there's anything you need or want to tell me, or just get off your chest, I'm here for you. And your secret, whatever it may be, will be safe with me."

Shit. Does she know? No. She can't. But the way she's looking at me, the way her eyes are trying to say something, makes me worry she knows.

But that's not what I need to talk to her about. At least, not yet.

"So the reason I wanted you guys to come out tonight was for you to give me your opinion on Jessica."

"My opinion?"

"Yes, your opinion." I reach over and take the beer the bartender just put down and take a pull. "I don't date much. And if I'm going to settle down, I want someone that will fit in with us. It's kind of a must. And I...I don't think she is. But I was worried I wasn't giving her a fair chance. I just need to know if you think my instincts are correct—that she's just not it."

Lucy places her hand on top of mine and gives it a few pats.

"I'm going to ask you three questions, and if you answer yes to any of them, I say stick it out. If not, then I think you know what you need to do."

I nod. "All right, shoot."

"One: is she the first thing you think of when you wake up in the morning?"

I'm silent, which we both know is a big old no.

"All right then. Now, number two: when she invited herself to my wedding, were you excited?"

Again silence. Again a no. Actually, that response was more under the shocked and appalled category.

"And last but not least: is Jessica the only woman you've thought about in a romantic way since you two started seeing each other?"

I'm silent again, and judging by the look Lucy's giving me right now, she knows exactly why. And exactly who.

Damn, she knows.

"I think you know your answer," Lucy says. "And, I know it's none of my business, and I'm not even sure if I'm on the right track here, but I think I am. If that woman you thought about happened to be the sister of a certain best friend, don't give up. In fact, I'd say it's a great time to shoot a shot."

My eyes go wide. "Really? What makes you say that?"

Lucy just smiles. "Best friend intuition. Now, let's get back to the table. And please, don't break up with Jessica now. I have a feeling she'd cause a scene, and I don't have the energy for that tonight."

"BRENNA? YOU HOME?"

Cole's voice almost makes me inhale the mask I'm currently putting on my face.

"Cole? What are you doing here?"

"Well, I do live here," he says, his voice getting closer. "I wanted to see... What are you doing?"

I turn to face him, my face covered in green slime. "A face mask."

He lets out a laugh, even though I can see he's trying to not laugh at me. "A face mask?"

"Yes!" I defend, crossing my arms. "The wedding is this weekend. I thought I'd pamper myself a bit and do a facemask. You know, remove all of those toxins and stuff."

Cole lifts an eyebrow. "Toxins and stuff?"

"Yes. Toxins and stuff." I let out a breath and tighten my robe a bit. Because yes, I just realized I'm only in a robe right now. And apparently still saying random things in his presence.

"What are you doing home? No hot date with your girl-friend tonight?"

I don't know why I'm bringing it up because the last thing I want to hear about is Cole and Jessica and their perfect dinner dates.

Not that I've been tracking their dates. It's just a little hard when she posts every single thing they do on Instagram.

Not that I'm following her. I'm not.

Fine. I am because I have a serious problem. I'm at least doing it under a fake account I created. So I'm not technically spying on them. Becky Cane is. Hey, the name worked on my fake ID in college, might as well bring her back for a second round.

"She's not my girlfriend. She might have been, but she's not anymore," Cole says. "Anyway, I'm ordering Chinese food and going to watch that new dragon show that I'm seeing everywhere. Want to join me?"

I blink a few times, because did I just hear what I think I just heard? They broke up? When did this happen? How did this happen? There is so much information I need to know. Actually, now that I think about it, this does now explain why Jessica posted a black and white profile selfie captioned by Taylor Swift lyrics.

"Brenna?"

"Yeah?" I say quickly, coming back to the present.

"What do you want to eat?"

"Um, yeah, lo mein and dumplings. Oh! And get some sweet and sour chicken. And maybe some crab Rangoon, but only if you'll help me eat it."

"That it? Maybe also a number five just in case?"

I open my mouth to protest before I realize Cole is teasing. His smile is small, but it's making me feel some big things.

"I think I'll be good," I say.

"All right, I'll go put in the order," he says. "Take your time here. I'd hate to interrupt the ridding of toxins and stuff."

"Shut up," I say as I close the door. All I hear is his laughter as he walks away from the bathroom.

Laughter I've missed hearing.

And not just the laughter, but him. I've missed him. So much.

Since he and Jessica reconnected, we've barely seen each other, mostly because I've made myself scarce. Now that I've quit denying the little voice in my head that always whispered about my feelings for him, I can't be in the same room with him without babbling like a lunatic.

So I figured out how I could limit my time as best as possible. I started going to school early to avoid any morning run-ins with him. There was a two-hour window between when I would get home and when Jessica would drag him off somewhere. I started spending that time using the apartment complex's gym.

Okay, fine. I would go to the gym and pretend to use the elliptical until he left. That's when I head back upstairs to start my nightly cycle of depression, knowing that I'm in his place, in his space, but he's with her.

The only comfort I had was that she never spent the night. And as far as I know, he never spent the night with her.

But now if they're not together, does this mean things will go back to normal?

I can answer my own question: no. Because pre-Jessica, I still believed that Cole was just my friend. Now I don't know how to act around him because when I see him, I want to climb him like a tree.

I wash the mask off my face and head back to my room. Pre-Jessica, I wouldn't have given two thoughts about what to wear for a quiet night in with Cole. Hell, most of the time it would have been a ratty T-shirt and a pair of oversized sweatpants. Do I wear that now so it seems like nothing has changed? Do I put on cute clothes? Do I put makeup back on? Would he notice one way or the other?

God, this sucks.

I wish I could text Lucy about this. But I can't. For one, I haven't admitted to her that she's right. Yes, she knows she is, but I'm not ready for the full "I told you so" speech. Also, it's the night before rehearsal dinner, and she and Bryce are having a quiet night, just the two of them.

Deciding to not overthink it, I grab a clean T-shirt and a pair of leggings then head back to the bathroom, where I give my hair a fluff and put on a minimal amount of makeup.

"Breathe," I quietly say to myself in the mirror. "It's just Cole. You've known him forever. Nothing is weird. Be natural. Be cool."

I let myself take one more deep breath before I head to the living room.

"Just in time," he says as he unpacks the unholy amount of Chinese food we ordered. "You get the drinks. I'll fire up the television."

Neither of us say anything for the first half hour of the show. I don't know why he isn't talking. Me? I'm trying to figure out what they're saying in their dragon language.

I'm also trying to ignore how freaking good Cole smells.

Do I try and talk? What would I say? I've never questioned talking to Cole about anything, and now all of a sudden I'm at a loss for words.

So I continue to not say anything. Instead, I lean down to grab an egg roll and accidentally bump arms with Cole, who is doing the same thing.

"Sorry," we both say at the same time, followed by awkward laughter.

"Is this weird?" I ask, because please let it not just be me.

He nods. "A little. When did it get weird between us?"

There are two answers to this question. I'm going to give just one. "I have a feeling it started about the same time I suggested you set up a date with Jessica."

Cole lets out a sigh. "Well that isn't going to be a problem anymore," he says.

"So what happened between you two?" I ask nonchalantly.

Cole grabs the remote and presses pause. "She's a nice girl. And she means well. But she isn't for me. She's a bit... intense. About a lot of things. She also kind of invited herself to Bryce and Lucy's wedding without asking me. That was the final straw."

My jaw drops. "No she didn't!"

He laughs. "She did. In front of Bryce and Lucy. When I asked her about it later that night, she said she just assumed I'd be taking her since we were an official couple and that she didn't know why it was a big deal."

"Oh..."

"Yeah. I had been thinking about ending things, but I didn't know if I was being too quick to judge. But that kind of sent me over the edge."

"I'm sorry," I say. "How'd she take it?"

Cole takes out his phone and tosses it to me. "You tell me."

I open up his text messages and holy shit... Jessica is not doing okay. And I'm talking more than playing sad song lyrics and eating ice cream. If I were Cole, I'd be worried about his tires.

> Jessica: So that's it? We're done? Just like that?

> Jessica: I can't believe you are breaking up with me. You're overreacting about the wedding thing. Let me explain.

> Jessica: I just wanted to go to the wedding with you. Don't you know how great for my career it would be if I was at their wedding? I even bought a new dress because I thought you'd like it and you'd finally want to be with me. Why don't you want to take me? Was I not good enough for you? I love you Cole! Why don't you love me?

"Wow. Love? Cole, I'm like, kind of worried about her," I say.

He looks over to see where I'm at. "Yes, at that point I did feel bad. But keep reading. The crazy is about to come out."

> Jessica: Do you know where I was last week when I couldn't see you? I was getting a tattoo. With your initials. It was going to be a surprise…

Oh shit...

> Jessica: Is there someone else? That's it. It's that roommate isn't it? I knew from the second I walked into your place she was more than what she said she was.

"Whoa! What did I do?"

Cole laughs. "Apparently you existed."

> Jessica: I mean, she's not even that pretty. And she's short. Does she even have a body underneath those T-shirts and sweatpants? I guarantee she doesn't have these.

"My eyes!" I yell as I toss the phone back to Cole. I suspected that Jessica's boobs were probably stellar compared to my barely B cups. But I really didn't need to see them for confirmation.

"Oh shit," Cole says. "I meant to delete that."

"Sure you did," I say, reaching for my dumplings. "Well, I'm sorry that it didn't work out. And, you know, for existing. But I think you dodged a bullet. She doesn't sound like a very nice person."

There. That was very diplomatic of me. Because what I wanted to say was, "Bitch, I'll fucking fight you in my sweatpants and your fake tits and red weave won't be able to help you."

But I didn't. I was nice. So two points for me.

"She definitely had two sides to her," Cole says. "Oh, and I don't agree with her."

"About what?"

"I happen to love your sweatpants."

Well, shit. I don't know if it's because it's coming from Cole, or I'm just not used to flattery, but that is the nicest and sexiest thing any man has ever said to me.

"Thanks," I say, suddenly feeling shy.

"You're welcome," he says. "I'm just glad I got out before it went any further. I can only imagine what she would have been like in the season."

"Likely accusing you of having different women in each city on the schedule."

"Or showing up at every hotel."

"You have a point. Though you can't say the woman wasn't head over heels for you."

Cole shakes his head. "True. Too bad she didn't check many of the boxes."

Well, now I'm intrigued. And also likely building myself up for heartache. But I don't see another time when this door will be open. So here goes literally *everything*.

"What are your boxes?"

Cole takes one of his hands and rakes it through his hair. "You want to know my boxes?"

"I do," I say, my courage amping up. "What would make Cole Campbell want to take a girl to his best friend's wedding?"

This makes him smile. "Well, she'd have to be smart. Funny. Someone not afraid to take a risk here and there. Someone who likes to go out but also embraces a night in on the couch. Someone who isn't afraid to speak her mind but also knows when to stop and listen to people. And she'd have to love football. Maybe a former cheerleader so she knows the basics of the game."

I nod, liking where this is going. "That's a good start."

"She'd have to get along with my family and friends. I can't imagine being with someone who doesn't fit seamlessly into my life. Oh, and she has to like kids."

I'm trying not to get my hopes up that he's talking about me, but I can't ignore the way his gaze is fixed on me as he's saying these words. His eyes are a piercing blue, and when they are looking at you, you feel like you're the only person in the world. And holy shit are they looking at me right now. I'm pretty sure a circus could be going on behind me and he wouldn't notice.

I swallow the growing lump in my throat. "Anything else?"

Cole inches closer to me and just with that little movement, I swear the temperature rises twenty degrees. His fingers are playing with a loose strand of my hair, and I'm ready to melt into a puddle on the ground.

"I'd love for her to have brown hair. Maybe be about a foot shorter than me so I could always help her reach stuff in the cabinets."

I lean into his hand, aching to feel his touch. "It's hard being short."

He smiles. "I'm sure it is. Oh, and she'd have to have the most beautiful blue eyes I've ever seen."

I bite my lip, aching to know what he's going to say or do next. "I'm a fan of blue eyes too."

Cole cuts the space between us down to nothing. His hand that was once just barely touching me is now fully holding onto my head, ready to bring me into him at any moment. His other hand is carefully tracing the line of my jaw. Up and down. Methodically. Like he's trying to memorize me.

"Brenna," he begins, letting his one hand drop down to hold mine. "Jessica was right about one thing." "Yeah?"

"You are more than just my friend. You're more than my temporary roommate. You're... well, I want you to be... what I'm trying to say is..."

I've always lived by the motto that if I want something, I have to go after it. Take it. I think that a person should do everything in their power to manifest their desire into existence. Because if they don't do it, no one else will.

So that's what I do. I put my hands on each side of Cole's face, and I kiss him. I kiss him because I know words can sometimes be hard. I know sometimes emotions are so big you don't know how to express them.

Plus, he's saying everything I'm thinking. Why not meet him in the middle?

Cole quickly follows my lead, lifting me up with ease so I'm on his lap. Now that I'm here, I never want to be anywhere else.

In all my twenty-five years, I never even had a glimmer of a thought about what kissing Cole would be like. That is, until three weeks ago. Since then it's practically all I've been thinking about.

Would it be weird? I mean, the man has been like a second

brother to me my entire life. Or would it be the best thing that has ever happened to me?

Well, now I know. And oh my God, it's the latter.

Our tongues are meeting in a perfect balance of give and take. His lips are soft and perfect as they begin trailing away from my lips and around my neck. And when he gives one last kiss on my forehead, I am melted into a sentimental puddle.

"So," he begins, brushing a hair away from my face with the gentlest of touches. "I don't have a date for the wedding this weekend."

I can't help but smile. "Actually, neither do I."

"Well, then. Would you like to be my date?"

I smile, giving him one more small kiss. "I would absolutely love to."

We share a smile before Cole leans back in. Only this time, he takes me back, pressing me into the couch. Cole is a big guy, and he's doing his best to keep his weight off me as he starts exploring with his mouth, but I want it. It's almost as if I *need* it.

I wrap my leg around his, wanting to feel him closer. He responds. He gently covers me a little more, and I can't help but gently roll my hips into him. His mouth feels too good. His touch feels too tender.

I don't want to rush this, but I also can't say no. And judging how Cole's kisses are becoming harder, I think he feels the same way.

I want to say stop, but how do you say no to the best feeling you've ever felt?

I start to wrap my legs around his body when the sound of his cell phone takes me away from the moment. But not for long, because Cole is kissing my body on top of my clothes, and I'm five seconds away from just telling him to rip them off.

But I don't. Because his phone goes off again. And again. And again.

I swear to God, someone better be dying.

"I guess I need to get that," Cole says reluctantly.

"You have five seconds," I say, already missing his lips.

He pushes himself up just enough to reach his cell phone. Just seconds into opening the screen, his eyes go wide, and he blinks so frantically I'm concerned he has something in his eye.

"What is it?" I ask, sitting up to see. And when he turns his phone so I can read the messages, I now understand the problem. Because I wouldn't have believed this if I didn't see it with my own two eyes.

> Jessica: I miss you.
>
> Jessica: If you take me back you won't regret it. I'll make you the happiest man ever.
>
> Jessica: Just imagine this in your bed every night.
>
> Jessica: Image…

"Oh my God!" I yell, squinting my eyes shut and putting my hands over my face for good measure. "How did she even put herself in that position?"

Cole furiously shakes his head. "I don't know but it's safe to say I need to block her number."

We look at each other, and I don't know why, but we both start laughing. Uncontrollably. It takes us a few minutes to calm down, and by the time we do, Cole has brought me back to his lap.

"I believe, before we were rudely interrupted, we were in the middle of something," I say.

Cole nods. "I do believe you're correct."

I'll never admit this, but Jessica's texts did serve a purpose that night. It slowed us down. Calmed us a bit. Instead of continuing wherever we were going, we spend the rest of the night slowly and lazily kissing, wrapped in each other's arms. I don't know exactly when we fell asleep, but I do know that it was the best sleep I've had in weeks.

I also now know there is nothing, and I mean nothing, like kissing Cole Campbell.

"YOU READY?"

The words seem like the right ones for a best man to ask the groom. They are also words that, at one point, I thought I'd never get the chance to say.

Bryce grins at me as we walk toward the altar, Luciano, Bryce's other groomsman, just behind us.

"I've never been more ready for anything in my life."

"It's a day that has always been meant to happen," Luciano says. "Now, let's go get you married."

I have to admit, this place is beautiful. It's at a historic house-turned-winery. The trees give the perfect amount of shade and almost serve as a barrier to the outside world. The white chairs are a stark contrast to the green surroundings. Between the trees and the flowers blooming, it's like Bryce and Lucy are getting married in a secret garden.

It's the perfect place for two of my best friends to finally start the next chapter of their story.

I hear the string quartet Lucy was able to find from one of the universities as we take our place at the front of the gathering. I double check my pocket to make sure I have the rings, which I do. I also feel the little piece of paper I found in my jacket when I put it on this afternoon. Somehow, Brenna snuck into the groom's room when we weren't there and slipped it in.

Remember to save me a dance. I'm the brunette in the gold dress. <3
Brenna

I've read it so many times now I've committed it to memory. Bryce nearly busted me reading it, but I somehow was able to convince him it was a note from the wedding planner telling us what time to be ready for pictures. He believed it. He's so happy today that I doubt he can think about anything else. Nothing's going to ruin his mood.

Except the news of Brenna and I. That could do it. For one, we've had one night together, and that was spent not talking. Sue me, but when the girl of your dreams won't stop kissing you, you let her. At some point, we fell asleep together on the couch, her little body curled up into mine.

It was perfect.

If I got my way, we would have spent all day yesterday continuing the kissing, and if I was lucky, maybe more. But the wedding craziness began bright and early. She had a mountain of things to do with Lucy, and I was on "keep Bryce busy" duty. And because of old traditions, Bryce spent the night at my place last night, and Brenna stayed with Lucy.

I love Bryce, but he is not the Donald I want to spend the night with.

Because of all of that, Brenna and I really haven't had a chance to talk about what we are, or what any of this is for us. So, until we are on the same page, and know that it's worth telling people, we are going to keep this between us.

We also know that telling Bryce won't be easy, and neither of us are about to do that at his wedding.

So for now this is a secret. But I don't mind. She's worth it.

"Here we go," Luciano whispers as the music changes.

The three of us straighten our shoulders as Bryce's mom is escorted down the aisle by one of our Fury teammates. Next is Mrs. Valenti, who is escorted by one of her nephews. Then comes Celine, and I don't have to look back to know that Luciano is beaming right now. Funny to think this was supposed to be him and Lucy at one point.

I can't let my mind linger on that for too long, because right behind Celine is Brenna, and everyone else just fades away.

I knew she was wearing a gold dress, but she wouldn't let me see it. The thin straps show off shoulders that I want to put my mouth on immediately. The neckline has a small scoop to it, not showing off anything, but teasing nonetheless. The dress is long and hugs every curve of her body. Her hair is wavy, sitting perfectly just below her shoulders.

She's a vision. I can't stop staring at her.

"You need to blink," Luciano whispers to me. "Or your eyes might fall out of your head."

I do as he says, realizing that if he is noticing I'm staring at Brenna, likely others are as well. That lasts a whole three seconds before I see Brenna give me a wink before she moves to stand in her spot.

I hear the music start to play for Lucy, but my mind is elsewhere. All of a sudden I can't get the vision out of my head of Brenna walking up the aisle in a white dress. She's glowing like an angel as she walks toward me. She's on Bryce's arm as he gives her away. That is, before he gives me one of his ridiculous man hugs before going to stand behind me as my best man.

Fuck...I have it bad. I mean, I knew I did, but if all it takes is a few looks and one night of making out on a couch to make me feel like this... I'm done for when it comes to Brenna Donald.

———

"Right here…one, two, three!"

I look at the camera for the umpteenth photo we've taken today. I never knew the bridal party was in so many of the photos. I also didn't realize that the normal, tough guy football player no-smile look wasn't appropriate for wedding photos. I wasn't trying to look angry, but apparently I was. Brenna whispered to me around picture twenty-five that if I tried to smile, she'd make it worth my while later.

I'm nothing if not goal-oriented.

"Okay, I think we're good out here," the photographer says as she scrolls back through her photos. "Bridal party, I hereby cut you loose. You can head to the cocktail hour. Bride and groom, let's head to the gazebo."

"You guys behave yourselves," Bryce says. "Don't get too drunk."

"We will be on our best behavior," Brenna says. "Now go take some more pictures with your wife."

Bryce looks at Lucy, smiling from ear to ear. "Wife. I like it."

The two of them walk toward the gazebo while Luciano and Celine waste no time heading to cocktail hour. I don't move, hoping that Brenna has the same idea as I do.

"I don't know about you, but I've never been one to be on my best behavior."

I smile as Brenna slips her arms around my waist. I quickly look to make sure we're alone as I turn around. We are. So I do what I've been dying to do all day—wrap Brenna into my arms and kiss the living hell out of her.

"Well then," she says when I release her lips. "And here I thought I was the troublemaker, out of the two of us."

"Oh, there's so much for you to learn about me," I say,

walking over to one of the chairs, where I promptly sit and bring Brenna to my lap.

She puts her hands around my neck. "I can't wait."

"Want to know what I can't wait for?"

"What's that?"

I lean in and quickly place a kiss on her shoulder. "The day when we don't have to hide."

"I know," she says, tipping her forehead so it's touching mine. "But this is for the best. At least for now."

She's right. It was the decision we came to, and it's the right one. Plus, Bryce and Lucy will be gone for two weeks on their honeymoon. That gives us fourteen days to make sure this is the real deal and to come up with a plan.

"At least I'll get to dance with you tonight," she says.

"I'm going to warn you, I'm a pretty good dancer," I say.

"Oh really? You've got moves?"

"More than you are prepared for."

Our lips connect again, and I know we shouldn't be doing this out in the open, but fuck, I can't help myself. She tastes too good. Her lips are too soft. Her body feels too right on mine. Unfortunately, our kiss doesn't get too deep, as we are interrupted by someone awkwardly clearing their throat, which immediately sends Brenna shooting right off my lap.

"Oh geez," Luciano says as Brenna tries to straighten her dress. "I'm so sorry."

"We...uh..." Brenna stutters before looking at me then back to Luciano. "It's not..."

This just makes him laugh. "Oh, Brenna, don't try to tell me what I didn't see. Plus, your man here was nearly drooling as you walked down the aisle."

I stand up and button my jacket, ignoring the drool comment. "What's up?"

"There's a woman at the reception asking for you. I told her you'd be there soon, but she wasn't happy with that answer and demanded I go get you. I feel like she also asks to speak to managers a lot. For the sake of not causing an incident, and also to escape her, I figured I'd come find you."

I give Brenna a bemused look because I have no idea who that could be. "Thanks, man. We'll be on our way."

"No problem," Luciano says. "And what I just saw? I didn't see anything. But I also think it's great. I also get why you're not saying anything. Your secret is safe with me."

"Thanks," I say as the three of us begin walking to the reception area. "We appreciate it. We're just waiting for the right time."

"No problem. I've been on the opposite side of having to deliver Bryce Donald news he might not like. I get it."

"Thanks, Luciano," Brenna says, giving him a quick hug. "Now, who in the heck is Demanding Debbie?"

We walk into the winery where the reception is being held and before Luciano can even point in her direction, I see exactly who he's talking about.

What the fuck is Jessica doing here?

"Are you kidding me?" Brenna says, though her voice is not as quiet as I think she thinks it is. "What in the actual wedding crasher hell is she doing here?"

Good question. "Let me go talk to her. See if I can get her out of here without a commotion."

I start walking away but feel Brenna next to me. "What are you doing?"

She looks up at me like I'm the crazy one. "You think I'm about to let you go over there and deal with a potential bunny boiler by yourself? Nope. Not happening."

"Bunny boiler?"

"*Fatal Attraction*. We'll put it on our movie list."

The fact that Brenna is having a seemingly normal conversation with me as she's shooting daggers with her eyes at Jessica is both impressive and slightly terrifying. However, it's not nearly as scary as Jessica turning toward us wearing a smile on her face like the damn Joker.

"There you are!" she says, quickly wrapping her arms around my neck to hug me. A hug I do not reciprocate.

"Jessica, what are you doing here?" I say, quickly removing her hands from me.

"I'm your date, silly," she says, turning to grab her flute of champagne. "Sorry I didn't make the ceremony. But I'm here now. Where are our seats?"

I turn to look at Brenna, who seems just as baffled as I am. Does Jessica not remember me breaking up with her? Is she choosing to ignore it? How do I handle this? Put a three-hundred-pound defensive tackle in my face, and I know exactly what to do. A redhead who won't accept a break up? No clue.

"We don't have seats, Jessica," I say as gently as I can. "You aren't my date. We broke up. Do you remember?"

In a reaction I wasn't expecting, she starts laughing. It has a shrill sound to it. It's kind of creepy. "Oh, silly. You didn't mean that. It was just a lovers' quarrel."

I blink a few times, because...*wow*. I'm speechless. I turn to look at Brenna for help, but all she's doing is mouthing the word "lovers."

She's going to pay for that later.

"Anyway," Jessica continues. "Where are we sitting? At the front table or maybe with the players and their girlfriends? I should start meeting them, you know. Before the season starts."

"Oh my God, what aren't you understanding?" Brenna whisper-yells. "Do you not realize that he broke up with you?"

Jessica's eyes get narrow as she focuses on Brenna. "I don't know what you're talking about, Breanne. Now, go be a dear and get some drinks for us. We're going to go and take a few pictures for my Instagram. I saw a beautiful gazebo while I was walking in!"

"Oh, hell no!" Brenna yells. Yeah, I knew the whisper yelling wasn't going to last. "One, I'm not your waitress. And two, you don't belong here. You weren't invited. He broke up with you. Get over it. Take your wannabe Ariel ass and get the fuck out of my brother's wedding before we call security."

I grab Brenna's hand, meaning to pull her back. Involuntarily, we link hands, which Jessica sees. How do I know this? It's the moment her face turns as red as her hair.

"I knew it was you!" Jessica shrieks, which definitely draws eyes. "No man lives with a woman and is just friends with her. You're the reason he left me! What do you have that I don't? I love him! I—"

"Whoa!" Bryce yells, coming in out of nowhere. "What seems to be the problem here?"

"Oh nothing!" Luciano says, running up next to me and separating Brenna and Jessica. "Just a little disagreement. Nothing to worry about."

"What are you doing here?" Lucy says to Jessica.

"What am I doing here?" Jessica yells, stepping back from Luciano. Every person in the venue has turned to see what is going on. "I thought he loved me! I thought we were going to get married. I'm meant to be a football player's wife! But no! He dumped me! And for her! She moved into his home and seduced him! She ruined my life!"

Jessica starts walking in Brenna's direction but Luciano and I each take an arm, holding her back. I'm also not sure about this, but I could swear Brenna is smiling right now.

Yeah, Trouble is grinning like it's her birthday.

"Oh, Jessica," Brenna coos, clearly stirring the pot. "I did nothing. This is all you. But maybe try wearing a pair of sweat-pants sometimes. I've heard he likes them."

"You bitch!"

Jessica flails between Luciano and me, but stops at the sight of two security guards.

"Let's go, ma'am."

"What in the fuck?" Bryce says as we watch the security guards guide Jessica away. "I knew she was crazy, but Brenna breaking you two up? She really is a nut."

"Yup," I say, taking a deep breath to regain composure. "Freaking hilarious."

As if nothing happened, everyone goes back to what they were doing five minutes ago.

Except me and Brenna. We just stand there staring at each other.

"Did that really just happen?" I ask.

"Yeah," she says. "I can't believe she showed up."

"I can't believe you egged her on like that."

Brenna shrugs as she takes a glass of wine from one of the waiters. "It's almost like you haven't known me my whole life."

I take a step closer to her so only she can hear what I'm about to say. "You know there are about three things that you said that you're going to have to pay for later?"

She smiles at me and ever so sneakily grazes her hand against my chest. "Only three? I must be slipping. Now let's go have some fun. Because ding dong, the crazy bitch is gone."

WHEN YOU'RE twenty-five and single, the wedding scene starts becoming repetitive. Especially if you've been to as many as I have in the past few years.

You go. You eat a meal that's either a chicken dish that just tried too hard or a steak that's overcooked. Sometimes you'll get a pasta plate you can stomach, but that's only because you know you need the carbs to help soak up the liquor you're about to drink. You drink watered-down vodka sodas, dance to one Bruno Mars song after another, and if you're lucky, the bride skips the bouquet toss. By the end of the night, you hopefully have a good buzz, start dancing a little more provocatively because the music has changed once the grandparents leave, and before you know it, you're singing "Don't Stop Believing" in a circle before being told that you don't have to go home, but you can't stay here.

Oh, and of course, when you're single, you skip the slow dances.

This is the recipe for every wedding.

Except for tonight.

I don't know if it's because I'm in the wedding party, or if it's because my brother and my best friend are finally starting their life together, or if because I've already snuck off twice tonight to kiss Cole, but this is the best wedding I've ever attended.

And that's not even counting the Jessica incident. That was just a bonus.

"Hey girl, why you sitting here all alone?"

My eyes go wide as I take in a whiff of a cologne I never wanted to smell again.

"Dexter," I say as he takes an uninvited seat next to me. "How are you?"

"Doin' my thing. How you been? You haven't hit me up in a while."

No shit, Sherlock. Is he that dumb? Did he think I'd actually call him again? Does he not remember me yelling at him about his small dick? What is it tonight with people forgetting being rejected?

"I'm...okay," I say, frantically looking for anyone I know to get me out of this conversation. "Are you having fun?"

"Not really," he says, leaning in closer. Oh God, that cologne is horrible. "Not many single ladies here tonight. I was hoping you'd join me on the dance floor and turn my night around."

"She won't be doing that."

For a mammoth of a man, Cole can be quite stealthy.

"Campbell," Dexter says, standing up. Though that doesn't do much; Cole still towers over him. "I believe the lady can speak for herself."

"You're right, I can," I say, standing up and immediately looping my arm around Cole's. "And I believe they just called the wedding party to the dance floor. Have a good time tonight, Dexter. Maybe go try the champagne. I hear if you keep drinking it, you'll eventually like it."

Cole and I walk to the dance floor, where Luciano and Celine, along with Bryce, Lucy and all of the parents, are already dancing. To play it cool, Cole and I keep our distance while dancing, even though every part of me wants to lay my head on his shoulder and let the words and melody of Etta James flow through me.

"Thank you for saving me from Dexter," I say.

"I don't care that he's my teammate, I hate that guy."

"No, you don't," I say, inching closer to him. "But thank you for saving me."

"Yes I do," he says, pulling me in even closer and bringing our joined hands over his heart. "Have I told you how beautiful you look?"

"Only ten times."

I look up at Cole, who is smiling down at me in a way I don't think I've ever seen before. His smile is soft and genuine. From a man who is always so serious, this smile hits me straight in the heart. His thumb is slowly making small brushes on the small of my back, but I feel like he's touching me all over.

How have I known this man for as long as I have and not seen what is right in front of me? I was so stubborn for so long, telling myself that he was just my brother's best friend.

Well, that ends now. I don't care how long I've known him or how long it has taken me to get here, no man has *ever* looked at me this way. And I'm not going to give that up no matter what anyone thinks.

Because *I* think there is something special here. Something I've been chasing my whole life.

And it was right in front of me the whole time.

"Cole?"

"Yeah?"

I want to ask him when we can take off, or at least find a

dark corner so I can kiss him the way I'm aching to right now, but we're interrupted by the couple of the evening.

Assholes.

"Whoa there!" Bryce yells. "Getting a little too close to my sister."

We both quickly step back, not realizing that at some point, we drifted so close together you could barely slide a piece of paper between us. And that the music has changed to some sort of upbeat group dance.

"Sorry," Cole says.

"It's okay, I know you didn't mean anything by it. I mean, you probably hate me already for making you dance with my sister all night."

"It's been torture," he deadpans.

"I figured as much. Anyway, come on, we're going to get a team photo."

Lucy walks over and grabs my hand. "Good. You boys head that way. I need Brenna's assistance in the ladies room."

Bryce grabs Cole while Lucy takes my hand and whisks us in opposite directions. I look back, trying to get one more glimpse of Cole. To my surprise, he's also looking back. And just before he's out of range, he sends me a wink, which hits me just as hard as that small smile did just a few minutes earlier.

"I'm waiting," Lucy singsongs as we enter the ladies room.

"For what?" I ask, hoping she's not going down the conversation path I think she is. "Because I'm waiting for a lot. Fat-free pizza. A woman president. All the streaming services in one convenient location."

"Don't be a smartass," Lucy says as she signals for me to sit on the couch in the ladies' room. "Are you ready to admit that I'm right and you have a thing for Cole?"

"I know you're the bride, and this is your day, but have you had a little too much to drink?"

"I've had two sips of champagne so cut the crap. I saw you two. You were trying to hide it, but you can't hide it from me. I know both of you too well. It melted my heart. It also made me want to jump up and down and cheer. So just say it, are you and Cole together?"

I don't say anything, because I have no idea how I want to play this. On one hand, this is Lucy. My best friend. The woman who has been there for me every day for the past five years. She's also now my sister. My family. She knows me better most days than I know myself. So of course I want to tell her every little detail about how crazy I am over this man.

The only problem is that Cole and I promised that we were going to tell Bryce together. We also want to make sure this is real before we do. No sense in poking the bear if he doesn't need poked.

He's going to freak out when he finds out. And we don't know in what way. And even though I love her and trust her implicitly, I don't want her to have to lie to her new husband. She shouldn't have to do that.

"No," I say, because, in some sort of weird justification in my mind, we aren't. At least, we haven't said it out loud.

Lucy gives me a look that screams that she clearly doesn't believe me. "So you're going to tell me with a straight face that there is nothing going on between you two? No flirting? No touches? Nothing."

I swallow because *shit*—I could justify the last lie. So I do the one thing I can think to do.

I grab her hand and start tugging her toward the door.

"How about we get you back to your reception?" My plan almost works until I open the door and see Cole. Waiting for me outside the ladies' room.

Lucy looks back and forth between the two of us, and even though we haven't been caught doing anything, I feel guilty as hell. Judging by the fact Cole is staring at the floor, he does too.

She *so* knows.

"All right you two, listen here," Lucy says in her best mom voice. "I don't know what exactly this is or what you two are doing. But I know enough to know that I freaking called this a year ago. I can tell. I know a guilty look when I see it. My husband might be a little dense on the subject, but you can't fool me."

"Lucy—"

"Stop!" she says, putting her hand up and stopping whatever Cole was about to say. "Let me get this out. What I was going to say was since you two are both stubborn mules and won't say words out loud for God knows what reason, I'm going to pretend I don't know that you two haven't been giving each other the googly eyes all night."

"Tha—"

"But!" Lucy says, cutting me off this time. "I won't lie to him. I won't tell him, but if he asks, I'm not going to lie."

"Thank you." I say. "We just—"

"No!" Lucy shushes me. "The less I know the less I eventually have to admit. So this conversation is going to stop right now."

I attack Lucy in a hug, fighting back tears. She's really the best.

"Thank you," I say. "We just need some time to figure a few things out."

"I know," she says. "Can I now say I was right?"

I step back, unknowingly into the waiting arm of Cole, who brings me into his side. "Yeah. Yeah, you can."

CHAPTER 15

COLE

ONE OF THE most memorable games Bryce and I played in college was a six-overtime nail biter that ended with us winning by running one of the craziest plays we ever drew up. It was a nearly five-hour game from which I never thought I'd emotionally, or physically, recover.

Somehow, I'm even more drained right now after Lucy and Bryce's wedding than I was after that marathon of a game.

"How could one day make you so tired?" I ask, quickly unlacing these uncomfortable shoes and kicking them somewhere they hopefully get lost forever.

"High heels are the devil, likely invented by a man, and I hope this pair in particular burn in hell," Brenna chimes in, throwing said high heels across the room before falling back into my chest.

I wrap my arms around her as she nuzzles into me. This. This is the moment I've been wanting all day. Just to be able to sit back, relax, and get lost in the feeling of my girl in my arms.

Hell, if we never move from right here, I'd die a happy man.

"I can't believe they're finally married," I say as my fingers gently stroke up and down her arm.

"I can't believe your crazy ex-girlfriend showed up."

I let out a groan, which only makes Brenna laugh. "Can we please never talk about that again?"

"Oh, I don't think so," Brenna says while she gets up and situates herself across my lap. "I don't think we're going to forget that one for a very long time."

"Well then, maybe I can distract you."

I wrap my arms around her center and bring her to me, pressing my lips against hers. Yes, we were able to sneak a few of these in during the day today, but it still feels like too long since I've kissed her the way I want to. Our tongues meet as I slowly lay her back on the couch, careful not to put all of my body weight on her. Which is hard as hell when one of her legs begins to wrap around me, pulling me closer.

"Brenna." I don't mean for that to come out as a groan, but I can't help it. The woman is not only trying to wrap herself around me like a vine, she's also kissing a spot on my neck that I didn't realize had a direct line to my dick.

"What?" Her reply comes out as innocent, but there is nothing innocent about this woman.

"If you don't stop that now, I can't promise I'm going to behave myself."

"Who said anything about behaving?"

Oh this woman...I've known for years she was nothing but trouble. I just didn't know how much I loved trouble until right now.

I jump off the couch and scoop her up into my arms. She's nothing but giggles as I hurry down the hall to my bedroom.

"What's so funny?"

"Someone's in a hurry."

Does she not know that I've been waiting for this moment for three fucking years? Three years of dreaming. Three years of waiting. Three years of trying to make myself believe there was someone else out there for me *not* named Brenna Donald.

It was all for nothing. It's her. It's always been her. It will always be her.

I gently place her down on the bed, but I don't follow. Not yet, at least. Because while I would love nothing more but to get lost in this woman until the sun comes up, I have to make sure she knows where I'm at.

"Is something wrong?" she asks.

I stand up next to the bed, keeping her hands in mine. "No, but, before we go on, we need to make sure we're on the same page."

She gives me a confused look. "About?"

"This. You know what this means, right?"

She nods, but right now, I need more than that.

"I need you to say it, Brenna. I need you to know that once this happens, there's no going back. At least not for me. This? You and me? I'm all in. I've waited so long for this. For you. For the chance of an *us*. I don't know what the future holds, but I know damn sure that if this happens right now, the future— our future—begins right now. So what do you say, Trouble? You in?"

I let out a breath as the last words come out. I don't know where all of that came from. I'm not that guy. I'm not the guy who puts his heart on the table or wears his emotions on his sleeve. Apparently when it comes to Brenna, all the rules are out the fucking window.

Just when I begin to panic because she hasn't answered me yet, she slowly raises herself to her knees and cups my face in her hands, begging me with her eyes to look at her. As if I could look anywhere else right now.

"I'm all in. On one condition."

Shit, at this point she could ask me for the stars, and I'd figure out a way to get them for her. "Anything."

"That you'll catch me when I fall. Because while you've

been waiting, I've been searching. I didn't know I was looking for you. But I was looking. I just didn't know I was looking in the wrong places. And now that I've found it—found you—I feel myself falling. I feel myself falling hard. And I'm scared. I'm scared in the best way possible. So, all I ask is that you catch me."

"Sweetheart," I say, picking her up so she is now standing in front of me. "That is one thing you will never have to worry about."

I lean down and bring her lips to mine, sealing our words with a kiss. I know there is still a lot to figure out. Frankly, that part terrifies me. But that's not tonight's worry. All I'm going to think about tonight is the fact that the woman of my dreams is here with me, and she wants this as much as I do.

The kiss starts slow but quickly speeds up. Brenna's hands are frantically trying to undo the buttons of my dress shirt and the knot in my tie. Our tongues are searching and begging for more while my hands begin to lower the thin straps of her dress.

The second they are off, it only takes one little push to make the gold dress fall to her feet. I stop the kiss, but only because I am fucking stunned to find her completely naked.

"Are you meaning to tell me that all day you've had nothing on underneath this?"

She shrugs, a devilish smile gracing her beautiful mouth. "I was hopeful you'd like this surprise."

"You are fucking trouble," I groan. "And I fucking love trouble."

I hear nothing but sweet giggles as I pick her up and take the two steps necessary to lie her back on the bed. And as much as I'd love to lie next to her and kiss every inch of smooth skin before me, that can wait.

I rip my tie off and toss it to the side as I lower myself to my knees. Like she can read my mind, Brenna slowly opens her legs for me. I have to remember to breathe when I see her lying in front of me. I always knew she was gorgeous. Hell, I've had to look at her every day of my life and keep my hands—and thoughts—to myself. But now? Now that she's lying here and giving herself to me like this? I don't have words.

"God, you are so fucking beautiful," I say before gently placing a kiss just above her knee. Her skin is just as soft as I imagined as I slowly kiss my way up to my desired destination.

"Fuck," I groan before letting myself take a long, slow lick around her wetness. I've barely touched her, and she's already soaked.

"Cole."

My name on her tongue does something to me that I've never felt before. Every cell in me leaps at the sound. It also spurs me on because I want to hear it again. I want to hear it every day for the rest of my life.

I grab her legs and throw them over my shoulders, diving into her pussy like this is about to be my last supper. My sudden change in pace makes her stiffen for just a second, but the second my tongue hits her clit, I feel her relax back into the bed.

Good. Let her relax. That gives me the ability to take what I please. To savor every drop. I've thought about this moment no less than a thousand times, and I'm not about to let a second go to waste.

There's only one problem. My brain and my heart want me to take my time. But my cock? The one that's hard as a rock right now and somehow growing harder with Brenna running her hands through my hair? It wants more.

And now.

"More," Brenna says, apparently in agreement with my dick. "I need more, Cole."

What the lady wants, the lady gets.

I pick up my pace, letting my tongue work in circles as I push a finger inside her. Her hips begin to press into my face, which only heightens my excitement. I insert a second, letting them explore for just the right spot as I suck on her clit.

"Yes!" she yells, her hands now all but pulling my hair out as my fingers work in tandem with my mouth. It's only a few more seconds of this before she explodes for me, her body shaking as I give one more kiss to her drenched center before slowly bringing her down.

Fuck. That was... I don't have words. I'm also not sure I have any hair, either.

I don't care, though. Let her pull. Let her yank. Hell, let her leave bald spots on my head. They'd be a badge of honor. I've never felt like this before. And I never want to go back to a time when I didn't know what a true win feels like.

EVERY INCH of my body is sore. My feet are aching. Hell, even my lips are swollen and chapped.

And I've never felt better and more relaxed in my entire life.

I'm going to name it the Cole Campbell Effect.

Because holy hell does that man have an effect on me.

I haven't opened my eyes yet, because I haven't fully committed this feeling to memory, and I want to remember this until I'm old and gray. His pillows and sheets are just as soft as they were last time I was here. The scent of his cologne—the one that drives me crazy in the best way possible—is hitting all the right senses.

But the best part? His arms around me, holding me like I might run away.

Not a chance in hell.

"You really need to quit doing that," Cole says, his voice a low and gravelly mumble in my ear.

"Doing what?"

He releases one arm from his hold on me, sliding it over to give one of my cheeks a good squeeze. Because yes, my ass might or might not have been rubbing against his growing erection.

"This. You know what you're doing, and it's not fair."

I don't open my eyes, but that doesn't stop the smile forming on my face. "I have no idea what you're talking about."

I have no warning before those strong arms lift me, pulling me up and over his body so I'm straddling him.

How did he do that?

And can he do it again?

"No idea what you're doing?" he asks as I feel his now hard dick nestled between my legs.

"How was I supposed to know you'd be so easy to wake up in the morning?"

I lean down, needing to feel his lips on mine. I don't remember when we fell asleep, but I do know that it was just about the perfect night.

"Mmmm, good morning to you," he says, locking his hands behind me. "Did you get any sleep?"

I place my hands under my chin, which Cole doesn't seem to mind. "A little."

Cole yawns. "Me too."

"Want me to put on clothes and let you get some sleep?"

His hands slide down from my back to my ass, his hands cupping one cheek in each. "Don't you fucking dare."

For being a big guy, Cole is surprisingly agile. And quick. That is just one of the many ways this man surprised me last night.

And now, apparently, this morning.

Cole quickly rolls me over and completely covers me while also kissing me like we didn't just spend all night tangled in each other. I don't mind, though; being buried under Cole is my new favorite place to be.

"What are you doing?" he asks, breaking the kiss that I thought was going very well.

"Huh?" I'm not even being coy. I'm genuinely confused.

"You keep doing that," he says, signaling to his arms. "I don't mind. It's just not something I'm used to."

I look at where he signaled, and apparently without even thinking, I've let my hands wander up his arms before taking hold of his biceps.

I can't help it. All I can imagine is them pinning me down. Or against a wall. Or holding me down as we sneak in a quickie someplace we shouldn't.

The possibilities are endless.

Arm test? He doesn't even need one. He's like the arm test cheat code.

"Is this the point where I admit my first semi-embarrassing thing to you?"

This gets me a soft laugh before a quick kiss on the nose. "I doubt it's embarrassing, whatever it is."

"You say that now." I take a breath, though I don't let go. "I kind of have a thing for arms."

He lifts an eyebrow. "Arms?"

"Yes. Specifically biceps."

"Really?"

I shrug. "What can I say? It's my thing."

"And you find mine…"

I bite my bottom lip, giving his arm one more squeeze. "They are one of my favorite parts of you."

"Oh really," he says, leaning in to kiss my neck. "What else do you like about me?"

This playful side of Cole was not one I expected. If you know Cole, you know him as serious. An old soul in a twenty-something body. The "dad" of the Nashville Fury because he's always the one who makes sure that business is handled.

Then there's this Cole. The playful one. The tender one,

who opened his heart to me last night. The one who is willing to fight a steep battle for us to be together.

I like that I'm the only one who knows this Cole. I hate that it took me so long to get here, but now that I am, I'm not going to take it for granted.

"Well, let's see," I say, letting my hands begin to explore. "I like your lips."

He moves his way up my neck to give me a kiss. "Well, that's good, because mine like yours too."

"I like your butt."

This makes him laugh. "My butt?"

"Hell yeah," I say, reaching around giving each cheek a squeeze. "I like that my man has some cake."

"Your man?"

I didn't even think about those words when I said them. But now that I have, I don't regret it.

"Is that a problem?"

"Not at all," he says as he begins to smile. God, I love it when he smiles. He doesn't do it a lot. In fact, I grew up thinking he didn't know how. So when he does? It melts me every single time. "You have no idea how long I've wanted to hear those words out of your mouth."

Oh now I'm curious. "How long?"

He shakes his head. "Nope. Not admitting that."

"Why," I say, wrapping my legs around his, trying to entice him a bit. "If you tell me, I promise you'll be rewarded."

Cole moves off me slightly, propping his head up with his arm. His other hand is gently stroking the outline of my face and if I wasn't so invested in this topic, I'd probably fall back asleep.

"The night we almost got arrested."

My eyes go wide. "In Clemson?"

He lets out a sigh. "Yes. In Clemson."

I can't believe this. That was just over three years ago. "Was this before or after I puked in the bushes? Or after the cop let us go because he had to go break up a party?"

"After the bushes, before releasing us," he says, pulling me in closer to him. "I took you out that night to make sure you were safe. I never expected it to be the night I realized that you were it for me."

I bite my lip, because it's all I can do to keep the tears at bay. That night seems like a lifetime ago. All these years and not a word?

"Why didn't you ever say anything?"

"Because... I don't know. At first I thought it would pass. I was off to the league and you were back in Laurel Heights. I thought it was just a crush and I'd get over it. Interesting fact, you are not that easy to get over."

"I don't know what to say." And that's the truth. I had no clue.

"Don't say anything," he says, placing a small kiss on my forehead. "We're here now."

"Yeah. But now I'm going to beat myself up thinking about all the time I was an oblivious idiot."

"Hey," he says, bringing me back on top of him. "I didn't want you to know. I wasn't ready. I was scared, and if I'm going to be honest, I still am. I think we both know what we have to figure out the second we leave the bubble that is this room. All I know is that you? Here? In my bed with me? Me getting to hold you and kiss you and call you mine? I don't care if I waited ten years for this. I'm here now. And this is the moment our future begins."

My lips are on Cole's the second he says that last word. For one, that was the most romantic thing I've ever heard in my entire life, and two, if I don't kiss him immediately I'm pretty sure I'm going to start crying.

Because who says that? Who truly means things like that? Cole. That's who.

I feel him grow hard again underneath me, which only makes my kisses more furious. Am I sore from last night? Yes. Is that going to stop me from having this man again? Hell no.

"You sure?" he asks, as if he was reading my mind. That or he was picking up on the signals I was clearly giving as I was rubbing my bare pussy against his cock.

"Mmmhmm," I mumble, letting my mouth trail across his jawbone over to his ear. I found a spot just underneath his neck that I think is his kryptonite.

"You really are nothing but trouble," he says, reaching over to his nightstand to grab a condom.

I take it from his hand as I sit up on him. I love being on top of him like this. He's so big and commanding in stature. But when I'm like this, and he's looking up at me with that fire in his eyes? I feel like the most powerful, beautiful, sexual being on the planet.

I rip the condom open with my teeth as I slide just far enough back to be able to roll it on to him. "I thought you said you liked trouble."

With my last stroke, he flips me over, pinning my arms above my head. "I'm starting to think I like it a little too much."

I wrap my legs around his, silently pleading him to enter me. "Show me."

He enters me with one thrust, which nearly takes my breath away. Maybe one day I'll get used to his size, but it won't be today. Secretly I hope I never do, because this man fills me like I never have been filled before.

Last night Cole took his time. And it was perfect. Exactly what a first time together should be. I felt adored and cherished and had orgasms that made me see stars.

But right now? Now I don't want to be slow and sweet. I

want him to fuck me so hard I feel him inside me the rest of the day. And judging by the way he's still holding my hands down while his thrusts are getting harder, he wants that, too.

"Fuck me, Cole," I say, wrapping my legs tighter around him. "Show me what kind of trouble I can be."

My attempt at dirty talk does the trick, because I see the second the fire turns up a notch in his eyes.

He lets go of my hands, but that's only so he can bring my legs up to his shoulders. Which, holy shit... That angle is hitting something that I didn't know existed.

"Yes." I let the word spill out of my mouth because no matter what he asked me right now, that would be my answer. His thrusts are the perfect blend of hard and fast. But I want more. I need more.

I let my hands trace up my torso until I reach my breasts. I watch Cole as he watches me play with myself, his eyes literally now burning.

"Fucking trouble," he groans, his thrusts becoming faster. "Is that how you want to play it?"

I nod, giving each nipple one last twist. "Show me what you got."

I feel like this whole time I've been playing with fire. That Cole is a spark that's one splash of gasoline away from becoming an inferno. Apparently, those words I just said are all the gas he needs to explode, because before I know it I'm on all fours and Cole is fucking me like a man on a mission.

And his mission is to make me scream.

He's about to get his wish. I can barely hold myself up, but I meet him thrust for thrust. I feel my orgasm building, and I am so close. Judging by the way he's gripping my hips, he's not too far behind either.

"Brenna," he groans.

"Yes, Cole!" I scream. I don't mean to, but the second I

opened my mouth, he hits the spot that sends me over the edge. My arms give out, and I sink back into the bed as I feel him push into me one more time. It's not long before he joins me, his big body covering me as we lie there in sated bliss.

Cole quickly tosses the condom into the trash next to the bed as he brings me into his arms, kissing me any place he can reach. How do we go from fucking to cuddling in five seconds? And how is it absolutely perfect?

Because it's Cole. The man of many layers. The man who one minute is the tough, badass football player and the next minute the teddy bear. The man who can go from grump to comedian at the drop of a dime.

The man I have a feeling I'm already falling for...way too fast.

"SO ARE we going to talk about it?"

Brenna doesn't acknowledge my words. Instead, she just keeps trying to get a glass on the top shelf that she knows she can't reach.

I walk up behind her, forcing myself to ignore her nakedness under my T-shirt, and easily grab it for her.

"You could just ask for help."

"But what if you aren't here one day and I need it?" she asks. "I have to be able to do it for myself."

"Has anyone told you that you're stubborn?"

She just shrugs as she takes the glass, rises up on her tiptoes to give me a kiss on the chin, which is the highest she can reach without me leaning down. "I like to say I'm independent."

"Sure, we'll go with that."

Brenna heads to the refrigerator to pour herself some juice. And I don't know what else she's trying to get, but it requires her bending over. The little minx is trying to distract me so we don't have to talk about the topic we know we have to.

"That's not going to work," I say as I take a seat at the kitchen island. But I might be lying.

She turns back to look at me, but doesn't bother standing up. "Whatever do you mean?"

"Do you really think tempting me with your bare ass is going to distract from the fact that we need to talk about the Bryce situation?"

She lets out a defeated sigh and closes the refrigerator. "A girl could hope."

"Come on," I say, standing back up. "The quicker we do this, the quicker you can get back to seducing me."

"Fine," she says, making her way to the living room and snuggling into "her" spot. I take a seat next to her and reach for her hand. I know if I get any closer we won't talk about a damn thing. But I can't not touch her. Now that I have, I can't imagine not touching her at every chance I get. "Do we think he has any idea?"

I shake my head. "He didn't give me any sort of hint yesterday that he did. And that's even after Lucy gave us her lecture. Your brother is clueless."

"Which is probably going to make things worse when we do tell him."

I let out a sigh, because yeah, this is not going to be easy. "Not only is he going to be pissed that you're my girlfriend, but the fact that I kept it a secret is going to only add fuel to his fire."

Brenna smiles and bites her lip in that cute way she does.

"What are you smiling at?"

"You called me your girlfriend."

Leave it to Brenna to turn a serious conversation into a moment where all I want to do is scoop her up and kiss the hell out of her. "Don't distract me."

"What? It was a significant moment. I wanted to make sure we properly acknowledged it."

I lean in and give her a kiss, though I fight the urge to start outright making out with her on the couch. "There. We've acknowledged it."

"Fine," she groans. "And you're right. Bryce is going to flip for many reasons. The problem is, I don't know what is going to set him off more. Since I moved here and he got sober, he has really tried to be more involved in my life. Which is great, but he tends to take it overboard. So when you combine that with the fact that his sister and his best friend are together, and that we hooked up behind his back, he's going to blow a gasket. Add on to that that you're his teammate and it's going to freak him the fuck out."

"You're right. He has this weird stance about the unwritten rules of football. And of course number one is don't fuck a teammate's sister." I let out a defeated sigh and throw my head back. "Is there any way we tell him this without him blowing up?"

"I doubt it," Brenna says. "You saw how he reacted yesterday at the wedding when we danced with each other. He didn't even think it was feasible. It's so far off his radar I don't think he's even comprehended it."

"He hasn't," I add. "One time I tried to hypothetically bring up the idea of you and me. He had no clue I was fishing for information. It was the night you were out with Dexter. He told me that not one teammate was good enough for you. I asked if I was. He all but laughed in my face."

"What an idiot," she says, now moving so that she is snuggled into my side. I quickly wrap my arms around her, loving the feel of her back to my front. "Well I hope you know, however we tell him, he's going to have to get over it. I'm my own woman. And you are a grown man who can see whoever he wants. Yes, it might take some getting used to, but he's going to have to suck it up. He might rule the football field, but he doesn't rule our lives."

God, I could kiss the hell out of her right now. "I couldn't agree more."

She turns to look up at me. "I hear a 'but' coming…"

"But we still need to find a way to gently tell him and try to minimize the damage as much as possible."

"You're right," she says, grabbing my arms and wrapping them tighter around her. "Any ideas on how to do that?"

"Not a clue," I say.

We sit in silence for a few minutes, both of us trying to figure out how to do this with the smallest amount of blood and the fewest casualties.

"What if we do it in private? Have him and Lucy over for dinner one night and just tell him?"

"No. Private means he could throw and break stuff. Which then leaves a public setting?"

Now it's my turn to shake my head. "Less chance of him causing a scene, but more of a risk of all of this coming out in social media. With our luck, someone would be ready there with a camera."

Brenna wiggles her way out of my hold, only to climb onto my lap. "How about this: We have two weeks before they get back from their honeymoon. The only people who know are Luciano, and now probably Celine, and they won't tell. So let's take these two weeks and figure us out while also taking our time to make sure we tell Bryce in the best way possible. That way, we know exactly what we're fighting for. He can't argue with us if we show him just how much we're both in this."

Two weeks. While I don't need time to know that she's it for me, I get what she's saying. If we sit Bryce down and tell him all the ways we work, backed by actual time spent together, maybe he'd be a little more willing to see things from our perspective.

Or maybe not. Either way, it's better than any other idea we've had.

"Two weeks, huh?" I say, pulling her a bit closer.

"Yup," she says. "So, what should we do with that time?"

I smile. "I have an idea."

"And what would that be?"

I pick her up, only to lay her back down on the couch. "First, I'm going to kiss you for a very long time. Then tonight, I'm taking you out on your last first date."

She raises her eyebrows. "Confident much?"

"Oh Brenna," I say, kissing my way across her neck. "You have no idea how confident I am."

WHERE IS Lucy when I need her?

Oh, right. On her honeymoon. With my brother. So even if I wanted to call her to properly freak the fuck out about tonight, I can't.

And oh boy, do I need to.

I usually have a solid panic before any date. And those are with men with whom I have little to no hope that things will go past the first date.

But this is Cole. COLE. Cole Campbell. Yes, I know we've already slept together. Yes, I know that he has seen me naked from every angle. But when it comes to a date, there is so much more to it than just sex. This is the time where we really find out if we're good together beyond the bedroom.

Believe me, we have that part covered.

And that's just one of the problems. Here's another one: normally before a date, I'd spread out every piece of clothing I own across my bedroom and overanalyze every outfit, all in an effort to find the perfect thing to wear.

Can I still do that? Sure. I mean, I did. It just feels a little different knowing the man you're trying to impress is right across the hall. And I don't know how much I can impress when I was told to wear something "comfortable and warm."

Considering my feet are still hurting from being in heels all day yesterday, I'm completely okay with that request.

I give myself one final look in the standup mirror I had to buy because—shocker—Cole does not own a mirror besides the one over the sink in the bathroom. I frown down at my outfit. I think I like it. Cute sweater that I can still get away with despite it being spring, paired with leggings and short booties. I kept my makeup natural and my hair straight.

Is this the look of a girl who potentially might be going out on her last first date? Who knows. But the thought of it being a possibility makes me smile in a way I don't remember smiling before.

Maybe this is another part of the Cole Campbell Effect.

"Here we go," I say to myself as I exit my bedroom. Cole isn't in his room, but I can smell his cologne lingering in the hall. I follow it like a trail of breadcrumbs to the living room, where I find him sitting on the arm of his chair.

How dare this man tell me to "keep it comfortable" while he has the audacity to sit there and look like a whole meal. He's wearing a white button down with the sleeves rolled up. If that arm porn wasn't enough, the jeans he's wearing hug every muscle of his tree trunk thighs but would never be considered tight or skinny jeans. His hair is styled, which he only does on special occasions, and then there's the cologne. The scent that I would follow to the ends of the earth.

Before I can get a word out, probably because my jaw is on the floor, Cole takes the few steps he needs to be only inches from me. His hand gently pushes my hair behind my ear before he brings me in for one of the sweetest kisses I've ever received in my life.

"You look amazing," he says.

"Not too shabby yourself."

"I was going for snazzy."

I laugh, remembering back to that night just a few weeks ago. Was it really that short a time ago? "Well, snazzy has been achieved."

"Good," he says, taking my hand and walking me to the door. "You ready?"

"I am. Can I ask where we're going?"

He shakes his head. "You'll find out soon enough."

We take the few steps we need to get to the elevator. But when it opens, I get my first surprise of the night.

"We're going up?" I ask as Cole pushes the button to go to the roof. "I didn't know we had access."

"Most people don't," he says, a sly smile forming on his handsome face. "Then again, most people don't hook up the building manager with Fury tickets for every home game."

"I like it," I say, stepping in front of him just so I can wrap my arms around his waist. I gave up trying to go around his neck. I barely reach his shoulders. "What other tricks do you have up your sleeve?"

He leans down, giving me a quick kiss on my forehead. "Just wait and see."

It doesn't take long for the elevator to make its way to the roof. In all the months I've lived here, either with Bryce or Cole, I've never been up here.

Though I doubt it looks like this on normal nights. The entire roof is strung with white bulb lights, giving it a soft glow as we look out over Nashville.

"Cole," I whisper, awestruck.

"Just wait," he says, guiding me toward the north edge of the building. When we get a few steps closer, it takes every ounce of willpower in me not to stop and cry. Because before me is a red and white checkered picnic blanket, a cooler, and enough takeout boxes to feed the Fury. It looks like something out of a Hallmark movie.

"What is all this? I ask.

"Well, I thought I could take you out for dinner, but I'm a bit selfish, and I wasn't ready to share you with the public yet. Then I remembered you saying you hadn't tried hot chicken yet. And I'm sorry, but if you're going to call Nashville home, you need a go-to chicken place. It will make our takeout nights much easier. So, I took the liberty of ordering chicken from five different places around town. That way you can try each and see what you like."

Okay, now I'm going to cry. Over fried chicken.

Who does this? Who remembers a specific detail in a lengthy rant that happened more than a month ago and turns it into a storybook first date?

This man. That's who.

"Thank you," I say, wrapping my arms around him and hugging him as hard as I can. "This is perfect."

"Good," he says. "Now, let's dig in. It's time to make you an official Nashville resident."

———

"Too hot! Too hot!"

Cole laughs as I grope desperately for a napkin to spit my mouthful of chicken lava into. I should have known his choices would be too hot for me. Early into this process, I decided I was a mild-to-medium kind of girl. But then Cole dared me to try a piece of his.

I don't turn down dares.

Damn my stubborn streak.

"You okay?" he asks, handing me a little glass of milk.

"How in the world do you eat that stuff?"

Cole puffs out his chest. "'Cause I'm a man."

I playfully roll my eyes. "Oh yeah. My big strong man likes his chicken *super* spicy."

"I'll show you a big strong man."

I can't help but giggle as Cole, from a seated position, picks me up in one motion and brings me across the blanket to his lap. I don't mind. In fact, this is probably my new favorite seat in the world. It's pretty much the only time I get to wrap my arms around his neck.

"Have I told you thank you for tonight?"

He kisses me softly. "Only about twenty times."

"Well then let me make it twenty-one."

I can still taste the spices from that crazy chicken on his lips, but right now, it's my favorite flavor. This night has been nothing short of perfect. And if it really is my last first date, what a way to go.

We talk. We laugh. We eat more chicken than I thought was humanly possible. I learn that just because I'm okay with medium spice at one restaurant doesn't mean I'll be able to take the medium spice at another.

The best part, though? It doesn't feel like a first date. First dates are so awkward. You're asking canned questions in hopes of finding anything you have in common with the other person. But with Cole, I already know him. I know about his family and his career. I know he will dip *anything* in ranch dressing but thinks mayo is the grossest condiment on the planet. I know he loves country music, and he would love nothing more than one day to live in a house that has a ton of land so he could get a few horses.

Of course, this would need to be next to Bryce. Ever since they were kids they've had this crazy idea of living next door to each other. Back then I thought it was stupid. Now the idea of maybe one day living with Cole in a house next to my brother and my best friend... Well, that's the stuff fantasies are made of.

The conversation of already knowing each other hasn't been just one way. Instead of a random guy asking me about being a science teacher, he asked me about the experiment that I did with the kids last week where we turned random fruits and vegetables into batteries. I didn't have to put on this grand show. I could just be me.

Best. Date. Ever.

"How did you put this all together?" I ask. "This screams Lucy but I doubt she came home from Italy to help you with this."

"Honestly, she was my first thought," Cole says. "Then I remembered that Coach McAvoy's sister was a party planner. So I called in a few favors."

I look around the roof for probably the hundredth time tonight. Each time I see something different. Like now, I didn't realize that if you look up at the lights, it almost creates this sense of being under a lit pergola.

"I still can't believe you did all this," I whisper.

"Hey," he says, taking my jaw in his fingers and bringing my head around so I'm looking him in the eye. "Do you know how many bad dates I've had to hear about you going on, either from you or your brother?"

I laugh, because holy shit, I had no idea this poor man was painfully enduring my dating stories while trying to bury his own feelings. "Probably too many."

"You are right. Too many. So you must be crazy if you think I was going to put myself in that category."

I tilt my head, because though this is the best first date in the history of first dates, he's getting off too easy. The man needs to work a bit. "Well aren't you cocky? You think you can roll out a super romantic picnic and feed me so much food I end up in a coma and then you aren't lumped in with the rest?"

My words spark that fire in his eye, which is exactly what I was hoping for.

"Fine. If I'm there, then no need for dessert."

My ears perk up. "Dessert?"

"Yup," I can tell he's trying to hold in his laughter, but I give him credit for keeping up the character. "But if I'm just another bad first date, then I guess we can call it a night."

He might be able to hold character, but I can't. "What was for dessert? You can't tease me with dessert then tell me no."

I give him a playful pouty lip, which apparently does the trick as he reaches behind his back and pulls out a small, perfectly plated chocolate cake.

"This is for you," he says.

"What about you?"

He leans in to give me the cake, which also leaves him inches away from my lips.

"You. You are *my* dessert."

I don't know if it was his low tone, or knowing what's coming, but all of a sudden my body is on fire.

"Maybe I can reconsider where you are in the standings."

He lifts me up and lays me down on the blanket. "That's what I thought."

Yup.

Best. Date. Ever.

CHAPTER 19

COLE

NO ONE in my life has ever described me as happy.

Grumpy? Sometimes. Serious? Without a doubt. Twenty-five going on sixty? I can say "get off my lawn" with the best of them.

So color me shocked today when not one but *five* of my teammates asked me what was wrong. Every one of them said I was smiling too much.

"Seriously, Campbell, what the fuck?"

This is coming from veteran tight end Wes Taylor. And I must be really smiling because this guy is the epitome of get in, do your job, and get out. After ten years in the league, he's all about just handling his business. He generally keeps to himself and rarely socializes with the younger guys. Except me. And that's probably because I barely socialize with the younger guys, and those guys are my age. This might be only my fourth year in the league, but I've been told I have the personality of a jaded veteran.

"I don't know what you mean."

We're walking back toward the locker room, both of us just having finished up our workouts.

"I think you do know what I mean, but I'm not going to push you. If you wanted to talk about something, you would."

"Thank you," I say, tossing my towel into my locker.

"But that doesn't mean I can't ask the question of who she is. Because only a woman puts a smile like that on a man. And whoever she is, I'm going to guess things are going *very* well."

I shoot a look at him, hoping I'm not giving myself away. I've never really needed a poker face. You don't need one when you don't usually talk or have anything to give away.

"Again, don't know what you mean."

I quickly grab a towel and shower shoes and head toward the showers. But before I get too far, Wes grabs my arm. "Hey. I'm just messin' with you. If you don't want to talk about her, I get it. If you want to ever, I'm here. I just want to say I'm happy for you, because that whole smiling thing looks good on you."

I give him a pat on the back. "Thanks, man. See you next week?"

"Sure thing. Have a good Easter."

I hurry and jump into the shower, hoping no one else stops me for smiling. Until today I never realized how rarely I did it. Don't get me wrong, it's not like I have been living in a state of depression for the past three seasons. But when I'm in the Fury facilities, I'm here to do a job. I'm an offensive lineman. I protect Bryce, I make room for the running backs to run, and I always have my fellow linemen's backs. That's my job. There is nothing I take more seriously.

Football has been my life since I was six years old. I remember that first game like it was yesterday. Bryce was the quarterback, and at that time, I was playing center. Apparently, I was the only one who understood how to snap the ball. Even then we were setting records. Well, at least that's what our coaches told us. I doubt they keep six-year-old football stats, even in a town as football-crazed as Laurel Heights.

I don't think I'll ever forget that first game, though. We were tied as the game wound down. We had the ball at the twenty-yard line, and when you're six, the end zone seems like a mile away. I snapped the ball to Bryce, recorded the first pancake block of my young football career, and Bryce went on to throw the game-winning touchdown. I was so excited I ran into the end zone and, for the first of many times in our career, picked Bryce up and twirled him around.

It was a great day.

Though now that I'm thinking about it, a new memory of that day is coming to light. As soon as I put Bryce to the ground I looked over to my right, and there she was. Brenna. Shit, I forgot that she was a Little Tigers cheerleader. But now that I think about it, I'm seeing her clear as day, jumping and yelling for us as we won our first game. I don't know if she was looking at me, but I was definitely looking at her.

And I remember smiling.

Shit, I had it bad for her even then. I just didn't know it.

I flip off the shower and head back to my locker, doing my best to keep a straight face. Enough guys were at the wedding that it would just be my luck for someone to connect the dots. Especially Dexter.

The only problem is my no-smile plan goes out the window when I see a text from Brenna as soon as I make it back to my locker.

> Brenna: Let the countdown begin: Two hours until a four-day weekend. I wonder what we can get into with four uninterrupted days. =)

Just as I'm about to text her back, my phone rings. And thank goodness I look instead of just assuming it's Brenna.

"Hey Mom," I say, switching the speaker to my AirPods so I can finish getting dressed.

"Hey, baby boy," she says. "How is everything? Catch me up. How was the wedding?"

My mom was devastated when she found out the date of Bryce and Lucy's wedding. She has loved Bryce like a son for so long, and she wanted to be there when he and Lucy finally got married. Unfortunately, the wedding fell right in the middle of my parents' thirtieth-anniversary vacation. They had saved for this for years—even though I could have paid for it in cash without batting an eye, and offered to. So, as much as my parents love Bryce, nothing was going to keep them from seeing the Caribbean.

"It was good," I say, slipping into my clothes to head out of the facility.

"That's it? Your best friend of twenty-plus years gets married and all you have to say is that it was good?"

"What do you want me to say, Mom?"

"I don't know. Make me feel like I was there. I mean, Lucy looked beautiful. And Brenna? Goodness. That dress was just perfect for her."

I make my way out of the facility and into my Jeep. "How do you know what Lucy and Brenna looked like?"

"Facebook, silly. I might not have been there in the flesh, but I made sure to look at every picture so I could make it feel like I was."

Fucking Facebook. Mom has been on me for years to get an account. I'm still holding out.

"Well then if you saw the pictures, what else can I tell you?"

"Maybe you can tell me why you were dancing so close with Brenna Donald when just a few weeks ago I heard through the grapevine you were dating some girl named Jessica?"

Thank God I haven't started driving yet, because I'm pretty sure I would have wrecked the car after hearing her say that.

"Mom, what are you talking about?"

"Which part?"

"Um...both?"

I swear I can hear her roll her eyes through the Bluetooth as I turn the car on. "Well, the Brenna thing was easy. Anyone with two eyes and an up-to-date glasses prescription could see that one. Hell, your granddaddy could probably see it, cataracts, and all. You love that girl, and we'll get back to that later."

Note to self: Find pictures of Brenna and me at the reception and make sure Bryce does not see them before we talk to him.

"As for the Jessica thing," Mom continues, "we have a Facebook group for families of Fury players. All of a sudden one day we get a request from this girl named Jessica, claiming she is your girlfriend. I had my suspicions, but she sent me a friend request and told me all about her and you. And I know you're not very comfortable telling me about your relationships, which I'm used to. I figured you'd tell me on your own time. At first, she was nice. Then... I don't know, Cole. I hope you're done with her, because I think she's a few McNuggets short of a Happy Meal."

This makes me laugh. "That she is, Mom. And don't worry. I broke up with her."

"Good. I'll make sure she's blocked from the group. And this works out great, because now you can bring Brenna home with you for Easter this weekend!"

I hadn't planned on going home for the holiday, especially now that Brenna and I are together. She has four days off, and I planned on spending at least three of them naked.

"Mom, I'm not sure..."

"About what? Seeing your family that you haven't seen since Christmas? Or is it a problem with Brenna? Does she not want to see her mama? *Is* there something going on between you two? Is there something wrong between you two? What are you not sure about?"

There is no guilt trip like the guilt trip of a mother. Thorough *and* unrelenting.

As much as I'd like to keep Brenna to myself this weekend, it has been a while since either of us were in Laurel Heights. Maybe she would like to see her mom? I know she didn't get to spend a lot of time with her around the wedding. And though I'll never admit this to my mother, it would be nice to bring a girl home as my girlfriend. Maybe telling Mom would be a good way to test the waters of how people will react to us being together?

"Fine. We'll drive up tomorrow."

"Good," Mom says. "But I have to know one thing first."

"What's that, Mom?"

"Is Brenna coming here as Bryce's sister? Or as something more?"

Fuck, there goes my stupid smile again. I can't stop it.

"Something more."

I think I hear my mom smiling. "Well, that's just wonderful. We'll see you tomorrow. Drive safe."

"Will do."

I pull up to the stop light and use the Bluetooth to send a text to Brenna. I have a feeling if I wait any longer, I won't be the one informing her that we are about to take a road trip home.

Cole: Change of weekend plans. How about a weekend trip to Laurel Heights?

The light doesn't even change colors before I get a reply.

Brenna: I like the sound of that. Let's go meet the parents =)

"ARE WE THERE YET?"

Cole gives me the side eye as he pulls off the highway that puts us on the road leading to Laurel Heights.

"You know exactly where we are. You've made this trip dozens of times. So why the question and why in the world is your knee bouncing like that?"

I look down to see that I am, in fact, bouncing my knee like an amped toddler getting ready to run out to see their Christmas presents. I didn't even realize I was doing it.

"I feel dumb even thinking it," I admit.

"Nothing you can say right now will make me think that."

I let out a sigh. "Fine. I'm nervous."

This gets me another side eye. "Nervous? About what?"

Does he really not get it? I swear...men. "Meeting your parents!"

Cole starts to laugh, but sees the glare I give him and wisely sucks it up. "Okay, I want to get this right. You, Brenna Donald, the most extroverted and daring person I've ever met, is nervous about seeing, not meeting, people you have known for more than twenty years?"

I let my head fall back against the headrest. "I knew you

wouldn't get it. And I know it sounds ridiculous. But this is totally different. They aren't just Susan and Jeff anymore. They are Mr. and Mrs. Campbell, the parents of my boyfriend. I'm not just the little girl who is coming over because I tagged along with my brother. Or the cheerleader who had to leave you your game day treat bag. I'm the girl who is corrupting their son."

"Hey, I'm not complaining about the corruption. And you always gave me the best treats."

"Focus, Campbell!" I yell, turning in my seat to face him. "And this isn't about just me. You have to meet my mother, as my boyfriend!"

I didn't expect calm, cool, and always-focused Cole to be as worried as I am, but I didn't expect him to laugh. And this time he doesn't hold it back.

Asshole. That will cost him later.

"It's not funny," I say.

Cole reaches over the console to take my hand in his. "Brenna. Your mother loves me. She always has."

"But as Bryce's best friend. Not as my boyfriend."

He brings my hand up to his mouth, kissing each of my knuckles. "You need to relax. My parents are over the moon about this. I could hear my mom smiling from Nashville. Dad might even hug you. And your mom? She will be just fine."

This takes me back. "I don't think your dad has said two words to me in my entire life."

"Now you know where I get it from."

I smile a little, but that doesn't erase the worry. "I can't believe we're doing this. What if people see us? You know how the gossip mill is around here. News of us together would literally set the Laurel Heights Facebook page on fire. What if someone tells Bryce before we have a chance to? What if our parents think this is a bad idea and we have to break up? What if—"

"Hey," Cole says, giving my hand a squeeze. "Where's all this coming from?"

I take a deep breath, hoping that Cole doesn't freak out when I say this. "Do you think this is a mistake?"

He doesn't answer for a second, which I don't blame him.

"What part? Us?"

I shrug. "I don't know. Maybe? It was one thing when we were in the cocoon of your apartment. It was just us and it was perfect. But now? Thinking about how many people this affects? Bryce and Lucy. Our families. They've been friends forever. Is this going to make it weird? What if it doesn't work out and all of a sudden our moms can't go to book club together?"

"Well, then they'll just have to find somewhere else to go to drink while pretending to read."

"I'm serious, Cole. I'm scared."

Cole slows the Jeep down and pulls over to the side of the road. He unbuckles his seat belt and does the same for me so we can turn to look at each other.

"Where is this fear coming from? That's not the Brenna I know. The Brenna I know isn't scared of anything."

"You're wrong. I'm also scared of spiders."

"Don't deflect. Tell me. What are you scared of? If it's going to Laurel Heights, I'll turn right around and tell Mom I got sick."

I shake my head. "No. I want to see everyone. I might have moved, but sometimes I miss it."

"Then what is it? Tell me. You know you can tell me anything."

I look into his crystal blue eyes, and they are filled with

nothing but concern—and maybe something more. And the something more has me scared shitless.

"This? This trip? This makes us real. Once we do this, we can't go back. And that makes me scared. I'm scared because this relationship isn't just about you and me. I'm scared because this feels more right than anything I've ever had. And I'm scared because you're the first thing in my life I'm afraid of losing."

Cole doesn't say anything. He doesn't need to. Instead he brings my face to his and kisses me with every bit of emotion and comfort he has in his body. It relaxes me. It lights a fire in me. It doubles down on the fact that I'm justified in being scared, because I never want to know what living without him would be like.

"I'm scared too," he says, keeping my face in his hold. "I'm scared that one day I'm going to wake up and find out that this was nothing more than the best dream I've ever had. But want to know what else I know?"

"What's that?" I ask, fighting back tears.

"I know that you're worth fighting for. That *we're* worth fighting for. And if our parents disapprove, then we figure it out. We'll make them approve. Because you? Me? Us? We're too good to go down without a fight."

I let out a big breath. "You're right."

This makes him smile. "Damn right I am."

"Okay, Campbell," I say, sitting back and re-buckling my seat belt. "Let's go see your parents."

———

"Brenna, I hope you saved room for some strawberry pie."

My stomach gurgles in protest. Or in desire. Mrs. Campbell's strawberry pie is legendary.

"Maybe in a minute," I say. "Or twenty."

I put my hand over my stomach and look down at my plate. I haven't eaten that much in... I honestly don't know how long. We might be from Southwest Ohio, but Cole's mom is from Mississippi, and her Southern cooking, and Southern sayings, have stuck with her even though she's lived in Ohio for nearly thirty years. We had pork chops, twice-baked potatoes, green beans, and corn. There might have been more; I'm not sure. All I know is that I'm going to need to be rolled out of here.

I'm just glad I wore leggings.

"Mom, it was delicious," Cole says as he starts picking up the plates around the table.

"I had to cook your favorites. I didn't know when I'd get to see you again."

He leans down and gives his mom a kiss on the cheek before taking her plate. "Your guilt trip is noted for the record."

I can't help but smile as I watch Cole interact with his parents. Adding to the many layers that make up Cole Campbell is the way he acts at home. With his mom, he is polite and loving. With his dad he is both of those things, but with a more formal delivery. This house is filled with love. I can feel it all around me.

Either that or it's the hug Mrs. Campbell gave me the second I walked into the house. I'm pretty sure Cole got some of his strength from his mama. The woman's hug was like a vise.

"Mrs. Campbell?" I ask, which only gets met with a stern look.

"Brenna, I told you to call me Susan. You have always called me Susan. I don't know why tonight you've decided not to."

Well, I can't tell her that reason. That reason is because I feel like if I call her Mrs. Campbell it will somehow be my way of saying sorry for the dirty yet delicious things her son does to me on a daily basis.

"I'm sorry. Susan."

"There, that's better. Now what do you need, my dear?"

"I was just going to ask if I could use the restroom."

"Girl," she says, tossing down her napkin. "Do you think you need to ask here? We're family. Just get up and go. You remember where it is?"

This makes me smile. "Yes. I do. Thank you."

I get up and walk up the few stairs in their split-level home to the restroom. Did I need to use it? Yes. But I also had a secret motive for coming up here. For some reason, I've wanted to see Cole's old room. I used to come up here a lot when I was in high school. It was tradition for the cheerleaders to drop in to the football players' houses and leave them treat bags. I always got Cole. I made sure of it. He was my brother's best friend, and I felt it was my duty.

Or maybe I felt something even back then? Who knows. All I knew was that over my dead body was that slut bag Moriah Marks going to give him treats. She used to say that if she were his cheerleader, she would leave more than candy on his bed.

Hell no.

I walk in, and it's exactly how I remember it. Football trophies line his dressers. There's a picture of him and Bryce when they were six, after they won their first of many league championships. It's right next to the one of the two of them the night they won the state championship in high school. Gosh, I remember that night. I was so proud of both of them. I had Bryce's number painted on one cheek and Cole's painted on the other. I remember after the game just trying to get through the fans and students who rushed the field after we won. Finally, I got a glimpse of Cole, and I gave him two thumbs up like I always did after a win.

If I only knew then what I know now, I would have done so much more. I would have rushed the field and rushed straight toward him. I would have jumped into his arms and given him the biggest hug and kiss I could muster. I would have told him how proud I was of him.

I probably would have told him something else back then. The words that have been rolling in my brain a lot lately, but I'm just not ready yet.

Soon. But not yet.

My eyes keep traveling around the room, and I can't help but notice a few drawings hanging up. Were those always there? I don't remember those from high school, but then again, I probably wasn't paying attention.

"He doesn't draw like he used to," Susan says, leaning against the door jam. "He was always so talented."

"I never knew he could draw like this. I knew he used to, but I never saw anything."

"Oh yes," she says as she signals for me to have a seat on the bed as she takes one herself. "He was always getting picked for art fairs at school as a kid. I think it was his way of giving his brain and body a break when the football got to be too much."

"Why did he give it up? I've never seen him draw, or even doodle."

"You know how kids are," Susan says. "Even when you're the biggest kid in the school, it doesn't mean you're immune to teasing."

When—not if—I find out who teased him for being able to draw, I will throat punch that person at the next reunion.

"Thank you again for having me," I say, not wanting an uncomfortable silence to take over.

Susan takes my hand between both of hers and gives it a

pat. "Oh, Brenna, don't you know how long I've waited for you to come through that door holding my boy's hand?"

I'm pretty sure my eyes grow two inches. "Excuse me?"

"Call it a mother's intuition, or maybe it was just hoping on hope, but whenever I thought about my baby settling down, it was always you who I pictured next to him."

Well, this is interesting news. "Can I ask why? It's not like we ever even flirted with each other back in high school."

"Oh, Brenna…" Susan trails off for a second, but then I realize she's looking at a picture on the wall I hadn't seen. It's Cole and Bryce in their uniforms. And right in the middle is me, smiling from ear to ear in my cheerleading uniform, my bow as big as my head. We are no more than eight in this picture. "I couldn't have asked for a better friend for my boy than Bryce. Was he a pain in the ass sometimes? Yes. But I knew from the moment those two played their first football game together that they were more than friends. They were brothers."

"They were," I say, knowing that's exactly how my mom and I feel about the two of them.

"But then there was you. It would have been easy to think of you as the little sister Cole never had, but there was one time, gosh, I don't even know why I remember this, but you guys were maybe ten years old. We were at the football fields, like always, and a boy came up behind you and pulled your ponytail."

I laugh, because even though I haven't thought about that in years, I do remember what she's talking about. "I was so mad."

"You were. I remember sitting back with your mama, both of us wondering how you were going to handle it."

"I was ready to punch him in the junk."

"That was our bet," Susan says with a laugh. "But you didn't need to."

I smile, the memory flooding back. "I didn't."

"Nope. Because my son was there in five seconds, lifting that poor boy off the ground by his shirt collar."

"I think I remember worrying he was going to pee himself."

"We all did. I remember thinking to myself that it was nice Cole did that for you. That it was a brotherly reaction."

I tilt my head, wondering where she's going with this. "I have a feeling there's a *but* coming."

"You're right. Because as soon as he dropped that pipsqueak, you ran up to my boy and jumped in his arms, giving him the biggest hug I had ever seen. You looked at him like he was your hero. And then when he put you down, that's when I knew. He wasn't looking at you like a sister. Nope, my boy had just rescued his princess."

I feel the tears welling up in my eyes. "Susan..."

She shakes her head. "I know neither of you realized it at the time, but that's when I looked at your mama and just knew in my heart we were going to be family someday. I know it took you both some time to get here, but I'm just glad you both made it."

I don't have any more words. Instead, I throw my arms around her neck, hugging her just as tight as she hugged me earlier.

"Thank you," I say, though I don't know what exactly I'm thanking her for.

"No, my dear. Thank you. Thank you for loving my baby."

"What are you two doing? Why are you both crying? I can't take you both crying." Cole's horrified voice cuts through the tears and makes both of us laugh.

"Don't you worry about us," Susan says as she stands up. "I'll leave you two alone."

She turns and gives me a wink as she walks out the door.

"Everything okay?" Cole asks, sitting on the bed where his mom just was. "What did she say to you?"

I shake my head and put my head on his shoulder. "Just shared some history with me, and reminded me of a few things."

This gives him pause. "History?"

"Yup. And guess what?"

"What's that?"

I turn and press a kiss to his shoulder. "I'm not scared anymore."

CHAPTER 21
BRENNA

Cole: What do you mean you haven't told her?

Brenna: I just haven't found the right moment.

Cole: You've been with her all day!

Brenna: I know. We're going to dinner now. I'll tell her then.

Cole: Do you want me to come with you? I've been with my sister and her crazy kids all day. I could use a break.

Brenna: No. They never get to see Uncle Cole. Go be the funcle.

Cole: We're going to see them tomorrow for Easter. I can come. No problem.

Brenna: While it would be nice for you to be here for backup, we're going out to eat at Celine and Luciano's place. I don't want the rumor mill to start up before we've told who we need to tell.

Cole: I get it. I miss you. But you got this. Call me if you need backup.

Brenna: Will do <3

I SLIP my phone into my purse as my mom comes back from the restroom at Lucine. I haven't been here since it first opened. I'm so glad for Luciano and Celine that it's just as busy tonight as it was opening night more than a year ago.

"So what looks good?" Mom asks as she opens her menu. "Did you order the pizza bread for the appetizer?"

"Yes, Mom," I say—like I'd forget that. Luciano's family owns the best pizza place in Southwest Ohio, Tripoli's. Also known as "what the Donald family has eaten for dinner every Sunday for nearly twenty years." When Luciano opened this place, he put Tripoli's pizza on the menu as an appetizer. It's a must-get.

"Good," she says, putting down her menu. "I'm so glad you came home this weekend. It has been too long since we've spent time together, just us."

We reach for each other's hands and give them a squeeze. "I know. And sorry I haven't been home more."

She waves me off. "No. I understand. You're starting a new life in Nashville. I can't expect you to be home every weekend just because of me."

"I know," I say, still feeling guilty. I hate that it's just Mom up here. Yes, she has her friends. Yes, she's still working so that keeps her busy. But knowing that Bryce and I are both away still stabs at my heart. "So what is new in Laurel Heights?"

"Ha. You're funny," she says. "You know nothing in this town has changed. But enough about here. Tell me about you. How are your students? Are you making friends? Maybe...I don't know... seeing anyone?"

A waitress comes to our table, and we put in our order. Her timing couldn't be more perfect. This now gives me a minute or two to decide how I want to enter this conversation.

Because it's now or never.

"Actually, Mom, I am seeing someone."

"Really?" she says, taking a sip of her water. "You didn't bring anyone to the wedding. Is this new?"

"Well, he was at the wedding. Though at the time, yes, it was very new."

She tilts her head. "I'm not following."

I suck in a breath, because here it goes.

"Cole. Cole and I are dating."

Mom doesn't say anything for what feels like minutes. I don't know if that's because she's processing what I just said or because the pizza bread was delivered to the table.

"Mom?" I ask, because her silence is killing me. "Do you have anything to say? You're freaking me out."

She shakes her head a bit, as if coming back to reality. "Oh, Brenna. Of course I'm happy for you. And I'm sorry if it sounded like I wasn't. It just...well, it took me by surprise."

"Believe me, no one was more surprised about how I felt than me."

"Wow," she says, like she's still processing. "I saw you two dancing at the wedding, and I thought for a second that you two looked cozy together. But I didn't think anything of it. Because it's Cole. And you."

"I know," I say. "Believe me, when I first realized I had feelings for him, I freaked out too. I mean, this is the guy who has been just as much a part of this family as anyone over the years."

"Can I ask when this started?"

I go on to tell Mom about the last few months as we munch on pizza bread. I tell her about my apartment flood, and I couldn't live with Lucy and Bryce. Though I kindly blame that on the wedding instead of the truth that my brother was loud during sex. He owes me one for that. I go on to say that I don't know exactly when it happened, but over the time spent we together, I started to realize he's more than just my brother's best friend, or the guy I've known since I had baby teeth. That he's Cole. And that every day I'm with him is better than the one before.

"Oh Brenna," she says, taking my hands in hers. "I guess now I do owe Susan a pie because she has been saying for years you two should be together."

"You can tell her that tomorrow over Easter dinner. She's invited both of us over."

"That would be lovely," she says. "So, since you said that this happened around the time of the wedding, and since I'm also just hearing about this, I'm going to go on a limb and say that your brother does not know yet."

I shake my head. "No. We didn't want to take away from the wedding, and we were still trying to figure out if this was real or not. No sense in telling him if it was just something that was going to pass by in a few days."

"And I'm guessing that it didn't pass."

I shake my head. "Not even a little bit."

Mom sits back against the backrest of the booth. "How do you plan on telling him?"

"That's the million-dollar question."

As our food gets delivered, my phone buzzes with a text.

Cole: Okay, I know you said you have this, but I don't feel right about you taking the bullet alone. Plus, I know your mom misses me. I'm on my way. Save me some pizza bread.

I can't help but smile as I dive into my bowl of shrimp Alfredo.

"If he makes you smile like that, then no way could your brother be mad."

I set down my fork and dab a napkin at my lips. "He's on his way."

"Oh good!" Mom says. "I barely got to see him at the wedding. I wondered why. Now I know. You must have been keeping him occupied."

I laugh as she wiggles her eyebrows. "Mom!"

"He's a very handsome man, Brenna. You have nothing to be ashamed about."

I feel the blush heating my cheeks. I was barely ready for this conversation. I'm definitely not ready to share details of my sex life with my mother.

I'll never be ready for that.

"I'm happy for you, Brenna, I really am," she pauses to take a sip of water. And I have a feeling I know why she did. "But, I still worry about how your brother is going to react. You know he doesn't take sudden news well."

A baritone voice answers her. "No, he doesn't. How about we send him up here so you can set him straight?"

I turn to see Cole standing next to the booth, looking just as handsome as ever in a fitted T-shirt and jeans. I also feel my heart melt just a little when I see the bouquet of flowers he's holding.

"Oh, Cole!" Mom says, leaping up from her seat to give him a hug. "How have you been?"

"No complaints at all, Mrs. Donald. Here, these are for you." He steps back slightly to give her the flowers before taking a seat next to me. I'm now thankful for the small amount of privacy we get from a booth. At least I can hold his hand under the table without the whole restaurant catching on.

"You didn't have to do that," she says, placing them down on the table.

He winks. "I didn't know what I'd be walking into, so I figured they couldn't hurt."

Mom just smiles at the two of us. "I'm so happy for you two. I couldn't ask for a better man for my baby girl."

"Can you make sure you tell Bryce that?" I say. "In those exact words."

Mom waves her hands in the air, as if dismissing the notion. "Bryce is stubborn. We all know this. And he's not great with change."

"Tell me about it," I mumble.

"He's going to feel like you both lied to him," Mom continues. "And though that's technically the truth, I understand why you both did it. Yes, he'll need some time to adjust. But if you show him that you're both committed to this relationship, and that it's more than just a fling, he'll have no choice but to come around."

"I don't know about that," Cole says. "He told me once that not one of his friends or teammates were good enough for Brenna. And when I brought up the idea of me, he all but fell over laughing."

Mom shakes her head, almost as if she can't believe it. "Oh, that boy. Such a dramatic. I always said if he didn't get into football, he would have been a great actor."

We all laugh at that idea. "We want to tell him," I continue. "We just don't know the best way. Any advice?"

Mom sits back into the booth. "I don't know if there is a best way, and unfortunately there might only be one way."

"And that is?"

"Rip the Band-Aid off. Don't drag it out. And don't expect his first reaction to be his last. Give him time to process."

We look at each other and nod. "That makes sense. Thanks, Mom."

"No problem. But there's one more piece to the puzzle."

"What's that?"

"Make sure Lucy knows and is ready to deal with the fall out. And buy her some wine. She'll need it."

"WHERE ARE WE GOING?"

Brenna points to the left from the passenger seat. "Turn here, then just follow the road."

I do as she says, though I have my suspicions about where she is asking me to drive her. "You know, if you wanted to make out with me, we could have just gone to my bedroom and pretended to take a nap."

"One: You know your nieces and nephew would not leave us alone long enough for any sort of kissing time. And two, who said anything about making out?"

"Are you not taking me back to Lake Laurel?"

"Yes, but what does that have to do with making out?"

I turn the car where she directs and head back to the spot that I only know exists because it's where Bryce used to come to clear his mind. It's also where he and Lucy used to go to get away from, well, everything. What they did there, I can only suspect. Though I do know that every time I saw him after a trip here his lips looked like they were just sucked by a vacuum.

"I guess I assumed that it was a Donald thing to come here for some privacy."

"Ew, gross," Brenna says, a visible shiver going up her spine. "I was more of a Heights Park fan. But no, we're not here because of that. Come on, follow me."

She gets out of the Jeep before I can even have a chance to go open her door. Hell, she's almost at a full-on sprint as she heads to a small, deserted picnic area. I mean, it makes sense given that it's Easter Sunday. But it's kind of eerie being the only ones here.

No, eerie isn't the right word. It's peaceful. Serene. Someone could get lost in their thoughts out here.

"Come on, Campbell!" Brenna yells, stopping at a picnic table. "You're getting slow in the off season."

"Excuse me for not sprinting for a race I didn't know I was in."

She shoots me a look for my sarcastic comment. "I'm going to let that one slide, but I should clue you in. You're with a Donald now. Everything is a competition. Now get over here. I have a surprise for you."

I can't help but smile as I make my way to the picnic table. I don't know if it's because I'm thinking of a lifetime of little competitions with this woman or the fact that somehow she's surprising me out of the blue. Maybe both.

"Okay, Trouble. What's up your sleeve?"

"Well," she begins as she starts pulling notebooks out of her bag, "I noticed something when I went into your room the other day."

"That my mom needs to take down the shrine she's made to me in there?"

She shakes her head. "No. I love that. Especially because there's a picture of me. What I was going to say was that I completely forgot you used to draw."

I feel a blush heating on my face. "That was a long time ago."

"I know. In my opinion, it's been too long." Brenna holds out the notebooks to me. When I take a closer look at them, I realize they aren't just normal notebooks. No, they are drawing and sketching books. And not only that—she also has an assortment of art pencils for me.

"What's all this?"

"I know they aren't the really good ones, but it was the best I could find on the fly. But I remember you telling me that you loved to draw, but that no one knew about it."

"You remembered that? I told you that when you were drunk in Clemson."

"I remember more of that night than you think," she says with a wink. "Anyway, seeing those pictures, I was blown away by how talented you are. And even if no one ever sees them, being teased years ago by asshole kids because they were likely jealous of you is no reason to let this talent go to waste. You're amazing at it. So, consider this your first step of picking back up an old hobby."

I'm not much of a crier. In fact, I can remember twice in my life when I ever cried.

This is very close to becoming number three.

"I don't know what to say."

Brenna puts her hand on top of mine. "You don't need to say anything. Just make me a promise."

"Anything."

"Draw one for me. I want something to look at in my classroom every day that will make me smile."

I set the drawings down and reach for Brenna. She immediately meets my hands and lets me pull her into me. Like it's the most natural thing in the world, she sits on my lap, looping her hands around my neck before bringing her lips to mine. We take our time savoring each other. Seeing family this weekend has been great, don't get me wrong. But that means we've only been able to steal a few moments with each other. I haven't been able to kiss her like this, slow and steady, where our lips and tongues are in no rush to take what they want.

"This is the best present I've ever gotten," I say as I push a strand of loose hair behind her ear. "Thank you."

"You are very welcome," she says, giving me one more small kiss. "Do you want to try them out? I thought this would be a good view for you to capture the sunset."

My hand travels down, only to go back up her shirt. I give her breast a squeeze, which immediately makes her squirm.

"I have a better idea."

———

"Cole! We can't do this!"

I pull my Jeep up to a tucked-away corner in Heights Park. "You said you were a Heights Park kinda gal. So here we are."

"Yeah, ten years ago," she says. "What if someone sees us?"

Brenna looks around for the people she thinks are going to see us, but she's not going to find anything. The park is completely empty.

"What happened to the girl I used to call Trouble?"

She shoots me a look. "You called me that an hour ago."

"Well, an hour ago I thought you were. Apparently, the rumors are true, the once-fearless wild child Brenna Donald has lost her spunk."

I see the moment the challenge enters her eyes. There's my girl. Yes, I'm crazy about the woman she has become. I love our nights alone when we're being lazy on the couch. I can see myself marrying the school teacher and spending weeknights with her grading papers and her wearing my jersey on Sundays. But a part of me has always wondered what it would be like to be with the wild child...the girl I first fell for all those years ago. She might not come out often, but I know she's still there.

"How dare you challenge my spunk," she says as she takes off her seatbelt and turns to me.

"I'm just saying," I say, pushing my seat back. "I call it like I see it."

"You play dirty, Campbell," she says, situating herself on her knees.

"I don't know what you mean?"

"You know exactly what you're doing," she whispers in my ear, her hand grazing over my cock through my jeans.

"I don't," I say, trying not to groan as she continues to stroke me. "I was a good kid. I never came up here like you troublemakers."

Brenna unzips the fly on my jeans and releases the button. It only takes a little adjusting to push down my jeans and boxer briefs to let my aching cock spring free. Brenna's hand is on it as soon as it does. Fuck, it feels so good. Her touch is so warm compared to the cool bite in the spring air.

"I guess it's true what they say then," Brenna says, adjusting herself so her mouth is now inches away from my dick. "You good boys should always watch out for us bad girls. We're nothing but trouble."

The second her mouth is on me I nearly explode. I have to take the deepest breath of my life to not come then and there. But fuck, she feels so good. Too good. Her mouth is working in tandem with her hand. There is never a point where some part of my dick isn't being felt or tasted. And her tongue? I don't know what she's doing at my tip, but I never want her to stop doing that.

I sweep her hair off her face, which gives me a fantastic view of her working every inch of me. "Yes, Brenna. God, you feel so good."

My words must hit the right chord because her tempo increases. She's like a woman possessed right now, and I can't stop staring at her. She's so fucking gorgeous. So fucking sexy.

So fucking mine.

I knew it before, but today has cemented it. I can't imagine her not in my life. I can't imagine her being with another man. I can't imagine not spending every day of the rest of my life with her.

She's it for me. And fuck anyone, especially my best friend, if he's going to tell me otherwise.

I gently bring her head back, surprising her, because I'm pretty sure my girl was about to make me see stars.

"What are you doing? I wasn't done."

I lean over and scoop her off her seat. Thank the fucking heavens she's wearing a dress today, so it only takes me a few seconds to hike it up and slip her panties to the side.

"I need to be inside of you. Right fucking now."

I lean over to the glove compartment to grab a condom, but Brenna puts her hand on my arm.

"No," she says, shaking her head. "I'm clean and get the shot. I don't want anything between us, Cole."

"Are you sure? I'm clean, too. We have to get regular checks. And I've never. Not with anyone."

She reaches down and lines my cock up to her center. Fuck, I can already tell I'm barely going to last.

"I trust you."

Those might not be the three words I've been fighting back, but they are the best three words I could hear at this moment. The second she lowers herself onto me, I crash my lips to hers. It's either that or scream so loud that everyone in town will know what we're doing.

Fuck, if I thought her mouth was warm before, that was nothing. She's so fucking hot. So fucking wet.

And now, without a doubt, mine.

My lips work down the side of her neck and across the top of her chest. My hands are working her tits through the fabric of her dress. There might not be any skin to skin, but the way her hips are answering every time I pinch her nipple, the effect is still there.

"You feel so good," she says, her hips working up and down to take every inch of me.

"Too good," I pant. "Not sure how long I'm going to last."

Brenna leans in to me. Our bodies are now flush as our hips continue to meet at a frantic pace. "Let go for me. Let me feel you inside of me."

Her words go straight to my cock. And I might want to do exactly that, but not without taking her with me.

"Lean back. Come with me."

She does as I ask, and my fingers begin to work in tandem with my cock. The inside and outside stimulation must be too much because in a matter of seconds, my girl stills on top of me a second before I feel her explode on my cock.

"Brenna!" I yell, because it's too much for me, too. I bring her chest into mine as our orgasms rip through us, holding her tight as we ride the wave together.

Fuck, that was intense. And judging by Brenna's heaving chest, and the fact that she is shaking in my arms, it was something special for her, too.

When we both come back to earth, I slowly lift her up off me, though I don't let her go. No, I'm not ready to quite yet.

"You're mine, you know that, right?" I whisper in her ear, leaving small kisses along her neck.

"Good," she replies. "Because I'm not going anywhere."

CHAPTER 23
BRENNA

"OKAY, let's practice what we're going to do one more time."

I think I hear Cole groan, but I choose to ignore it. He can pout all he wants, but tonight is important.

Tonight we're telling Bryce.

We didn't pounce on him and Lucy the second they got home from their honeymoon. Granted, we were still in Laurel Heights when they got back, so they had a few days without us. But Cole and I both know we won't be able to hide it from him, so it's best to do what Mom suggested— rip off the bandage of denial and tell him tonight.

"We're not going to bring it up right away," Cole says. "We're going to talk normal. Eat dinner, then bring it up."

"Correct," I say as we step onto the elevator to take us up to Bryce and Lucy's. "I'm going to take Lucy into the kitchen to get us all drinks, and you're going to begin bringing up the conversation."

"And then when you come back you're going to sit next to me. I'll either hold your hand or touch you in some way, and then I'll tell him, gently, that we have been seeing each other. That it's getting serious, and we wanted him to know."

"Then when he asks how long it's been going on?"

"We'll be honest and say the wedding, but we didn't want to get in the way of his day or honeymoon."

"And when he starts going insane?"

"We let Lucy handle him."

"Perfect," I say, letting out a relieving breath. "I have a good feeling about this."

Cole leans down and gives me a small kiss. "You really are a glass-half-full girl, aren't you?"

"I am," I say, returning the kiss. "But let's be real. Tonight's glass is going to be full at all times. That's the other part of the plan."

Cole holds up a six-pack of Dr Pepper. "Cheers to that."

The elevator stops and opens, bringing us face-to-face with Bryce's door. I might have been confident thirty seconds ago, but now that we're here, that confidence is draining fast.

"We got this," he says, giving my hand a squeeze.

I look up at him and give him a wink. "It's you and me. Of course we do."

I hear us each take one last deep breath before Cole knocks on Bryce's door. Cole lets go of my hand, and I miss the contact instantly. But it's necessary, because after tonight, we'll never need to sneak around again.

"There are my two favorite people!" Bryce yells as he swings open the door.

"Hello, brother," I say, giving him a hug and a kiss on the cheek. "How was the honeymoon?"

"Perfect in every way," he says, walking over to Cole to give him their weird man-hug-slap thing. "Come in. Dinner was just dropped off."

Cole and I make eye contact and give each other a nod. He sneaks in a wink, which nearly makes me giggle, but I hold strong.

"There she is!" Cole says as he sees Lucy walking toward

the dining area carrying plates. He takes them from her, sets them down on the table, and wraps her in a big bear hug.

"I've missed you too, Cole," she says, giving his chest a pat as he lets go of her. "Have you been holding down the fort while we've been away?"

"I have," he says as he turns his eyes to me. "I've been holding it down pretty good, if I do say so myself."

My eyes go wide and I hurry and look at Bryce to see if he caught onto that little innuendo. Luckily, and predictably, Bryce is in his own world, playing with something on the television.

"Brenna, can you help me bring the rest of the food out?" Lucy says as she not-so-subtly summons me to the kitchen.

I don't say anything, though I do shoot Cole a "you better watch it" look before I head back to the kitchen. Though the second I step foot in it, maybe I need to be telling Lucy to chill out, judging by the way she's bouncing up and down.

"Are you okay?" I ask. "Did you come back with some sort of weird European disease?"

"Oh my gosh!" she squeals, running into me for a hug. "You two are so damn adorable together. Which I knew all along. Ahh! This is so great."

"Shhh!" I whisper-yell. "You're going to blow it."

"Well then you two better quit giving each other the fuck-me eyes," she says as she goes into the refrigerator to pull out the wine for us. "I mean, you can't help the 'we had sex an hour ago' energy. He's smiling, which—let's be real—Cole isn't exactly a smiley guy. And you? I think you're floating on air. Which, by the way, is a very good look on you."

I smile, because it does feel like I'm floating. "I'm so happy, Lucy. It's... I don't even know how to put it in words."

She smiles and gives my hand a squeeze. "That's when you

know you have it. When you have all of the words, yet none of the words can do justice to what you're feeling."

My best friend is so damn smart. "So, I wanted to give you a heads up. We're telling Bryce tonight."

Lucy nods. "I think that's a good idea. He's in a good mood from the honeymoon. And even if he resists at first, how can he hold out when he sees how in love you two are with each other?"

"Whoa, love?" I say. "I never said love."

Lucy picks up a few containers of whatever she ordered and gives me a wink. "You didn't need to."

————

"Who's ready for dessert?"

All three of our stomachs lurch at the sound of Bryce's question.

"How can you even think about dessert after what we just ate?" I ask. Cartons of empty Chinese food litter the table at Bryce and Lucy's. I think Lucy ordered one of everything. And there isn't a noodle or grain of rice to spare.

"Fine," he says as she stands up to start clearing the table. "I just figured we'd want a little something to snack on as we looked at wedding photos!"

"How do you have wedding pictures already?" Cole asks. "I thought those took months to get ready?"

"These are just proofs, but we couldn't wait any longer," he says. "Now, you two grab a seat. Lucy and I will clean up and bring out drinks and snacks. It's picture time!"

Cole and I do as Bryce asks and take a seat on his couch, panic both shooting through our eyes.

"This wasn't part of the plan," I whisper.

"I know," Cole grumbles. "Leave it to Bryce to get as excited about wedding photos as he does about game film. I guarantee we are going to break down and analyze every photo."

"Shit! What if photos are there of us?"

His eyes grow wide. "The ones my mom saw…"

"Exactly," I say. "What if they are there and he puts the puzzle together?"

"Then that's how we tell him. That's our Plan B." Cole reaches for my hands and gives them a squeeze. "And if he doesn't then we're on to Plan C."

"What's Plan C?"

He shrugs. "Run."

"Personally, I'm waiting to see if the photographer got any of Cole's crazy ex trying to crash the wedding."

Bryce's comment startles us so much we nearly leap back from each other like two teenagers who just got caught making out. "Yeah," I say, trying to cover our reaction up. "That would be hilarious."

"No," Bryce says, firing up the television. "The hilarious thing was that she thought you were the reason Cole dumped her."

Lucy gives me a sympathetic look as she takes a seat next to Bryce.

"Why would it be so crazy?" I ask. I mean, he brought it up. "I'm living with Cole. We've known each other for years. It wasn't a preposterous assumption on her part."

Bryce looks at me, then at Cole, then back to me. "Yes, it was. You're basically family. So for one, it's gross to even think about. And two, there's the code."

The fucking code. I hate the fucking code.

"Is that really a thing?" I ask. "Or something that football players believe in that doesn't exist. Like a weird superstition?"

"The code is sacred," Bryce says, pushing the final buttons to connect the computer to the television. "You don't date a teammate's sister. Nothing good ever comes from it. The relationships rarely work, and all they do is cause drama in the locker room. It's just better to never have them."

I don't even look at the pictures as Bryce goes through each and every one of them. How can I, when all I can do is replay what Bryce just said on a loop?

I don't want to be that person. I don't want to be the person who causes drama. I just want to be with Cole and have my brother be on board with it. Is that too much to ask?

"Oh, look!" Bryce says. "Here's a picture of the bridal party dance."

I look up and immediately push back the tears. The photographer has a wide shot of the dance floor, letting us see every couple dancing. Bryce and Lucy are looking at each other like they are the only two in the room. Celine and Luciano are blissfully smiling at each other. Then there's me and Cole. I'm guessing this had to be toward the end of the song, because my head is on his chest, and he's holding me like he's never going to let me go.

"Everyone looks so happy," Lucy says, laying her head on Bryce's shoulder.

"They do," Bryce agrees. "Except Cole and Brenna. I'm pretty sure he's trying to figure out a way to move her head from his body."

"Actually," Cole says. "That's not at all what I was thinking. Not even in the slightest."

Bryce gives him a questioning look. Lucy pops her head up suddenly from Bryce. I stop breathing.

Holy shit, here we go...

"Dude, why are you all of a sudden so serious?"

I don't know if Bryce means to, but the television screen changes to the next photo. It's of the same dance, only this time, the photo is just of Cole and me. My head is still on his chest. My eyes are closed. He's holding my right hand against his heart as his other hand is completely around my waist. His eyes are also closed.

We both look so peaceful. Like nothing in the world that could ruin this moment for us.

Bryce looks at the television then looks back to Cole.

"Dude. What the fuck?"

In a move I wasn't expecting, Cole reaches over and takes my hand in his, linking our fingers together.

And that's all we need to say.

Because before I know it, Bryce is jumping over a coffee table and punching Cole in the face.

ONE PUNCH. I always knew in my heart of hearts that when Bryce found out, I'd give him one punch. I figured it was fair since I was doing things with his sister that no brother should ever have to imagine.

And I have to give my best friend credit; I didn't know he could throw a fist like that.

"Bryce!" Lucy yells as she does her best to pull him off me. "What are you doing?"

I stand up and put a little bit of distance between us. "It's okay, Lucy."

Brenna comes over and looks at my eye, which is going to surely have one hell of a shiner there tomorrow. Again, if it wasn't this situation, and I wasn't on the receiving end, I'd be pretty impressed with Bryce.

"No, it's not!" Brenna yells. "Bryce, I know this is a shock and might be hitting you out of left field, but that's no reason to punch him."

"A shock?" he yells. "A shock would be telling me the Fury got sold to the highest bidder. This? This... I can't even fucking *think* right now I'm so mad."

I look at Brenna, who is currently fighting back tears. I

know we talked about his reactions, and this was one of them. But I don't think either of us knew how much worse it would be in person.

"Let's all sit down and try to relax," Lucy says, coming out of nowhere with two bags of frozen vegetables for me and Bryce. "We're all adults, and I think it would be wise of us to remember that right now."

Brenna and I sit down, and after Lucy gives his sleeve a tug, so does Bryce. None of us say anything for minutes. It is, without a doubt, the most uncomfortable stretch of silence I've ever experienced. But hell if I'm going to be the one who says something. Bryce is the one with the problem right now.

"How long?"

His question is so muffled I barely heard him. "Right before the wedding," I answer. "The reason we didn't tell you was because we didn't want anything to take away from your day."

"Bullshit," he says, pointing to the picture still on the screen. "That's not the face of two people who started fucking days before. So how long?"

"Sorry that we don't fit your timeline standards, brother, but Cole is telling you the truth," Brenna says. "We kissed the night before the rehearsal dinner. That was the first time anything happened between us."

Bryce looks at me, then to Brenna, then back to me again. "Brenna? Lucy? Can you excuse Cole and me? I want to talk to him. Just the two of us."

"Absolutely not," Brenna says as she stands up, almost daring to get in Bryce's face. "Whatever you want to say to him you can say in front of me."

I put a hand on her arm, bringing her back to me. "It's okay."

She looks between the two of us. "This is our fight. Together."

"I know," I say, standing up and kissing her forehead. "But let me take this round."

"Get a room!" Bryce roars. "Let me talk to my *supposed* best friend!"

Lucy steps in front of him, and I can tell she's trying to stay calm. "You're allowed to be angry. You're allowed to have your feelings. But just remember, anything you're about to say to him, you can't take back. Do you understand?"

I've always called Lucy the Bryce Whisperer. She was the only one who was ever able to bring him back when he hit his low points. And apparently, she's the only one from stopping him from grabbing a kitchen knife and stabbing me.

"I'm fine, Lulu," he says. "I just want to chat with Cole."

Brenna grabs her purse and gives me a kiss on the cheek before she and Lucy leave the apartment. We both sit back down. I hold the frozen vegetables to my eye as he holds his against his knuckles. I plan on telling him anything he wants to know, but fuck if I know at this point what he's the most upset about.

That's the problem with being Bryce Donald's best friend. On the field? The man can handle pressure and blitzing defenses like it's nothing. Real life? That's never been his strong suit. He has trouble processing a lot of things at once. So something like this? I knew it was going to throw him.

I guess I just didn't realize how much.

"I'm going to ask you again," Bryce says. "How long? And not that you've been together. How long have you had feelings for my sister?"

I sit back in the chair and take the veggies off my eye. "That I can remember? Senior year at Clemson. That's when I first realized it."

"But?"

Figures my best friend could hear the unsaid word. "But

now that we've been together, I think it was a long time before that. It was just—she was Brenna. She was your sister. That's what I thought it was. Now that we're together? I think it's always been her."

"That's it, though!" Bryce yells, standing up so he can start pacing. "She's a sister to you. Or at least she should be. You've known her as long as you've known me. This just... It isn't right."

"Or," I say, also standing up, which I don't know is a smart move on my part, but I'm going with it. "Maybe that's why it *is* right. I've known her forever. She knows me. We fit. There was no weird first date chatter. Hell, my mother was already picking our wedding invitations."

"Wait!" Bryce yells. "Your mom knows?"

I swallow, because here's the second low blow of the night. "Yes. And so does yours."

"Fucking wonderful!" Bryce yells, throwing the bag of vegetables against the wall. "Am I the last one to fucking know?"

"Yes, but not by design," I say. "We really weren't going to tell anyone. Then Luciano caught us at the wedding. And Lucy caught on, 'cause she's Lucy and you can't get anything past her. As for our families? Mom invited us home for Easter, and she just knew. We also talked to your mom so there were no secrets between our families. This wasn't done on purpose. It's just kind of how the hand played."

Daggers. That's what are shooting out of Bryce's eyes now.

"I'm sorry," I say.

"For what?" he asks. "For which of all of betrayals are you sorry for? Or is this some half-assed blanket apology?"

"Bryce, listen."

"No, Cole. *You* listen." He stops his pacing, which might be more frightening than wondering if he's going to punch me again. "You're my best friend. And, in a matter of minutes, I not only find out that you are fucking my sister, but that you also lied to me about it, and lied to me for years about having feelings for her. Then, to top it off, you tell me that everyone in my life knew except me, and you want me to listen? Fuck that, Cole. I've listened enough for one night."

"I understand," I say. "Please know though, we didn't mean to hurt you."

"Good fucking job on that one," he says.

I take the few steps I need toward his door but turn back to look at him. He's slumped down on the couch, his head resting on his fists. Usually this would be the time I'd try to coax him out of it. I'd try to help him figure out what's going on in that brain of his. And if I couldn't do it, I'd send in Lucy.

Thank God he'll have her tonight.

"One more thing," I say as I open the door. "I know this is a lot. But whenever you're ready to talk more, or to ask questions, or to figure out whatever you need to figure out, I'm here. But also know this. I love her, Bryce. She's not a fling, and I'm not just another guy. This isn't the fuck buddy of the week. I'd die before I let something happen to her. I promise to protect her at all costs. No matter who it is, that's who you should want for your sister."

Bryce looks up to me, his eyes more sad than I've seen in a very long time. The last time he looked like this involved Lucy, Luciano, and the worst months of his life. "You said that to me once. That you'd protect me. Funny how you end up being the one stabbing me in the back."

"Bryce—"

"Leave, Cole. Just fucking leave."

Realizing that this isn't going anywhere, I do what he asks and shut the door behind me.

"WAS THAT A GOOD IDEA?"

That is the eighth time Lucy has asked that question since we left the penthouse and came back down to Cole's apartment. Also known as the Neutral Zone.

"I mean, it's been a half hour," I say, setting down freshly refilled wine glasses for the two of us. "Either they are hugging it out, into the fifth round of their boxing match, or they are not speaking and uncomfortably staring at each other."

If I were a betting woman, my money would be on the last option. I would be utterly shocked if Bryce came around to the idea of Cole and me after one conversation. And while I'm sure Bryce felt better after getting in that punch, he's smart enough not to try to actually go rounds with a man who has six inches and more than a hundred pounds on him.

"Well, at least you get to stay here," Lucy says. "I have to go to the lion's den and admit that I knew about you two."

"Ah but there is the hypocritical difference when it comes to my brother," I say, tipping my wine glass to hers. "You are Lucy. His Lulu. You can do no wrong. You will be forgiven the fastest in this whole debacle. Yes, he might pout for a night.

Maybe get a little angry when you have to rein him in, but you two aren't going to bed tonight fighting."

"I don't know," Lucy says. "He was pretty mad. Then again, if I knew what he was really angriest about, maybe we could end this sooner rather than later."

"Everything. He's mad about everything."

I don't even hear the door open as Cole walks through. His eye is already swollen, and he looks mentally exhausted, but he seems otherwise unharmed.

"Hey," I say, running into his outstretched arms. "Everything okay?"

He leans down and kisses the top of my head. "I guess that depends on what your definition of okay is."

We walk back to the couch together as Lucy brings him over a bottle of water. "I'm so sorry, Cole," Lucy says. "I really thought he'd handle it better."

Cole shakes his head. "You have nothing to apologize for. In fact, I'll apologize to you because he knows now that you knew before him. So for that, I'm sorry for whatever you're about to endure."

She leans over and gives both of us a hug. "Don't worry about me. I've learned how to handle an angry Bryce Donald."

"Thank you," I say as I get up to walk her to the door. "I'll text you tomorrow."

"You better."

I start to turn away, but Lucy grabs my arm. "Just so you know, my idiot husband might be against this right now. But me? I'm in. I'm all in. I always had a feeling about you two. And I couldn't be happier. I know this will all work out. Just give it time."

I bring my best friend in for the hug of her life. "Thank you," I whisper. "Now please go work your magic on your husband."

She gives me one more squeeze before letting go. "I'll do my best."

I shut the door as Lucy heads back up the elevator. "Well, we did it."

Cole lets out a humorless laugh. "Something like that."

"Can I get you anything? Your eye doesn't look so great."

He shakes his head and reaches out his hands. "All I need right now is my girl in my arms."

I smile, because that I can do. I walk back over to him and climb on his lap, him cradling me like he's holding a baby. Which sometimes I feel like he is, considering he's a full foot taller than me. "So, we told him."

This makes him laugh. "Yeah, we did."

"Should I ask how it went?"

"Well, I didn't come back with another bruise."

"If that's the best thing that happened, then I don't know if we should consider that a win."

Cole brings me in a little tighter. "There wasn't going to be a win tonight."

"Yeah, I know." I sigh. "I love my brother, but wow, he does not process news and change well."

"He never has," Cole said. "I told him when he was ready to talk, or to ask any more questions, that I'd be here. That the ball is in his court."

"That's good," I say. "I just wish I knew what he was the most mad about."

"I don't even think he knows."

I let out a frustrated breath as Cole and I sit in silence for the next few minutes. On one hand, I feel the weight off my shoulders now that Bryce knows. No more sneaking around. No more asking people we love to keep this secret. Cole and I can now really begin our relationship with nothing between us.

On the other hand, Bryce took this way worse than I thought. Did I think he was going to get mad? Yes. But I never expected him to punch Cole. Or to have such rage in his eyes.

"Did anything you say to him get through?"

I can feel Cole shrug. "I'm not sure. I told him everything he asked. I apologized that we kept it from him, and that others found out before him."

"Oh, I'm sure he loved that."

"It definitely cranked up the rage factor," Cole says. "But I also told him that when he calmed down to remember that this isn't just a fling."

I feel my eyes welling up with tears as I look up at Cole. "It's not a fling for me, either."

"I know this is still new," he says. "I know we've not had the most conventional start to a relationship. Hell, the majority of our relationship has been spent in this apartment. But I need you to know that I love you. I love you, Brenna Donald. I've loved you since you nearly got me arrested in college. Hell, I think I might have loved you long before that. Whatever happens with Bryce, I don't care. Because that's how much I love you. I know you might—"

I cut him off, putting two fingers on his lips. "My turn."

He gives me a small smile as I remove my fingers from his lips. "You're right. This isn't normal. We're not normal. But that's what I love about us. I love that I didn't have to get to know you by playing twenty questions. I love that you knew me in my awkward stage. And in my crazy stage. And in my even crazier stage. I love that I know I can call your mom right now and she will give me every incriminating baby picture that exists of you."

"She would. She likes you better than me."

I can't help but smile at that. "I love everything about us. And I love you, Cole Campbell. Yes, you might have known it first, but I got here eventually. And I'm going to spend my life making sure you know every day how much I love you."

Cole brings our mouths together and...wow. That's all I can say. I've always known Cole doesn't wear his heart on his sleeve. But what he doesn't say he tells me in other ways. Like this kiss. If a kiss could talk, it would say that we're in this for the long haul. That no matter what's thrown our way, it doesn't matter. We love each other. And that's going to be enough.

It has to be.

And I don't care if my brother has a problem with this. No one, not even the mighty Bryce Donald, is going to come between us.

Because a love like this? This isn't normal. Which is what makes it perfect.

CHAPTER 26
COLE

I REMEMBER my draft night like it was yesterday, not three years ago.

Since I wasn't projected to go in the first round because of a knee injury I suffered senior year, I wasn't invited to the live event. Which was fine by me. I was content watching my name being called in my childhood home with my family surrounding me.

But a part of me wondered what it would have been like to be at the event on draft night. What it must have been like to be someone like Bryce, who had the red carpet rolled out for him as the eventual top pick.

Well, now that the draft is being held in Nashville, I'm here as part of the pomp and circumstance, and I can safely say I'm just fine with how my draft experience went. Yes, you can feel the energy and adrenaline from the fans lining the streets and the cameras and the lights. Yes, it's a pretty cool feeling knowing that in just a few short hours, football players' lives are about to change forever.

I'm still glad I got to do it in sweatpants while sitting on my parents' couch.

"This is insane," Brenna says, her eyes wide as she takes in the production set and the draft stage, which is situated at the end of Broadway in downtown Nashville. "I didn't know they closed the streets for anything other than country concerts."

"I mean, it kind of is." I nod to the stage, where someone is entertaining the crowd, singing what sounds like a Luke Coombs cover. Leave it to Nashville to throw in a concert between the sports.

Brenna turns to me and fixes my jacket. "Are you sure you're okay to do this?"

"For the twentieth time, I'm fine," I say, taking her hands because I know for a fact nothing is wrong with my jacket. "It's just a television interview."

"But it's with Bryce," she says. "Speaking of, where is that brother of mine?"

We both look around, but neither of us see him. Since the draft is in Nashville this year, a bunch of Fury players are doing television hits and interviews. My agent, Dean, who also represents Bryce, thought it would be a good segment to put the two of us on camera together to talk about our draft experiences. Even though we've told our story a billion times, apparently people never get tired of hearing about the two guys who have played every level of football together since they first laced up their cleats.

Then again, it would require Bryce to be here.

"He'll be here," I say. "He might not be talking to us, but he knows better than to skip out on a media engagement. Dean and Coach McAvoy would have his ass."

"Whose ass am I having?"

Dean Braxton pops through the curtain that shelters us from the crowd gathering next to the stage. Because he's always in agent mode, he's wearing a full suit and tie, cell phone in hand. I swear the man never takes a day off.

"No one's," I say. "Bryce is running a few minutes late is all."

"No worries," Dean says, turning to Brenna and extending his hand. "I don't believe we've ever officially met. Dean Braxton, agent to this guy, your brother, and another twenty Fury players."

Brenna returns the gesture. "Brenna. Nice to finally meet you."

Dean looks at Brenna, then to me, then back to Brenna. "So the rumors are true? You two are an item?"

"Rumors?" I say, all of a sudden feeling protective. "What are you hearing?"

Brenna puts a hand on my chest, instantly calming me down. "Easy, Papa Bear. All Dean means is that he heard that we are together, and he's now seeing it for himself." She turns to face Dean with an apologetic smile. "You'll have to excuse him. Because my brother is a jackass and isn't taking this well, my boyfriend here is under the assumption that everyone is going to have the same reaction."

Dean holds his hands up in defense. "Hey, I'm happy for you two. As long as Bryce doesn't do anything stupid, everything in my world is A-Okay."

As if he was waiting to hear his name, Bryce approaches us from around the stage, Lucy at his side. The three of us are staring at him, waiting to see his reaction. I know Dean is worried this is going to push him off the ledge again. I don't blame him. Considering his history, it makes sense.

As for Brenna and I? Neither of us know what to expect. We told him to sit on the news for a few days. That was a week ago. I never thought he would be butt hurt for this long. Then again, I should have known this was Bryce Donald we are talking about. The man has a flair for the dramatic.

"Dean," Bryce says as the two shake hands. "How long until we're on?"

Okay then, Bryce is going to go with the strictly business route today.

"I'm not sure. Let me go find a producer, and we'll get you two mic'd up."

Dean walks away, leaving the four of us alone. Staring at each other in awkward silence.

"So, how've you guys been?" Brenna says.

"Fine," Lucy replies. "Just getting situated. How about you?"

"Well—"

Brenna starts to answer, but Bryce cuts her off.

"This is really what we're going to do? Make small talk like we're fucking strangers?"

"Really?" I say, now just angry. "You're the reason we're all walking on eggshells. So you don't get to snap at us when this is your fault."

"My fault?" Bryce looks genuinely shocked. "I'm not the one who decided to start fucking around behind my back."

"Oh my God, Bryce! Why are you so dramatic?" Brenna says. "How many times do we need to tell you—"

"Hey!" Dean yells, startling all of us. "I don't know if you realize how loud y'all are, but I'd tone it down unless you want to be front-page news on the gossip sites."

We all take a step back and hang our heads.

"Better," Dean says, handing Bryce and I wireless mics. "Now here's how it's going to go. They want Bryce first for a segment. Bryce, they are just going to talk to you about your draft year. What it was like being the top pick. All that shit. They have promised me they aren't going to bring up the mental health year. After they break, Cole, you'll join him on stage. You'll tell the story y'all have told a hundred times. Deal?"

Bryce and I look at each other and nod our heads.

"Good," Dean continues. "Now, I don't give a flying fuck who is dating who and who feels what way about it. That is a *you* problem that shouldn't have to be a *me* problem. So you two go up on that stage and act like the two best friends you are. If one of you acts like something is off, it will only stir the pot. So put this shit aside for ten minutes, deal?"

I look at Bryce, who refuses to make eye contact with me. "I'm fine."

Bryce doesn't say anything for a second, until Lucy elbows him in the stomach. "Fine."

"Good. Now, Brycc"—Dean gives him a push on stage—"Go make everyone fall in love with you even more."

Bryce enters the stage and I see the minute he puts on his media face. He learned it early. People knew Bryce was going to be special before he played one snap of varsity football. He was doing newspaper interviews in middle school.

As for me? I was just the guy who blocked for him. Offensive linemen don't make headlines. We're just the guys who do our jobs so the quarterbacks can get the glory.

And I'm fine with that. Even now, when he's pissing me off, I'm still okay with that. He's my best friend. I've laid my life on the line for him, both physically and metaphorically, for twenty years.

Which is what infuriates me the most about how he's acting. I've been there for him through everything—through his college decision, through his ups and downs with Lucy, through the drinking and the women. Apparently, this is the thanks I get.

"If you need me to say anything to him, let me know," Dean says to me as I continue to watch Bryce on stage.

"Thanks," I say. "I don't know why he's acting like this."

"It's Bryce. Do we ever know?"

It's funny because it's true. "What do you need, Dean?"

He turns to look at me like I'm nuts. "What? Can't an agent stand next to his client and just take in the moment."

I raise an eyebrow. "He can, but he doesn't. So what's up?"

"You're a smart one, Campbell," Dean says. "Which is part of the reason why the Fury wants to offer you a contract that is going to make your head explode."

Now both eyebrows are up. "Contract? I mean, I know this is the last year of mine, but I didn't think we'd start negotiating this early."

"It's informal," Dean says. "The Fury just want me, and you, to know they are going to be serious when it comes time to sit down and nail this out. The way the front office was talking, I'd expect to see somewhere around twenty-three a year."

Now my jaw is on the ground. "Twenty-three? As in million?"

Dean smiles. "Per year. Probably six years. It would make you the highest paid lineman in the league. I just wanted to let you know that's your future, if you want it."

I have to blink a few times, because I'm trying to imagine what that kind of money would even look like.

It means paying off every bill my parents have. It means my nieces and nephews are going to be set for college or whatever the hell they want to do with their lives.

Then I catch Brenna out of the corner of my eye. I know Dean was talking about my professional and financial future, but she's the only future I care about.

I'm going to build us our dream home. I'm going to give her the wedding and honeymoon of her dreams. She'll want for nothing. She's going to have everything she's ever wanted or dared to ask for.

"You staring at me?" she says as she makes her way to me.

"What if I was?"

"You know it's rude to stare," she says as she fixes my jacket one more time.

"What if I wasn't staring?"

"Then what were you doing?"

I take both of her hands in mine. "I'm looking at the future."

This gets me a smile. "And what does this future look like?"

Dean signals that I'm about to be up, so I lean down and give her a quick kiss on the forehead. "It looks perfect."

"I FEEL like I'm in high school."

I look over to Lucy, wondering what in the world she's talking about. "What do you mean? You never snuck around in high school."

Lucy's blush takes over her face. "Well, I mean this is what I guess it would be like. The most sneaking around I did was when your brother would ask me to stay up past my curfew."

"You rebel."

We both laugh as we take sips of our margaritas. There is nothing quite like a girls' day filled with shopping, laughs, tacos, and margaritas. If this were any other day, I'd file this under a perfectly lovely day with my best friend.

Instead we've nicknamed it "Operation Hard Head." As in, my brother is being a hard head. And that's the nice way of putting it.

Why did we have to give a code name to our girls' day? Because my brother still isn't talking to me or his best friend. Lucy and I talk, but only through discreet text messages. I wanted to run up to her last week at the draft interviews and give her a big hug because I miss her. It was then we decided we needed a day all to ourselves.

"So, we've not talked about it long enough."

Lucy shakes her head at my statement. "Nope. A little longer. For just a little longer I want to pretend everything is fine and this a normal day. So, right now, I'm going to sip on this delicious margarita, and you're going to gush about Cole to me the way you've been dying to for weeks."

I laugh a little at her enthusiastic denial. "Who said I've been wanting to gush?"

Lucy raises an eyebrow while simultaneously taking a drink. "Because you never stop smiling, and that says a lot when it comes to you. And, even though it's in the eighties today, you are, for some reason, wearing a turtleneck. Want to tell me what that's about?"

I feel the blush coming over my cheeks. "Cole might have been a little extra...*bitey*...last night."

Lucy lets out a shriek that I'm pretty sure the whole restaurant heard. "Cole is a biter?"

I shake my head. "No. He likes to kiss. And nibble. And last night it just got a little much. And that might or might not have had to do with the fact we were having sex in the parking garage."

"Brenna Donald!"

I shrug, while reaching for my glass. "I have found that I might not be wild in the ways of my past, but there is something about Cole that makes me feel a little...daring."

"Daring how?"

I smile and lean in, because this has to be whispered. "We might or might not like to have sex in places we're not supposed to."

"Brenna Marie Donald!"

I shrug, leaning back into the booth. "What can I say? Roofs. Jeeps. On the open road. We like to keep it spicy."

She furiously shakes her head. "I'm never going to be able to look at Cole now."

"Good," I say. "Now you understand how I feel knowing the kind of sex noises my brother makes."

"Fair," Lucy says in defeat. "So let's review: Cole passes the arm test. He also passes other tests I didn't know you had. Now, for the biggest question of them all, what, my dear Brenna, have you nicknamed him?"

This catches me off guard because I honestly hadn't thought about it. Maybe because other guys have been so bad so quick, the only thing to get me through the date was to figure out what I was going to nickname them for future stories. But with Cole? A nickname hadn't even crossed my mind.

"Can I sound cheesy?" I ask.

Lucy smiles. "The cheesier the better."

"Now don't laugh."

"I would never."

"He's Mr. Perfect."

In any other situation, I would vomit in my mouth if someone said that to me about a guy. Hell, I'm fighting back the urge just listening to myself. But it's true. The man is perfect. And yes, I know we're still in the honeymoon stage where everything is new and great. But even when things settle down and become normal, I can't imagine him not being perfect.

Because he's perfect for me.

"That is..." Lucy says, fighting back tears. "The sweetest thing I have ever heard you say. Which means now more than ever we have to get your brother to get his head out of his ass."

"Ugh," I moan. "Why is he my brother? Why not your husband?"

"Because I'm slightly still mad at him. Therefore he's your brother. He can be my husband later when he clues in."

I let out a sigh of disappointment. "I really didn't think he'd be mad for this long."

"Well," Lucy begins, then stops to take a healthy sip of her margarita. "I have at least got out of him the why."

"Really?" I nearly yell, but I don't care. This has been what has bothered me the most. "Please tell me. At least then we can know what to focus on so we can get past this."

"Well, that might be easier said than done."

"Go on…"

"So at the end of the day, it's a little bit of everything. He does think it's weird that you two are dating, and admits that he could get over that with time. He also said that he might put in a no PDA policy."

"That's fair," I say. "I know how weird it is when I see you two kiss, and we've only been friends since college."

"Exactly. So he has admitted to me, though the stubborn ass won't say it to the two of you, that the physical part will be an adjustment for him. The bigger thing for him is that he feels you both lied to him."

I sink into the booth a little bit. "I mean, he's right. But it wasn't this great conspiracy theory."

"And therein lies the disagreement."

I quirk an eyebrow. "I'm not following."

"In Bryce's head, Cole has been lying to him for years."

"Well, by that way of thinking, I should be mad at Cole too because he didn't tell me either."

"That's neither here nor there," Lucy says. "All that matters, at least to Bryce, is that he feels that his best friend lied to him and that it was ongoing."

"Cole won't apologize. In his mind, Bryce thinking that this was some massive conspiracy is unreasonable."

Ugh, I feel like both sides have a point and the answer is somewhere in the gray. And the problem is, both Bryce and Cole are very literal people. They prefer answers in black and white. In their minds, gray isn't an option.

Which sucks because this whole situation is fifty shades of gray.

And not in the kinky way.

"I hate this, Luce. For the first time in my life, I'm in a relationship that I want to shout from the rooftops about. This should be perfect. We should be the happiest couple of couples in Nashville. Two best friends dating other best friends. We should be double dating and having dinners with each other. We should be making silly videos on ForU where people get jealous of how amazing we are at being couples. This just sucks."

Lucy nearly slams down her drink. "Brenna! That's it!"

Now I'm confused. "What's it? The videos? I mean, it could be fun, but I doubt I could get Cole to do viral couple challenges."

"No—actually, if you could, that would be hilarious—but that's not what I'm talking about."

"Then please tell me what made you slam your drink down so hard it shook the whole restaurant?"

"A double date."

Hmm... I might have just said it in passing, but I like where this could go. "Continue..."

Lucy sits up straight like she's about to give a presentation. "Bryce used to always give Cole shit about not having a girlfriend because that meant they could never double date."

"Well, I mean, you guys did get to go out with him and Jessica."

Lucy rolls her eyes. "Don't remind me."

I laugh. "She was a bit crazy."

"Off her rocker, but that's not the point. What if we convince both of them to go on a double date? Something super casual. Let them let loose so they can remember their friendship. Maybe, just maybe, it will melt some of the frost, and we can start making our way back to peaceful times."

My smile grows wider with every word that comes out of Lucy's mouth. "That, my dear Lucy, is why you are the smart one out of our bunch. Absolutely brilliant. Do you have anything in mind?"

Lucy nods. "Of course I do. But let me make sure I can get Bryce on board. I don't want to lie to him; that would only put me on his shit list. He has to be willing to come for this to work."

"That's fair," I say. "And how are you going to get him to agree to this?"

Lucy's smile becomes devious. "Let's just say if he says no, I'm about to have a long string of headaches that come on just as we're about to go to bed every night."

I hold my glass. "Lucy Donald. You are a genius."

She clinks her glass with mine. "Some call it a genius. Some call it desperate times calling for desperate measures. Now, let's get our hard-headed men back together."

CHAPTER 28
COLE

"STRIKE! THAT'S MY MAN!"

I chuckle and shake my head at how excited Brenna gets when I get a strike. It almost makes me want to do a little victory dance.

Almost.

"Lucky."

I hear Bryce mumble from the other side of the seating area. If we were on good terms, I'd throw back some remark about how I'm going to get lucky with his sister later. But I know my audience, and now is not the time for that joke.

I'm starting to wonder if it ever will be.

"No luck needed," Brenna says. "Just admit it. Cole and I are better bowlers than you two."

"Hell no," Bryce says, not an ounce of humor in his voice. "Give me the damn ball."

Bryce stomps up to the lane, ball in hand and flings it down the lane straight into the gutter. Now, Bryce is not a good bowler. Yes, the man who gets paid millions of dollars to throw a football to a moving target has trouble rolling a ball sixty feet to attempt to knock down ten stationary pins. However, every other time we've been bowling, it's usually been with teammates in some sort of team-building scenario. His terrible bowling has always served as a good joke among the guys. And he's leaned into it.

Not tonight. Tonight he wants to beat me. Decimate me.

He forgets that in high school, I was an all-state bowler and have rolled four perfect games in my life already.

And maybe if I were in a more generous mood, I'd take it easy on him. But considering he has barely looked my way tonight, I'm not.

"Maybe bowling wasn't the best idea," Lucy whispers from across the way.

"No, it was a good idea," Brenna says. "Nothing opens the lines of communication more than a little competition."

I give the girls credit; they are trying. They can both see how hard this is on everyone. If I thought Bryce was at all coming around, maybe I'd put in an effort. But as far as I see it, I'm not about to go killing myself for him when he would rather pout in a corner.

"Order number ten, your food is ready at the pickup window. Order number ten!"

"That's us!" Brenna yells, jumping up from her seat. "Lucy, why don't you come help me carry it?"

Lucy looks back and forth between me and Bryce. "Sure! I'd be glad to."

The girls leave, letting the two of us sit there in silence.

"I forgot how good you were at bowling," Bryce mumbles.

"And I forgot how much you stink."

For the first time in weeks, my best friend cracks a smile. "God couldn't have made me a good bowler too. It just would have made me too powerful."

I chuckle. "Yeah. That must have been it."

The silence falls back on us, though it doesn't feel as

awkward as it did just minutes ago. Maybe this whole bowling/date night was a good idea?

"So how is married life?" I ask, hating how the small talk sounds, but not knowing what else to say.

"Great," Bryce says. "I mean, not much has changed. We started to look at property down in Franklin."

I can't hide the shocked expression on my face. "Wow. Already?"

He shrugs. "Yeah. I mean, it will take a while for the house to get built. Might as well get a move on it since we know that's where we want to be."

I swallow the response I want to say—which is "gee, thanks for including me." I mean, if we're still going to build next to each other, I should have been a part of that. But apparently I'm not a part of those plans anymore.

"Good for you," I choke out, looking to see if Brenna and Lucy are on their way back. Sneaky women are nowhere to be seen.

"You know they did that on purpose, right?"

I look back to Bryce. "Of course I do. But hey, at least they are trying to get the ball moving."

"What's that supposed to mean?" he asks.

Really? Is he that self-absorbed? "It means that I have tried to reach out to you to talk. The girls put this whole night together to at least try to break some ice. Then there's you, playing the Bryce Donald pity-me card. Well, guess what, buddy? It doesn't work on me. And you should know that after all the shit we've been through. I'm not going to fall for your woe-is-me, feel-bad-for me act."

"At least I'm not playing the holier-than-thou card."

"Excuse me?" He can't be serious.

"You're acting like you're innocent in all of this. You aren't, buddy. Not by a long shot."

I can't believe what I'm hearing. "Do you think I'm apologizing just to say the words? I know I did you wrong. And I've been trying to apologize for weeks, but you won't listen to me."

"What are you apologizing for?"

Bryce's question throws me. "What do you mean?"

"It means, what exactly are you apologizing for?" Bryce asks. "Sleeping with my sister? Breaking the bro code of not only friendship, but of a locker room? The sneaking around? Or the fact that you've been lying to me for years? Which one, Cole? Or is that one 'I'm sorry' supposed to make up for it all?"

Wow. I didn't realize I committed so many cardinal rules just by wanting to be with Brenna. "I don't even know where to begin with all that."

Bryce leans back, extending his arms out on the chairs at the alley. "Wherever you want to. I mean, you do that anyway, might as well continue."

"First of all," I say, trying my best to keep my voice and tone low. "It would be good to remind you that your sister is an adult. It's not like I kidnapped her and made her fall in love with me."

"Love?" He says it in almost a laughing tone.

"Yes, Bryce. Love. I love her. She loves me. I've told you this isn't just sex. Do you think we'd risk all of this for just sex?"

Bryce throws his hands in the air. "How the hell should I know? It seems that you did to start with."

"Are you going to be reasonable and try to listen to me or are you going to have a snarky comeback for everything?"

"Fine," he says, though I think he barely means it. "Go on."

"As for the sneaking around? It was three days. And the other part of it was when you were on your honeymoon. How can we sneak around when you were out of the fucking country?"

"Oh, well, then that brings up another point," Bryce says,

now leaning toward me. "How about the fact that I was the last one to know? That's fucking nice."

"Get over it, man," I say. "It wasn't on purpose. In fact, everyone we told we specifically asked to keep to themselves because we wanted you to hear this from us. We didn't want to sneak around. We didn't want this to be weird. We wanted nights like tonight, you know, except without the fact that we are five seconds from punching each other."

This makes Bryce laugh, but not in the humor-filled way. "You have an excuse or a reason for everything. Yet in all of this, I still haven't heard an actual 'I'm sorry.'"

This man is going to be the death of me. "What do you want me to be sorry for? Just tell me so we can get on with our lives!"

Bryce just shakes his head. "We've been friends for twenty years. Twenty years of blood, sweat, and tears. Twenty years of sharing things with each other that will go to the grave. You were my brother in more ways than I thought was fathomable. Then I find out one day that you've been lying to me for seven years. And not just about something little. Something that affected us both. That's a hard pill to swallow, Cole."

"I'm sorry, Bryce. I'm sorry that's how you see it," I truly mean those words, even if he doesn't believe me. "I honestly never thought that's how you would see it. Because in my mind, I wasn't lying to you. If anything, I was trying to stop myself from feeling it. Do you know how many nights of sleep I lost because I felt like the worst friend in the world for wishing that I was with Brenna? How many events I skipped out because I knew she would be there, and it would be too much for me to handle? How many nights I drank myself stupid because I knew she was with another man? So you might see it as lying, but to me it wasn't that. If anything, I was trying like hell to make it so I was lying to myself."

I look back and I see the girls standing next to the seats, food in hand. By the looks on their faces, they heard at least my last rant. I know Brenna did. The tear escaping her eye gives her away.

"Hey," I say, standing up, taking the food from her hold, setting it down before I wrap her in my arms. As soon as I do, her one tear turns into many. "Shh. Don't cry. It's in the past."

I look back at Bryce, Brenna still in my arms. This. This has to be his turning point. Can't he see it as I can? That every step of the way I thought about him and our friendship?

"Can we call this?" I ask. "I'm tired of fighting. I'm tired of consoling. I'm tired of apologizing. Can't we start this over? Can't this *be* over?"

We all look at Bryce, who is just staring at Brenna in my arms. She's unsuccessfully fighting back her tears, but she hasn't let go of me. Can't he see what he's doing to us? To his own sister?

"I'm sorry," he says, walking toward Lucy and taking her hand. "But I'm not ready. Lucy, let's go."

She drops the tray of food she's holding as she lets Bryce lead her away. She turns back to mouth that she's sorry, which I know she is. I can't imagine being her right now, being torn like this.

"I thought that was going to be it," Brenna says.

I kiss the top of her head and squeeze her tighter against me. "So did I, Trouble. So did I."

THE ONE THING I always loved about my relationship with my brother was that we had what many twins have—the intuition. The twin brain sharing.

Except now. Now I don't know what the hell is going on in that thick skull of his.

Which is why I'm marching up to his apartment now and demanding that he tell me, once and for all, what the hell his problem is.

"Bryce!" I yell, pounding on his door. "Open up! I know you're in there!"

I hear him grumbling before he swings the door open. "Geez. What the hell, Bren?"

I walk through without waiting for a formal invitation. "Funny, that was the question I was about to ask you."

It's been three days since the blowup at the bowling alley, and I've decided I've had enough. Cole is sitting back doing nothing, as if he and Bryce are playing a silent game of chicken. But not me. Nope. I'm taking action.

"If Cole sent you up here, tell him it's no use," Bryce says.

"Cole didn't send me here," I say. "In fact, if he knew I was up here right now he'd probably tell me not to waste my breath. Too bad for him I'm a hard-headed woman, and I don't give up that easily."

Bryce walks to his oversized couch and takes a seat. "What do you want me to say, Brenna?"

I go and sit next to him. "I want you to quit acting like a jerk. I want you to actually try to be happy for us. I want you to stop acting like the whole world was out to get you."

He smiles. "Is that it?"

I shake my head. "No. My list is very, very long. But that's where we're going to start."

Bryce leans back, looks up at the ceiling and lets out a deep breath. Which is fine. Let him gather his thoughts. I have no place to be and all the time in the world.

Especially for something this important.

"I can't get over that he has been harboring something for you for years. Years! And he didn't tell me. Or you."

"Why does that bother you so much?" I ask, genuinely curious. "Don't you see he didn't tell you because he tried to put you and your friendship first? And think of it, what would you have said?"

"Huh?"

"What would you have said? He told me he first knew after I came down and visited y'all at Clemson your senior year. What would you have done if he had said, 'Bryce. I think I'm in love with your sister.'"

"I—" Bryce starts to speak, but quickly stops. "I don't know what I would have said."

"Neither do I, but I guarantee it wouldn't have been anything good."

He laughs. "Probably not."

"If I were to guess, you would have gone on and on about that bro code—that, by the way, is not a real thing."

"It is so."

"It's a convenient excuse for you to be mad."

"It's real."

"Okay then," I say sarcastically. "Whatever you need to tell yourself to sleep at night. But back to the point, if he would have told you then, don't act like you would have been 'Great! Let me set you up with my sister!' Because we both know you wouldn't have, so quit acting like you would have reacted differently if you had known."

Bryce nods, but doesn't say anything. Which in my book right now is a win.

"So tell me. Just you and me. What's the real reason? Is it really the lying? Is it something else? Because I miss my brother, and I know Cole hasn't said it, but he misses you too. And frankly, I'm not very good at Call of Duty, so I need you two to kiss and make up."

Bryce almost smiles before shutting it back down. "I just feel like this was slapped in my face and everyone else in the world had time to process it."

I nod. "That's valid."

"I mean, Cole had years. You—well, I don't know about you, and I'm not sure I want to. There's still some brother waters that I'm not sure how to navigate here."

I let out a little sigh, my shoulders starting to relax, because the more he keeps talking, the more he sounds like my brother.

"I mean, Mom knew. Luciano and Celine knew. Hell, even crazy Jessica knew. And it was right in front of my face, and I didn't see it."

"In your defense, you were kind of staring at your wife."

This gets me a smile. "I was. But I feel like I should have realized that for years my best friend was in love with my sister."

"So you missed some signs? So what? You're here now. You're in the know."

"Yes but..."

"But what?"

"Never mind," he says, trailing off. "It's not important."

I don't know whether or not to press right now. I feel like if I do, it's only a matter of time before I step on a wire. So I'm just going to sit back and let Bryce navigate this conversation. Which is why it makes me jump a little when I feel Bryce's hand on mine. Bryce and I are close, don't get me wrong. And I know since he quit drinking and started seeing a therapist consistently, one of his main goals is to be more present for his friends and family. But this? His whole reaction to me and Cole? This feels like I'm entering a new sibling territory of protectiveness.

"This wasn't how it was supposed to be," he says.

"What do you mean?" I ask.

"I just...it wasn't supposed to be like this. We had plans."

"Yes, I know," I groan. "You know it's not normal for two men to plan to build houses next door to each other?"

This gets me a smile. "I mean, it just makes sense that if we want to raise our boys to play football together then we should live next door to each other. How else are they supposed to practice together?"

"And didn't you always bug him about finding a girlfriend so you guys could double?"

He rolls his eyes at that one. "Yeah, but I didn't mean my sister."

"Well then you should have been more specific."

"I tried," he said. "But he didn't listen."

Now I'm smiling. "No, he didn't. Not at all."

We sit in silence for a minute or two, and for the first time in weeks, I feel the air is a little lighter. That I might have made a breakthrough.

"I'm sorry I've been acting like this, but you know I don't process things in normal ways," Bryce says.

"If that isn't the truest thing I've heard today…"

"I get what you're saying. I know I need to get over it. And I'm close. I promise I am. But I need some time alone to process it all."

I nod. "That's okay. I'm okay with that. As long as I know we're going in the right direction."

He wraps me in his arms and gives me a tight side hug. "Lucy and I have been talking about going away for a bit. Get out of town before the season starts."

"Didn't you two just go on a honeymoon?"

"Yeah, and that was nice. But we're going to go home for a few weeks. Maybe take a trip with Luciano and Celine. Maybe another few weeks just the two of us. Give me that time, and I promise when I come back, I'll be in a better place, and I can talk to Cole with a better head on my shoulders."

I give him another tight squeeze. Progress. It's not the end, but I see the light at the end of the tunnel. And I'll take it.

"You go do what you need to do," I say. "We'll be here. Always."

KEY TURN IN: Check.

Equipment inventory: Check.

All of my fun science posters that I insist the kids love, even if they pretend they are corny, off my walls: Check.

Another year teaching science to seventh graders: Check.

I throw up my arms in victory as I walk out of school for the last time this year. Technically, yesterday was our last day with students. Today was the teachers' last day. Summer vacation is here.

And boy, do I need it.

Don't get me wrong, I couldn't have asked for a better first year at this school. But no matter where you teach, middle schoolers are exhausting. Add on to it the drama with Bryce, who has also been acting like a twelve-year old boy, and it's safe to say I'm going to relish every second of this summer break.

Maybe I can even convince Cole to take a vacation with me. Somewhere warm. With a beach. Where we can have drinks with little umbrellas, soak up the sun during the day and soak up each other at night.

Yes, that's going to happen.

I smile thinking about our hypothetical vacation as I make my way to my car. I'm so in my head thinking about bikini shopping that I almost don't realize my six-foot-four hunk of a man leaning against my car.

Holding a bouquet of flowers.

"What are you doing here?"

He hands me the flowers, but, of course, not before pulling me in for a kiss that is borderline inappropriate for a school parking lot.

"It's your last day of school. I wanted to surprise you."

I look around to make sure we're not being watched before I jump into his arms, kissing him again. I find it funny that I once used to give men the arm test. Like anyone else's could ever compare to Cole's. Especially when he's holding me like I weigh nothing.

"How about," I whisper in his ear, while also leaving small little kisses on his neck, "we go home, I put on a little something that I've been waiting to surprise you with, and we celebrate the end of the school year with orgasms?"

This gets me a chuckle, which wasn't exactly the reaction I was looking for.

"While that does sound good, I thought we'd celebrate in a different way."

I bring my eyes back to his. I love his eyes so much. They are the clearest and brightest blue I've ever seen. Yes, I have blue eyes, but nothing like his.

I wonder what our kids' eyes would look like? I've never thought about that before. A little girl with our shared brown hair and his crystal blues? Or maybe a little boy with blue-gray like mine? I can see both so clearly. The four of us at a little league football game. Cole coaching on the sidelines while I get the cheerleaders ready. Our son geared up while our little girl jumps up and down with her pom-poms.

It's the most perfect thing I've ever dreamed about.

"Earth to Brenna. Did you hear any of that?"

I shake my head, coming back to the present. "Sorry. I was daydreaming."

Instead of being annoyed, Cole just smiles. "Well, then you're really going to be surprised, because I'm not going to tell you again what's in store for the rest of the night."

Now this surprises me. "The night?"

"Yup," he says, slowly putting me down. "Brenna Donald, your summer of fun begins right now."

———

"What are we doing here?"

My body doesn't know whether to cringe or smile as we pull up to Fire Lights. On one hand, this was the scene from my awful date with Dexter. On the other hand, Cole had to come pick me up that night. It was the first night I spent in his bed, even if it was without him. It was the night I became addicted to his smell and comfy pillows.

"You're not very good at surprises, are you?" Cole jokes as he gets out of his Jeep. He comes around to my side to open my door before giving his keys to the valet.

"I'm a curious person."

Cole takes my hand and leads me toward the door. There is a line around the block of anxious people waiting to get in, but all he does is nod to the bouncer, who unclicks the velvet rope to let us through.

Well, isn't that fancy.

When we walk inside, the sound of live music overtakes my body. I don't remember having this experience when I came here with Dexter. Then again, he hauled me so fast up to the third floor, I don't even know if this was going on. But now that I'm here, I want to take in every second of it.

I let go of Cole's hand as I wander to the stage. I've always loved live music. There is just something about the energy in the room that is different from anything else. Take this band right now: They are no one anyone would recognize, but that isn't stopping them from treating this like they are headlining at Madison Square Garden. They are playing like tonight is finally the night some Nashville hot-shot producer is going to change their lives forever.

Also, this lead singer is belting the hell out of this Carrie Underwood cover, and I am here for it.

I'm swaying to the music, singing right along with her, when I feel Cole's arms snake around my waist. He doesn't say anything. Instead, he just stands and dances with me. I rest my head against his chest, loving every second about this moment. Our bodies are swaying to the beat, changing tempos with each song. I must say, this band is damn good. Either that or I'm just a sucker for 2000s country covers.

"Are you having fun?" Cole asks, his mouth right next to my ear.

I nod as I turn to him, his hands still firmly around my waist. "How did you know this is exactly what I needed?"

"Can I just say I know you that well?"

"You can, but even you aren't this good."

"Oh, but I am," he says, taking my hand and leading me toward the elevator. It opens and we quickly step in as he hits the button for the second floor. "I know how stressed you've been, so I wanted to give you a night that you didn't have to think about anything. Then, I remembered one conversation when you said that, more than anything, you wanted to experience Nashville. You wanted the food, and—"

"The music and the line dancing," I say, finishing his sentence.

Cole smiles as the elevator opens. "So, we crossed off the food on our first date. I knew no matter what there would be a band here, so that checks off the music. So now, there is only one more thing to do."

I look around and it's like every video I see on ForU of line dancing bars. Guys and girls mixed in together, somehow all knowing what to do at the same time. It's fascinating to watch.

"Oh my gosh, Cole!" I squeal, jumping quickly to give him a quick kiss. "This is amazing."

We take a few more steps toward the floor when the song changes to a pop song that for some reason has taken over line dancing culture. At least, that's what I gather from videos I watch. I mean, I can't blame them, the song is catchy as hell, even if it is sung by a redheaded guitarist who is usually known for his ballads.

"Oh I love this one!" I squeal. "I'm going to go out and try!"

I don't wait for Cole as I make my way onto the floor. For one, I'm too excited to try this dance in person. Second, Cole isn't a dance kind of guy. At the wedding I never saw him on the dance floor except when we had to dance together.

So color me shocked when he follows me onto the floor. And not only does he follow me, he jumps right into the dance like he made up the damn thing.

"What are you doing?"

Cole gives me a sexy smirk as his feet and body move effortlessly with the music. "What does it look like I'm doing?"

I'm frozen as I watch his feet move to the beat of the song. He's doing it perfectly. Believe me, I have watched no less than a hundred videos of people doing this dance. Yes, I will admit I have found a few of the men doing it hot as they hit every step to the beat. But watching Cole move like his body is in perfect sync with the music as he holds eye contact with me? It is by far the sexiest thing I have ever seen in my life.

I start moving my feet, though I have no idea if I'm doing it right. I can't possibly concentrate right now. "How did I not know you could dance like this? I feel like I should have known this."

He smiles again, but doesn't answer me right away. Instead, he waits until after the signature part of the dance where everyone jumps three times on a specific beat.

"I'm a man of many talents," he says.

"Obviously," I say, my feet now finding the rhythm and pattern of steps. Before I know it, Cole and I are in perfect unison. We even improvise a bit, changing the direction so we can look at each other. This isn't supposed to be a partner dance, but somehow we've made it one. Our eyes are locked as our feet continue to move to the music. I swear my body is on fire right now. Between the way Cole's body is moving and the way he's looking at me, I'm about ready to fuck him in the middle of this dance floor.

The song changes to a slow one, but instead of walking off the floor, Cole takes my hand in his, pulls me closer, and dips me so low I think I'm about to fall. But I know I'm not. Cole would never let that happen.

Ever.

The last time we were here, I trusted him to carry me to safety.

Little did I know then that he was carrying me to our future.

"Can I ask for one more thing?" I beg as he brings me back upright.

"Anything."

"Take me home."

CHAPTER 31

COLE

"PANTS OFF, CAMPBELL. NOW."

I barely have the door closed before Brenna is furiously trying to undo the button of my jeans. In her defense, she at least listened to my request not to undo them in the Jeep during the ten-minute ride back to the apartment—or do anything else that would make me recite football stats from 1994 in my head.

What I have in mind for her is going to take a lot longer than ten minutes. And I can't be wasting precious restraint on whatever her naughty mouth had in mind.

"It's cute you think you're in charge," I say as I take both of her hands in mine and place them above her head. "But I'm not done with your surprises yet."

She bites her lip, which drives me absolutely insane. I don't know why. Then again, everything this woman does drives me crazy in the best possible way.

"Now, you have to be tired of wearing these pants all day," I say as I lower myself to my knees. I slip off her shoes before slowly unbuttoning her jeans, which, by the way her hips are moving, is driving her crazy.

Good. Exactly how I want her.

I slowly slide her jeans and panties down her legs. She steps out of each leg with ease, leaving her hands exactly where I told her to. Brenna might be as independent and hard-headed as they come, but in the bedroom, my girl is nothing if not obedient.

"Cole," she moans. I know that tone. She wants more.

Who am I to keep my girl from having anything?

I waste no more time, taking one leg and resting it on my shoulder, giving me perfect access to bury my face in her sweet pussy, sucking on her clit like my life depends on it.

I hear Brenna gasp, her hands all of a sudden tugging on my hair. Yes, I know I told her to leave them up, but I'll allow this. She doesn't know this, but I love it when she does that. The feel of the pull lets me know how much she loves my mouth on her. If anything, it makes me want to give her more.

And I do. I continue to suck, my tongue getting in on the action, flicking the swollen bundle of nerves as her hips begin to move circles on my face.

"Fuck, Cole!" she cries out, her one knee starting to wobble.

I know I should lay her down, let her enjoy this without having to keep standing. But I have a better idea.

My other hand scoops up her other knee so she's now sitting on my shoulders, the only thing holding her up is the door and my hands holding onto her for dear life. I feel her relax into my hold. Good. Because I am a man on a mission and like hell am I going to stop now.

She doesn't have much time to relax before my tongue starts working overtime. I'm a strong guy, but I don't know how long I can hold her here. Not because it's too much, but because with every second I taste her sweetness, it gets harder for me to concentrate. She's like a drug. I can't get enough of her. I crave her daily. And when I get a fix like this? All I want is to taste every drop I can get.

Brenna's grip tightens on my hair just as her legs begin to squeeze around me. "I'm close, Cole. I'm so close."

Her words send me into overdrive. My mouth is sucking and nipping while my tongue is flicking furiously on her clit. I know the combination is working because I am one nibble away from Brenna ripping half of my hair out.

"Yes!" she yells just as I feel her pussy begin to contract. My tongue slowly begins to ease its feast on her before I lay her back down on the ground.

I can't help but stare at her. God, she's beautiful. Her hair is a mess. Her face has a beautiful flush. The top she's wearing is now completely wrinkled and somehow missing a button. Her breathing is heavy, and I think she could pass out right here.

She has never looked more beautiful than she does right now.

I lean down to kiss her, knowing she'll be able to taste herself on me. She knows it too, as her fingers slide through my hair, bringing me in even closer to her.

"I love you," I say, brushing a loose strand of hair away from her face. "I love you so fucking much."

"I love you too," she says. "But you know what would make me love you even more?"

"What's that?"

"If you were to take me to our bedroom and let me show you how much today meant to me."

I don't know if it was the words "our bedroom" or knowing that when Brenna wants to be in charge in the bedroom I'm never disappointed, but I don't waste a second. I jump up from the ground and pick her up like she's nothing more than a lap dog. This, of course, makes her giggle as I all but run to our room, which is only twenty feet away, and nearly jump onto the bed with her in my arms.

"Anxious, are we?" she asks as she gently pushes me to my back.

"For you? Always."

I lay back and smile as she finishes the work on my pants she started the second we walked in the door. She then straddles my legs to get a better angle to work on the buttons of my shirt.

"Do you know how many places I wanted you to fuck me tonight?"

I smile, because even though I have an idea, I want to hear her dirty little mind and mouth at work. "How many?"

"Well—" She begins slipping the shirt over my shoulders. I sit up just enough to take it off, and of course steal a kiss. "I considered going down on you in the school parking lot when you surprised me there, but I figured I'd probably lose my job."

"We wouldn't want that now, would we?"

She shakes her head as she lifts her top off over her head and tosses it to the side. "Then there was at dinner. I figured there I could sneak under the table. It was a dark restaurant. No one would have noticed."

My hands trail up her smooth stomach to her perfect tits, which are covered by the sexiest lace bra I have ever seen. "I like that restaurant. Probably best we don't get kicked out for public indecency."

"That's what I thought too," she said, her hands trailing behind her back and quickly undoing her bra. "Then there was the club. I know we could have done it there."

"I'm sure I could have bribed my security guard friends to clear us a dark corner."

Her back arches as I start pinching her nipples. I know she wants to be in charge now, and I want to let her be, but fuck, if she doesn't hurry this up I can't promise that I'm not going to flip her over just so I can suck her tits for as long as I want.

"I bet they could have," she says, taking my cock in her hand and stroking it. "But as much as I love being adventurous, tonight is just about us. Because, Cole Campbell, I'm not sure if you realize this, but I love the hell out of you."

That's it. That's all I can take. I flip her over and cover her body with mine in point two seconds. Before she even realizes what I've done, my mouth is on her, kissing her like I've never kissed her before.

We don't say another word. Our mouths are too busy taking what they want. Without separating, I line up my dick to her core and slowly press in, filling her inch by inch as our mouths and hands touch each other everywhere and anywhere.

"Cole!" she yells as I push all the way in. "You feel so good."

"Not as good as you," I say, meaning every word. Her warmth surrounds me, and as much as I'd love to take my time and savor every moment of this, I can't. I'm too worked up. She's right. We've had a whole day of flirting and foreplay. It's more than time.

I scoop her up off the bed and bring her to my lap.

"What are you doing?" she asks.

I take each of her tits in my hands, giving them a squeeze as I quickly suck the nipple of each one. "Seeing what I missed earlier?"

She raises her brow. "Earlier?"

"Earlier," I say, continuing to slowly work my dick inside her. "Show me how you would have let me fuck you at the club."

The fire in her eyes is immediate. "Really?"

I nod. "You heard me. Tell me how you wanted to be fucked. What kind of bad girl was Brenna ready to be tonight?"

She gives me a hard kiss and bites on my bottom lip just hard enough to send a shot of electricity straight to my dick as she climbs off me. She walks backward toward my wall, never taking her eyes off me, even as she turns to the wall and puts her hands against it.

"What are you waiting for?" she asks, slowly bending over.

It takes me three steps to get to her. I press one hand down on the small of her back as my other hand guides my dick back to where it's aching to be. She's so wet it's no problem sliding into her, and I know this was my idea, but it's taking every ounce of energy I have to hold myself up.

"Fuck, Brenna," I say, letting my hands wrap around her stomach, traveling up to her tits. I take one in each hand as I take her from behind, twisting her nipples as I begin to pick up my pace.

She meets me thrust for thrust. Her hands are the only thing keeping her from hitting her head against the wall. I take my hands and bring them up higher, holding her away from the wall.

"I got you, baby," I say. "I got you."

Her back is arched, and it only takes a few more thrusts before I feel her start to contract around me. Furiously, I pick up my pace, wanting to give this to her more than I want to take my next breath. It doesn't take long before her body freezes, nearly collapsing back into the wall.

"Fuck!" I yell, my balls tightening the second I feel her orgasm begin. I don't know how we both don't fall to the floor in that second. Somehow, we hold each other up and clumsily stumble back to the bed.

"That was..." I begin, though I don't know how to finish it.

Brenna turns to look at me. She looks thoroughly fucked— flushed and fucking beautiful. "That was us. And I wouldn't have it any other way."

I HAD SO many plans for Cole and I this summer. We were going to go on vacation. Go and visit our parents. Have lazy days by the pool. Go to the huge country music festival that takes over Nashville for a week in June.

Finally get Bryce and Cole talking again.

We did three of those things. We had plenty of lazy days by the pool. We made it to the country festival for one night. We got tickets in the Fury's suite and had it all to ourselves.

We made the most of it.

Twice.

We also made it back to Laurel Heights, and I don't know if it was a good or bad thing, but we missed Bryce and Lucy being there. It has officially been more than two months since Bryce and Cole have said a word to each other. They have never gone that long without speaking. Hell, before this fight they used to text more than teenage girls.

But now the summer is over—at least for the guys it is. Camp opens tomorrow, and it's officially football season again.

Which means tonight is the night. Lucy and I have it all planned out. If we need to, we're going to lock them in a room together until they kiss and make up.

We refuse to let them go to camp without speaking.

"You didn't have to go all out," Cole says as I put the final plate down at the dining table. "It's just Bryce and Lucy."

"Exactly, it's Bryce and Lucy," I say, straightening the centerpiece I picked up the other day. "Maybe if he sees how much this place has become ours, he'll realize this is for real between us, and he needs to suck it up and get over it."

"Speaking of ours," Cole says, tossing me a letter. "This came for you today from your apartment complex."

I take the letter and rip it open.

"What does it say?"

I hold up a finger as I quickly scan the letter. "It says that the renovations are finally done."

"Took them long enough."

"They also say that they realize since it took weeks longer than expected, that if we need out of our leases because of agreements we had to make, we have until the end of the week without being penalized."

I look up at Cole, who is doing a very bad job of containing his smile.

"What are you smiling at?" I ask, putting the letter on the table.

He reaches for me, and as always, I give him my hand so he can pull me into him. "I mean, I did buy you a bed."

I chuckle. "You mean the one I don't use?"

"And you've overtaken my closet. Seems silly to move all of those clothes back to your apartment when we both know that you are going to miss my sheets and pillows too much to not stay here every night."

I smile, because he's one-thousand-percent right. "This is true."

"So I think you should call your landlord and tell him that you won't be needing that apartment anymore."

I'm pretty sure my smile right now could light up Nashville during a power outage. "Are you sure?"

"Am I sure?" he asks, picking me up so we're eye level. "This coming from the woman who barged in here in the middle of the night and never left?"

"Hey! I gave you an option."

He tilts his head, giving me the "you're out of your mind" look. I get this look often. "As if I could have said no."

"I'm so glad you didn't."

I lean in to kiss him. I meant for it to be a small one. But like many kisses with us, it quickly grows deeper. My fingers start traveling up to play with his hair, which is usually my signal for let's-go-sneak-in-a-quickie, when I hear my phone alerting me to a text message. I unwillingly separate from him only to see the worst possible message on my phone.

> Lucy: Plan is off. I can't get him to come. I'm so sorry.

"What the fuck?"

I scan the text message again because there's no way I read what I just read.

"What's going on?" Cole asks.

I nearly throw my phone at the wall. "It's Lucy. She can't get Bryce to come. I'm so mad I could scream!"

I start pacing around the dining room mumbling swear words I didn't even know I could string together. It takes all the restraint in my body to not pick up one of these plates and hurl it against the wall.

But I don't. Because the only thing that needs bashed into a wall is Bryce's head.

"That's it, I'm going up there," I say as I start marching to the door. Somehow Cole gets in front of me and cuts me off, slamming the door shut as soon as I open it.

"You are not going up there," he says.

"Like hell I'm not!"

I try to maneuver around Cole, but it's impossible. He's just too damn big. First time I've ever said *that* about him.

"Brenna, you aren't going to get anywhere talking to him this mad. Now, go sit down on the couch and take a second to breathe."

I let out a huff but do as Cole asks. "Why is my brother so fucking ridiculous? I knew he was going to be weird about this, but we are going on *three months* of him being a fucking toddler. And camp is opening tomorrow, and if you two aren't speaking what does that mean for the team? This is all sorts of fucked up, and all because Bryce can't get his head out of ass."

Cole doesn't say anything as he sits next to me, which in this situation kind of surprises me. I mean, I wasn't expecting a "Brenna you're the smartest woman in the world" response, but a "you're right" would be nice.

Instead, he just sits there. Silent.

"Don't you think he's acting ridiculous?" I ask again.

Cole puts his hands together as he rests his elbows on his knees. He's looking at the floor, and all of a sudden I get this feeling in my stomach that I'm not going to like what I'm about to hear.

"I think he's acting like Bryce."

"What's that supposed to mean?"

Cole sits back up and turns to face me. "It means I get why he's acting like this. I didn't before, but I do now. Especially now that he's had time but still isn't ready to talk."

I shake my head, because now I feel like I'm in Crazyville: Population Brenna. "You're taking his side?"

"I'm not taking his side. I'm just saying I get it. I get him."

"And you're saying I don't?"

"I'm not saying that," Cole says. He lets out a breath, which

I'm pretty sure is his way of trying to figure out how to calm me down. "What I'm saying is that yes, he's your brother, but he's been more than that to me for years. I know him better than anyone. Hell, there are things about him that Lucy doesn't know but I do. And if there's something that I'm sure of, it's that sudden shifts in his life? That is something that your brother is shit at. Hell, look at how long it took him to figure things out with Lucy. Or how far off the rails he went when he found out she was engaged? Brenna, I'm pretty sure the only reason he isn't in the bottom of a bottle right now over us is because of Lucy. So, I get it. I get that he needs his time."

"But he promised!" I yell. "He promised after this summer he'd come back and be ready. He promised me, Cole."

I can't hold back the tears anymore as I fall into Cole's arms, letting months of frustration, anger, and sadness flow out of me. I cry because I want Bryce to be okay with this. I cry because I hate that because Cole and I found each other, it means that the man I love doesn't have his best friend anymore. I cry because I just want things to be how I know they can, and I don't know how to get them there.

"I hate this," I say through tears. "I hate that it's like this."

Cole kisses my head and squeezes me a little tighter. "I do too. I never thought I'd say this, but I miss him. I just got him back from whatever the hell the last two years were, and now he's gone again."

This makes me cry all over again. "How do we fix this? Because right now, I don't see a way we can be together and have my brother be okay with it."

"No," Cole says, bringing me to his lap so he can look me in the eye. "Don't even think like that. I love you, Brenna Donald. I love you so much it fucking hurts. And yes, it hurts that my best friend is taking longer than I'd like to get to a space where he's okay with it, but we just have to let him take his time.

When he's ready, he'll be ready. But you and me? Sorry, baby, you're stuck with me."

I want to smile, but I can't shake one nagging thing off my mind. "What if he doesn't come around?"

Cole takes my face in his hands and brings me in for a long kiss on my forehead. I close my eyes and let the feel of his lips soothe every part of me that hurts right now.

"He will. Just give him time."

I LOVE PLAYING FOOTBALL. I don't know what I would have done with my life if this wasn't my career. And knowing that, I will never take for granted a single day of the job I get to do for these few years of my life.

But training camp can suck my left nut.

"How do I forget every year how bad the first day sucks?" Wes asks as we finally make it back to our lockers after what might be the longest training camp day I've ever experienced.

"I mean, you've only had twenty training camps," I joke. "Maybe they are starting to meld together in that old man brain of yours."

"Watch it now," he says, grabbing a towel. "And it's only been ten."

We laugh as we both sit and take a breath. The locker room is silent except for muscle-weary groans and occasional swear words. We've just wrapped up our second session of the day, and I don't know what is up with Coach McAvoy, but he wasn't messing around today, first team practice of the season or not.

I look up for just a second, and like the world is trying to remind me that I'm not speaking to my best friend, Bryce walks past me to get to his locker. I nod my head at him, but it's only returned with an icy glare.

"What the fuck is up with you two?" Wes asks.

I shake my head. "There isn't enough time or beer to cover that."

He tosses me a towel. "Well, I don't have the beer, but I bet the story could make the time in the ice bath go quicker."

I nod and stand as we walk to the training room, where multiple ice baths are waiting for the team. They might sting, and I might never get used to the cold, but I can't deny that they do wonders for my body after a hard day of practice.

"So tell me," Wes says, easing into his tub. "Why is the Fury's favorite bromance seemingly on the outs? What did you do? Sleep with his sister?"

I don't answer because I'm not quite sure how to say yes to what Wes thought was clearly a joke. Apparently, by the look on my face, I don't need to.

"No, you fucking didn't!" he says. "Dude, what were you thinking?"

I shake my head. "No, it's not like that."

"Did you not sleep with his sister?"

"Well, yeah. But it's more than that," I say as I submerge myself in the icy hell. "We're dating. She just officially moved in with me."

"Wow. Congrats. That's a huge step. Wait! Was she the reason you were all smiles this summer?"

"Yeah. It was her," I say. "And I still want to be excited, but it's hard when everything else seems to be shit right now."

"I mean, how bad is it?"

For the next five minutes I fill Wes in on the events since the wedding, which he was unable to attend. I try my best to not paint Bryce in a bad light — he's still this team's quarterback, and the last thing I want to do is divide the locker room.

Plus, if he's refusing to talk to me, I'm sure players will start picking up on it sooner or later. Wes just happened to be the first.

"Fuck," he says after I catch him up. "He's not speaking to you at all?"

All I can do is shrug. "Nope. Brenna and I tried to have him and Lucy over for dinner last night to try and clear some air, but he refused to come over."

"Shit, that sucks," he says. "I wish I had some great words of wisdom."

"You don't? Isn't that your role as our team's elder statesman?"

Wes tosses a towel at me, which I easily avoid. "Listen, just because I was playing in the league before your balls dropped doesn't mean I have all the answers. Hell, I'm dealing with enough crazy in my own house."

"Really? Everything okay?"

Wes shrugs. "I don't know. As you so nicely pointed out, I'm getting up there in years. I brought it up to my wife in the off season that there aren't going to be too many more of these. I have three years left in my contract and when that's up, I'm done."

"You? Retire?"

Wes nods. "Yeah, my body can't go through this for many more years. But when I bring up the R-word to the wife, she freaks out. Asks me what kind of job I'm going to get if I'm not making millions a year. As she so kindly put it, she has become used to a certain lifestyle."

My eyes go wide. "Wow. She said that?"

"More or less. But enough about me and my crazy wife. You and Bryce. We have to fix this. I don't know if you realize this, but if you two aren't talking, that could create some serious problems on the field. And in the locker room."

"I know, I just wish I knew what to do."

"I wish I could help," Wes says as he starts to stand up from the ice bath. "You broke the pro-football locker room bro code. Which I think is a load of shit, but I know others don't. Clearly, Bryce falls into that camp."

I stand up and step out of the bath, quickly grabbing a towel to dry off. "Bryce is a very black-and-white person. He's always had trouble seeing the gray area in anything. So in his mind, we betrayed him."

"I get that," Wes says as we start making our way back to the locker room. "But on the other hand, if I had a friend like you, I couldn't pick a better guy for my sister to be with."

"Thanks man. That's…"

He holds up his hand, clearly not wanting me to get too emotional about this. "I'm just saying, there are bad men in the world. You aren't one of them."

As if on cue, Dexter struts into the locker room. I still can't believe Brenna even went on one date with this ass hat.

I need the hell out of here. I need to go home and fall into bed with Brenna next to me. Maybe if I'm lucky she'll do that head scratch thing that puts me to sleep instantly.

My girl has magic fingers.

"How is Mr. Cole Campbell doing?" Dexter says, stopping at my locker. "How was your summer?"

I give a skeptical eye to Dexter. The question seems innocent enough, but this man rarely talks to me. He has his crew—the young guys who like to party and flash the kind of money they make. Yes, I'm only a year older than him, but that's not my scene, never has been.

"What do you want, Dexter?" I ask. "You've never once asked how my day is going."

"Can't a teammate care about another?" he asks, clutching his chest in mock pain. "Just asking how your off season went."

I know what he's fishing for, but I don't want to cause a scene.

"It was fine."

He pretends to be shocked by that answer just as Bryce walks behind him. "Just fine? Damn. If I were with the dime piece known as Brenna Donald, I'd hope my summer was more than fine."

I feel the temperature of my blood starting to go up. I can also feel Bryce staring at me, obviously having heard what Dexter said. And I'm sure that's exactly why Dexter said it.

Play it cool, Campbell. Don't give anyone any reason to blow this up.

"We had a great summer," I say as I finish getting dressed. "Now if you'll excuse me, it's been a long day."

Dexter puts his hand on my chest. I swear if we weren't in our locker room right now, I'd be forcefully removing it myself. "Listen, I just want to clear the air."

What is he talking about?

"Clear the air about what?"

"You know," he says, clearly liking that an audience is starting to form. "My history with your girl. I know it can be weird being teammates who have both...you know."

Apparently, this man woke up today and chose violence.

"There will be no—what did you say, weirdness?—because there was nothing between you and Brenna. You went out on one shitty date and I had to come rescue her."

"Excuse me, *what?*" Bryce yells, jumping in the middle, looking back and forth between us. "Brenna did what?"

Now I don't know if Dexter seriously didn't realize this or if he's just a decent actor, but he seems shocked by Bryce's reaction. "You didn't know? Yeah, man. Me and your sister were hot for a second."

"Oh for fuck's sake, no you weren't," I yell over a still-stunned Bryce. "You got her drunk off her ass, and she still proceeded to tear you down a peg. If that's what counts as hot on your dates, then you clearly need some help in the female department."

"You got her *what?*" Bryce yells, though Dexter seems to be ignoring him.

"I don't need no fucking help," Dexter says, trying to step closer to me. "Believe me, ask your girl. She'll tell you."

That's it. He can egg me on all he wants, but I refuse to let him make shit up about Brenna just because of his ego. "She'll tell me what? You two didn't do shit, so quit acting like you did. And if you're mad that she picked me over you, that's something you and your therapist need to work on. How about you go buy another sports car? I'm sure that will help."

Dexter lets out an annoyed breath. "Whatever. That bitch ain't worth—"

He doesn't get a chance to finish that sentence. I push Bryce out of the way and load my fist back. I'm inches from hitting his smug face before I feel multiple people holding me back.

"Get the fuck out of here," I say. "And I swear on my grandmother's grave, if I ever hear you say one fucking word about Brenna again, no one will dare try and stop me."

Dexter points to me then looks over at Bryce. "This the kind of guy you want with your sister?"

Bryce doesn't answer this, but takes a few steps into the locker room, where we have now accumulated quite the audience. "Has anyone else here gone out with or done anything with my sister that I need to know about?"

I look back at Wes, who was the one who came to grab me, and nod that he can let me go. I take a look around the room, filled with my teammates, who are all wide-eyed and slack-jawed at the events of the last few minutes. None of them is going to say anything to Bryce. Hell, Brenna could have dated the entire defensive line right now and no one would say a damn word.

Bryce looks back to me and Dexter. "See? These are true teammates. They know the code. And this? This pissing match between the two of you? This is why the rule is in place. You don't date, screw, or do anything with a teammate's sister. It never leads anywhere good."

"Whatever," Dexter says, now seemingly bored with this conversation. He tries to step away, but I don't think he really understands me yet.

"Listen here and listen good," I begin as I step in front of him. "This will be the last time you ever say her name. You see her? You don't look at her. You don't say hello. You pretend she's a stranger. Got it?"

"Or what? What are you going to do? Coach McAvoy will fine your ass if you hit me."

I step a little closer, which allows me to look down at him since I have a few inches on him.

"Let him. Hell, he can have my whole damn check. It would be worth it."

"Whatever, man. I ain't scared of you."

"I would be if I were you."

The words shock me because, yup, my ears didn't play tricks on me. They came from Bryce, who I didn't realize was standing next to us.

"Walk away, Dexter," Bryce continues. "If you ever want me to throw you another pass again you'll listen to what this man says. And considering I know you have a performance clause in your contract, it would be best for everyone if you took Campbell's advice."

Dexter looks back and forth between the two of us before

turning away like a kid who didn't get his way. Good. Let him go.

I turn to Bryce. "Thanks, man."

The look he gives back to me sends a chill down my spine. Hell, it's colder than the ice bath.

"Are you happy now?" Bryce says.

I tilt my head in confusion. "What are you talking about?"

"This," he says, waving his hand around the locker room. "This is your fault. I hope it's worth it."

And before I can say anything else, he walks away.

"ARE you sure it's okay we're here together?"

I look over my shoulder to Lucy, who looks as nervous as I've ever seen her. "Why wouldn't it be okay?"

"I don't know," she says as we walk toward the practice field at the Fury's training facility. "Bryce said things got pretty heated this week. I don't want him to see us together and have it set something in motion."

"Oh please," I say. "If my brother is also going to try and tell me who I can and can't be friends with, then we might as well just throw in the towel. He can get over it. You're my best friend. The men we love play on the same team. It's the first open practice we can go to, so guess what, we're going. Together. And if he doesn't like it, he can suck an egg."

"You're right," Lucy says as we show our passes to the security guard. "Let's just go in and have a nice night and pretend that everything is great and right in the world."

"Sounds like a plan."

Pretending is as close as we're going to get right now. It has been a week since the near-fight in the locker room, and things aren't getting any better according to Cole. Each night he comes home looking more and more drained, and I know it's not just his body getting used to the rigors of the season again. He's mentally exhausted. I don't blame him.

"I hate this, you know," I say as we make our way to the seats.

"Everyone does," Lucy says. "Bryce said that when he and Cole are in the locker room at the same time, everyone just stops talking."

"Cole said that too. He even overheard a few of the defensive guys asking each other if they were on Team Bryce or Team Cole."

Lucy's shoulders slump. "This is horrible. What if this goes on through the season?"

"I don't know if it can," I reply. "I don't know why, but I feel like the volcano is about to erupt."

Lucy nods. "I completely agree."

Lucy and I take our seats in the impromptu Fury family section just as the teams start to run out onto the field from the locker room. Today's practice is the first that's open to the public, which means it's also the first time the families can come watch. Normally, a night like this would give me all the warm fuzzies. Dads bringing their sons and daughters to come watch the players, fans getting excited about the upcoming season, kids of players watching their dads in awe and amazement. But unfortunately for me and Lucy, all we can do is hope that our guys get through another day without killing each other.

We both put on fake smiles as we watch wives and girl-friends of players come up and take their seats. No, we don't have assigned seats, but everywhere we go, we seem to all gravitate toward each other. Probably because we want to be as far away from the fans as possible.

We appreciate them, but they are a tad crazy.

"Hey, Lucy! Brenna!"

We both wave as Sadie, Coach McAvoy's wife, and Bethany, who's married to Coach Davis, come up the stairs and make their way toward us. Bethany is carrying Charlotte, who I believe is now about eighteen months old. Her hair is dark like her dad's, but I'm guessing by the all-pink Fury outfit she is wearing that she is one-hundred-percent just like her mama.

Then there is Sadie, who just looks like she's carrying a basketball under her shirt.

"Let me help you," I say, standing up and offering her a hand.

"Thanks," she says, taking it before she plops down onto a bleacher seat. "I didn't realize how hard these stairs would be."

"I told you," Bethany says, sitting next to her and arranging Charlotte on her lap. "Everything is hard when you're about to pop."

"When are you due?" Lucy asks. "I thought you said at the wedding he was due before camp started."

"He was," Sadie says, her eyes all of a sudden looking angry. "Because of course, we tried to plan a child around football season. Then the doctor said he got the date wrong, and that he was a week off. Now on top of that, the little guy is two days late."

"Oh no," Lucy and I say in unison.

"Oh no is right," Sadie says. "I'm hoping that since this boy is the product of Hunter and me, that he would want to come watch football practice and be so jealous he'll decide it's time to vacate."

Bethany shoots her a look like she's insane. "Yup. That's exactly how it works."

"Oh shut it, Miss-I-had-my-baby-three-weeks-early," Sadie says.

Bethany just shrugs. "Hey, at least your baby daddy will be there when he's born."

"Davis ended up making it. Barely. But he was there."

Bethany laughs. "Let's not replay that night."

The two sisters continue to joke back and forth as the guys warm up on the field. Lucy and I look at each other, and as if we're thinking the same thing, grab each other's hand and give it a squeeze.

This should be us. Laughing and sharing inside jokes. Holding each other's kids, not just because the other needs help but because the child desperately wants their aunt to hold them. To have husbands who are best friends, so we could live our lives together as the family not only of blood but of choice.

That's what we should be having right now. Not senseless fighting that is going on for so long at this point I think we're forgetting what even started it.

I hurry up and brush the stray tear that has somehow leaked from my eye. But unfortunately, Sadie sees it and grabs my free hand.

"Hey," she says, giving my hand a squeeze. "Everything is going to be okay."

"You know?" I ask.

Both Sadie and Bethany nod. "Yeah," Sadie says. "The guys might think they're being sly about it, but the coaches know. Between us, they are trying to stay out of it and let them work it out."

"By the way, Brenna, you and Cole are just adorable," Bethany says. "The picture on Instagram of you two at Country Fest? It's everything."

"Thanks," I say, all of a sudden feeling a little bashful. Or because I'm remembering what we did about a half hour after that picture was taken.

"I knew you two were together at the wedding," Sadie says. "I love you both and think you're a great couple, but you were shit at hiding it. I called it then. Hunter didn't believe me. I won twenty bucks and a week of foot massages."

I laugh. "Glad to help. I just wish I could help fix this with Bryce and Cole."

Sadie looks out to the field where the offensive players and the defensive players have split now and are running individual drills. "I wish I had an answer, because believe me, Hunter wants it to end. He wants to let them work it out, but he's about two practices away from locking them in a room together."

"We wanted to try that," Lucy says. "Bryce wouldn't come."

"Doesn't surprise me," Sadie says. "Bryce is an emotional guy. I mean, look at everything he's had to learn to overcome the last few years. And now everything he's known is different. Not saying he shouldn't get over it, because he needs to, but for years it's been him and Cole. Now it's not. And I think that scares him."

"It does," Lucy says. "Even if he won't admit it."

"Then why can't they talk about it?" I demand. "I feel like if they just sat down and fucking talked this would all be over."

"Ah, and that's where you try and apply logic," Bethany says. "They are men. Logic does not exist."

Lucy and I can't help but laugh at that. Because it's the damn truth. "I had hoped by now this would be said and done," I say. "Because at this point, if it were a relationship, I'd tell them they'd either need to fight or fuck."

As the words are coming out of my mouth, I see a whirlwind of commotion on the field. Arms are flying. Guys are trying to hold their teammates back.

And not just any teammates—Cole and Bryce.

"Holy shit!" Bethany yells, pointing to the field where Cole and Bryce are now inches away from each other.

"Looks like they chose to fight." Sadie says, holding her

belly as she stands to get a better view. "Bryce does know that Cole has a hundred pounds on him, right?"

I don't answer Sadie because I can't. I'm frozen. I want to go down and break this up, but I can't move.

Which is why I get to watch in real time as Bryce reaches back and punches Cole straight in the face. Again.

CHAPTER 35
COLE

TEN MINUTES EARLIER

"OFFENSE, break for water. Make it quick! Two-minute drills when we're back!"

The offense runs over to grab a quick drink before the big show: the offense versus the defense in a game-like simulation.

"Everyone ready?" Bryce asks.

Most of the offensive guys nod or give him some sort of acknowledgment. I just continue to drink my water. I'm not about to say something that will ruffle his panties. Especially in front of fans.

"What about you, Campbell?" Bryce says. "You ready?"

I look at him, wondering why he's calling me out like this. "Of course, I am. You know I'm always prepared."

"How the hell am I supposed to know?" he asks. "I thought I knew you, but apparently, I never did. So, since it's your job to make sure I don't get my clock cleaned, I just want to make sure you're ready."

I want to roll my eyes because for one, he doesn't get hit in practice. The shiny red practice jersey he wears makes sure of that. And two, why the fuck is he starting shit in front of every-

one? This isn't the time nor the place. Not in front of teammates. And certainly not in front of fans.

"I'm ready," I say, wanting to put an end to this. "Let's get
out there."

Everyone must get the tone of my voice because the rest of
our teammates start to disperse and head back to the field. But
not Bryce.

"The girls are here," Bryce says, nodding toward the stands.

I turn to look at them, and I can't help but smile. They are
each wearing Fury clothing and smiling at something Sadie,
Coach McAvoy's wife, is saying. Coach Davis's wife is next to
her. They all look happy. Content.

Like they should.

"I'm glad they can at least figure this out," I say, though
that probably wasn't the best thing to say if I'm trying to
diffuse this conversation.

"They shouldn't need to," Bryce says.

"That I can agree with," I say. "Because this shouldn't be an
issue."

"Just the opposite," he says. "It shouldn't be an issue
because it should have never had to be one. You started it. You
chased after Brenna. It's a thing because of you."

That's it. I'm done. I'm fucking done. I've held this in for
months now. I've tried to be reasonable with him. I've tried to
take into consideration his past and how I know he copes with
things. But now he's just being a child, and I'm fucking done
with it.

"Why is what I did so fucking wrong?" I ask. "And don't
give me that locker room, bro code bullshit. That has been a
convenient excuse for you this entire time, but that's all it is. So
tell me, honestly, what the fuck is your problem with me
dating Brenna?"

"You really want to know?"

"Yes. Fucking tell me."

"Brenna has never had great taste in men," he begins. "Probably has something to do with our dad, but I'm not a shrink. And she picks horrible guys. Guys that don't deserve her. She's an amazing woman who deserves an amazing life. Not a life where her husband is on the road half the year with groupies surrounding him. Not a life where she has to come in second to a guy's career. She deserves better. She deserves better than you or any other guy on this team."

I feel my blood start to boil.

"Fuck you, Bryce. Just fuck all the way off."

His eyes go wide. "Excuse me?"

"You heard me. I said fuck off." Apparently, the rest of the team heard me because we're starting to gather an audience. "Fuck you for thinking that I'm the kind of guy who would cheat on Brenna—or any woman for that matter—with some cleat chaser. What does that say about our friendship that you would even think that?"

"Can you blame me? You've never been in a long-term relationship. How do I know how you'll act on the road? Or that you'll give my sister the life she deserves?"

I step closer to him, because he needs to hear this loud and clear. "I have been your best friend for twenty fucking years. I have protected you from linemen and life. I have stuck up for you when your sorry ass didn't deserve it. I picked your head out of toilets. I made sure you weren't dead in ditches. And you think that I would hurt not just anyone, but the woman I love? If you really think that then we were never really friends."

"We must not have been, because a true friend wouldn't have put us in this situation."

I feel my fists balling at my sides. "You're ridiculous. And a fucking hypocrite."

"A hypocrite? How so?"

I take another step toward him because I want to make sure he hears this nice and clear. "Take a look in the mirror, Bryce. Everything you said? It's the pot calling the kettle black. So by your logic, you're not good enough for Lucy either. Oh wait, we always knew that one."

I expected the punch Bryce threw at me when we first told him about us.

But this one? This one I didn't see coming.

Even though I should have with that last dig.

I feel the punch before I can react to it—a right uppercut right to my jaw.

That is when all hell breaks loose.

Teammates can't get to me fast enough as I dive for Bryce, driving him to the ground. I'm on top of him and before I can even consider whether or not this is a good idea, I punch him square in the face. I cock my arm back again, ready to deliver another one, but feel at least three sets of hands pulling me from him. At the same time, a group of guys are lifting Bryce off the ground as Coach McAvoy and Coach Davis come between us.

"What the hell is going on?" Coach McAvoy yells. "Both of you, in my office. Now."

We stare at each other for another few seconds before we shake off the teammates holding us back. We all start walking to the office, which is probably a good thing. If we weren't escorted, I might be up for round two.

"Sit your asses down," Coach McAvoy says. "I knew things were off between you two but fighting? What in the hell is going on?"

Neither of us say anything. Or look at each other.

"So it's going to be like that, huh?" Coach McAvoy says. "Do you know how bad this is? How could you do that? In front of fans and media, no less!"

That I will speak up on. "I'm sorry, Coach. We shouldn't have let our personal issues interfere with the team."

Bryce huffs. "If you really thought that you wouldn't be fucking my sister."

I snap out of my chair, because apparently he wants me to break the other side of his nose.

"Sit down!" Coach Davis yells, which I do, reluctantly. "My God. You two are the last ones I ever thought would be in this situation. Fighting at practice? Dividing the locker room? We hoped that you two would work it out like men, but apparently not."

"I don't even know what to do," Coach McAvoy says. "You two have put us in a real shitty position. You understand that, right?"

"Yes, sir," we both say in unison. I know it's not the appropriate time, but this reminds me of back in high school when Bryce and I orchestrated a prank on the freshmen. Our high school coach pulled us into the office and read us the riot act. I wish I could smile back at the memory.

"We're going to have to put out media statements. I'd ask you both to not do any interviews for the time being, do you understand?"

I nod. Out of the corner of my eye I see Bryce do the same.

"Second, we need to figure out what's next. You two are to stay away from the facilities and from camp until further notice."

"Coach!" Bryce says. "It's camp. We have to be at camp."

Coach McAvoy stands up from behind his desk. "Well, you should have thought of that before you cold-cocked your left tackle. We'll have meetings with both of you and then we'll figure out the best thing to do moving forward."

"Yes, sir."

We both try to stand, but Coach immediately waves his

hands down at us. "No. You are not leaving together. I can't risk another blow up. Donald, I see your wife in the locker room. Go to your locker. Get your things and leave out of the back. Don't talk to one reporter, do you hear me?"

"Yes sir," Bryce says, giving me one more glare before he leaves the office, Coach Davis following him. That doesn't surprise me. The two have a bond after the last few years. Maybe he's the one who can get through to him.

"Put some ice on your chin," Coach McAvoy says.

I nod. "He got me good."

"You know I lost twenty bucks to my wife because of you?"

I look at my coach curiously. "Excuse me?"

He sits back down. "She bet me twenty bucks at the wedding that you and Bryce's sister were together. I said no way. No way would Campbell risk his friendship with Bryce. Turns out I was wrong."

I want to laugh, but it hurts. Shit, Bryce got me good. "Yeah, you were."

"Is she worth it?"

I look over at the locker room, where Brenna is standing, doing her best to hold back tears. "She's worth every punch."

Coach McAvoy nods. "All right. Then let's fix this."

CHAPTER 36
COLE

IT TOOK FOREVER to get home.

Even worse, I was by myself because Brenna drove her and Lucy to the practice.

Coach McAvoy made me wait more than an hour after Bryce left before he released me, so I told Brenna to go home. No sense in her staying.

Though now as I open the door to our apartment, maybe I shouldn't have done that. Because all I see before anything else, is the sight of suitcases.

"Brenna?" I say, closing the door and dropping my keys. "Breanna, where are you?"

She doesn't answer, but I hear a sniffle come from the guest room.

"Brenna?"

When I walk into the guest room, she's sitting in the middle of a pile of clothes, holding onto one of my white T-shirts, tears falling down her beautiful face. In two steps I'm sitting next to her, bringing her into my arms, kissing the top of her head. Anything to give her any sort of comfort.

"This wasn't how it was supposed to be," she says through heavy tears. "This wasn't how it was supposed to be at all."

"I know," I say, rocking her back and forth. "This isn't how I imagined it."

"We were supposed to be a family. You, me, Bryce, and Lucy. It was supposed to be the four of us. We were supposed to go to dinners together and concerts. Go back to Laurel Heights and finally bring all of our families together like they should have always been. Bryce and you should be looking at properties together so you could build your houses, and Lucy and I were supposed to not comment about how ridiculously excited you two were about it. But it's never going to happen, is it?"

I don't say anything, because I don't want to lie to her. A month ago? I probably would have said that everything is going to be just fine, because I honestly thought that. Now? Now my hope is dwindling day by day.

"Brenna," I say, already regretting the words that are about to come out of my mouth. "Why are there suitcases in the living room?"

"Because," she says, but not before a huge wave of tears hits. "Because I need to leave."

My heart sinks to my stomach in an instant. "What do you mean *leave*? For the weekend?"

She shakes her head against me. "I need to go back to Laurel Heights. For good."

My heart continues to free fall out of my body. "For good? You can't leave."

"I have to, Cole," she says, trying to pull away from me, but I won't let her. No. I just have to hold on to her. If I don't let her go she can't leave.

Because she can't. She can't leave me.

"Why are you saying that? You can't."

She pushes again, and I reluctantly let her go. "I have to. I've thought about this every way I can. And the only way for everything to be okay again is if I'm not here. I'm the problem, so I'm taking myself out of the equation."

"Okay," I say, taking a deep breath. "We can do long distance. That's doable in the season. If you go back to Laurel Heights maybe Bryce not seeing us together every day will help him ease into this. Then you can come back when he's had a little more time."

Brenna shakes her head. "No, Cole... I need to leave. And we need—"

"No!" I yell, cutting her off. "Don't you dare say what I think you're about to."

"Cole, let me—"

"No!" I yell as I jump to my feet. I begin to pace in circles because no, I'm not even going to acknowledge what I think she was about to say. "Brenna, he'll get over it. He has to."

"No, he doesn't. And if tonight is any indicator, he never will," she says. "Seeing you two tonight? Fighting? Punching each other? It broke my heart. Not for us, but for you two."

"Don't worry about us."

"No, Cole, I can't. I can't *not* worry about you two. I never had a best friend growing up. I had a lot of friends. I was never lonely. I always had someone to sit with at lunch or go to the mall with. But I never had that person. I never had a Bryce until I met Lucy. And I know that because I watched you two grow up, and I was jealous of you. I was so envious of what you two had. And you didn't care that it wasn't normal for guys to be that close. You two ran with it."

"Maybe we shouldn't have."

Brenna shakes her head. "No, it was beautiful. You two have the kind of friendship everyone should have. And look where it got you. You two made a pact to get to this level of your careers together, and you're here. You're playing profes- sional football together. If I were to go back in time and tell the seven-year-old versions of you two that you made it... I'd give anything to see those little faces."

I reach for her hands and pull her off the ground. "Do it. Go back and tell them. And tell a young me that the feeling he has when his best friend's sister comes over, that it's actually a crush. And not to pull her pigtails."

This gets her to laugh a little through her tears. "You and my brother have dreamed of this your entire lives. There has never been a day when this wasn't the end goal. And I'm not going to ruin it. I'm not going to be the reason you two don't fulfill the dream. I can't do it. I *won't* do it."

"Brenna," I say, though nothing else comes out. I just reach for her and bring her in, hugging her to my chest where I'm pretty sure she can't breathe.

"This is going to be for the best, Cole," Brenna says into my shirt. "I know it hurts now, but it won't forever."

I shake my head. "You're wrong. Because I don't know if you realize this, but I'm head over heels, crazy in love with you. This? Us? It's worth more than football. It's worth more than a pipe dream of a kid from Ohio. It's worth more than anything in this world. Don't you think that? Isn't our love worth more than that?"

I feel her lips against my chest before she steps away. "I love you too. That's why I'm doing this. Because I love you. I love you so much that I can't be the one who stands in the way of what you were meant to do. I won't stand in the way of destiny."

"What I was meant to do is love you. That's what I was meant to do."

She shakes her head. "No, Cole. I wasn't the Donald that you were destined for. You and Bryce still have the football world to conquer. But I want you to know... I will never forget this. I was done dating before you. I had given up. I thought that finding someone just wasn't in the cards for me. But how you loved me? How you opened me up to love you? It's something I'll never forget. And I'll always love you, Cole. I just— I can't be selfish. I can't let this continue when it's tearing up our lives."

"Selfish!" I yell. "You're not the selfish one. Your prick of a brother is the one who is being selfish. Don't you see, you leaving means he wins."

"But if I stay, everyone loses."

Brenna walks to the closet and grabs another handful of clothes. "I still have my apartment for another week. I'm going to go sleep there tonight. I'll come by tomorrow and grab the rest of my things."

I'm frozen as I watch her pack her bag. This can't be it. This can't be the end. This isn't how it's supposed to go. I'm not done yet. I'm not done loving her yet.

She is supposed to be it for me. My end game. The reason my jaw fucking hurts and the reason my heart beats.

She exits the room, and I follow behind her.

"There has to be another way," I say.

She turns to look at me, nothing but sadness in her eyes. "There isn't, Cole. I have thought about this from every angle, and in every angle someone gets hurt."

"So you're choosing to hurt us? To hurt me? Is that it?"

Her tears start falling again. "I don't want to choose anyone. Don't you see I hate this? But what do you want me to do? I won't sit back and watch you and my brother destroy everything you've worked for. I won't do it."

"I won't let you go without a fight."

It takes me two steps to cut the distance between us. Before she can object, I kiss her hard. I kiss her with desperation. She doesn't resist as her hands cling to my shirt, pulling me closer. My hands are gripping her head because she needs to feel how much this is killing me. Tears are spilling from both of us as we kiss each other with every bit of grief and love in us.

Eventually we stop, though neither of us loosens our hold.

"There has to be another way," I say. "I'll find another way."

She shakes her head, slowly letting go of my shirt. "I wish there was."

And with that she backs away, grabs her suitcase and keys, and walks out of my apartment.

She doesn't look back. She doesn't say anything else.

She just leaves me. Standing in the middle of my apartment. Heartbroken and empty.

I don't know how long I stand there. Eventually I end up sitting down on my couch, though I have no memory of physically doing it.

I look down, sure that I'll see blood leaking from my chest. But I don't. All I see is that damn blanket that Brenna loves. I'm sure if I bring it to my nose I'll smell her sweet scent. How many nights did we sit here, her wrapped up in this thing while she snuggled into me? Those were the perfect moments. When it was just the two of us. None of the bullshit from the world.

No. This isn't over. It can't be. I'm not done holding her. I'm not done loving her. I'm supposed to marry her. We're supposed to have kids and dogs and memories for the rest of our lives.

Then it hits me. She didn't see another way—but I do.

I pull my cell phone out of my pocket and dial the only number that can fix this problem.

"Hello? Cole?" Dean says. "Are you okay? I was going to call you. Did you and Bryce really get into a fist fight at practice tonight?"

"Dean, when is my contract up?"

Judging by my agent's silence, that wasn't the question he was planning on getting from me tonight. "Excuse me, what did you ask?"

"My contract," I repeat. "When is it up?"

"Um, technically the end of the season. But the Fury wants you to renew before then. Remember the number they floated around? They are serious about it. Why do you ask?"

"Call around. See who needs a left tackle. I want a trade. Maybe see if Cincinnati is in the market. But no matter what, I want out."

"A trade?" Dean asks. "Cole, have you thought this through? You remember how much money the Fury is offering you, right?"

I look at the door that just shut. The one that isn't opening back up. And I look at the blanket, the one that I'm going to have to burn if she doesn't come back.

"I have. And it's not about the money. Hell, I'll take a pay cut. Do whatever it is you need to do. Get me out of Nashville. Immediately."

CHAPTER 37

BRENNA

COLD AND EMPTY. Those are the perfect two words to describe the last eighteen hours.

That was my heart when I walked out of Cole's apartment. That was *my* apartment when I walked into it for the first time in months.

And today, as I make my way back up to the place where I found true love for the first time, it's what I'm feeling.

Nothing but emptiness.

"Stay strong, Brenna. This is what you have to do."

I take one last deep breath as I open the door. Cole sent me a message that he had to go meet with the Fury, so he'd be gone for the next few hours. Thank goodness he's not here. Leaving him last night was the hardest thing I've ever had to do. I don't think I could do it twice.

I managed to stop crying about an hour ago, but as soon as I open the door, the waterworks hit me all over again.

Because there in the middle of the living room are the rest of my suitcases, all packed. The blanket I used every day is lying on top of one. And propped up on one is a letter next to a single red rose.

Trouble,

It took me all night, but I understand why you think you have to do this. Do I like it? No. Do I agree with it? No. But I understand it. Because what you are doing is why I love you so much. Because you are the most selfless person I know. So you go. For now. But just promise me that you won't give up on us. That you won't forget me. Remember how I said there had to be another way? Well I'm working on it. So go to Laurel Heights. See your mom. But know this. I'm coming to get you. Because we're not done yet.

Love you forever,

Cole

"Where are you going?"

Bryce's voice startles me as I finish reading the note. What is he doing here?

"What does it look like?" I say with a bite as I push back the tears. "I'm leaving."

"Good," he says, entering like he owns the place. I bristle. "I know you thought you loved him Brenna, but really this is for the best."

Oh, that's it. I'm done. I'm so fucking done with him. Maybe I'll punch him too. And mine won't come with a league fine.

"Look at me!" I yell as I step in front of him. "Does this look like someone who is happy with the decision she's made?"

"What do you mean?" he asks. "You're just going back to your apartment. Don't act like it's the end of the world."

"No, you dumbass! I'm leaving Nashville. I gave up my apartment. I'm moving back home. I can't do this. I can't be here anymore."

"You're what?" he asks. "You're moving back home?"

Is he really that dense? "Yes Bryce. I'm moving back home."

I march into the bathroom to make sure I didn't forget to

grab anything last night. Like a puppy, Bryce follows. "Are you and Cole done?"

"Yup. I broke up with him last night," I say, tearing through drawers. "Thanks for that, by the way. First healthy and real relationship of my life and you shit on it every chance you got because for some reason it's an inconvenience to you. I'll remember everything you did for me these past few months at Christmas."

Bryce takes a few steps toward me and tries to put a comforting hand on my shoulder. I shew it away immediately.

"Brenna, I know you don't see it now, but this is for the best," he says. "You'll see that I'm right."

I turn to him, hoping he can see the anger and near-hatred in my eyes. "What am I supposed to be seeing, Bryce? Tell me. What in the world was so bad about us that you insisted on making our lives hell every day for the past few months?"

"You know."

"No, actually I don't," I say, pushing past him and heading back to the living room. "Because your story has changed sixteen times. First it was the so-called lying."

Bryce's eyes go wide. "Are you really going to tell me you didn't lie to me?"

"It was for two days before the wedding when we didn't even know what was going on with us. As soon as you got back we told you. How did we lie?"

"You didn't. Cole did. For the years that he had a thing for you."

"And how would that have played out? I can picture it now," I say, stepping to the side so I can play both of these roles. "Cole: Bryce. I have a thing for your sister." I step to the other side. "Bryce: Hell yeah man! Let me set you up!"

Bryce stares at me, not happy with my dramatics. "We

won't know how I would have reacted. I never had the chance."

"Well then let's go with a situation that's a little fresher," I say. "What was this bullshit I heard last night that you don't want Cole with me because of the fact that he *might* cheat on me? Seriously? Do you have that little faith in the man?"

"You don't know what it's like being on the road."

"Do you know something I don't?" I ask. "Is Cole going from city to city picking up every woman who waits outside of your hotels? I thought Dexter was the manwhore of the team."

Bryce shakes his head. "Oh, and we need to talk about that."

"No, we don't. Stay focused. Have you ever seen Cole hook up with a cleat chaser?"

"No."

"Then why all of a sudden was his dick going to get bored and need to nail a woman in every city?"

"I just—"

I hold up my hands for him to stop. "You just nothing. You are grasping at straws. You have been for months, and you still are. So level with me, Bryce. Be honest with me once and for all: why the hell does this bother you so much? Especially because I distinctly remember hearing you say repeatedly last year that you couldn't wait for Cole to find someone. Well, he did. So was it me? Was I not the right pick? What was wrong with me?"

"No, that's not it."

"Then what is it, Bryce? I can't figure it out. Please, help me understand your madness!"

He takes a deep breath before answering. "It's not me I'm worried about. Or Cole," he says. "It's you."

"No," I say, shaking my head. "No, it's not. Because if it was about me you would have found a way to be okay with this.

You would have seen how much I love this man. You would have tried harder because you would have seen that I'd marry him tomorrow if I could. But I'm not. And you want to know why? Because this hasn't been about me or Cole. It's been about you."

"Don't put words in my mouth, Brenna."

"Then do me the courtesy of telling me the truth. Because I'm over this. I'm so fucking over this."

He doesn't say anything, so I start to walk to the suitcases. I grab them and turn to leave when I hear Bryce whisper something that I almost don't catch.

"What did you say?" I ask.

I turn to look at him and for the first time in months, I see a true sadness in his eyes. "You just changed everything."

Is he serious right now? "What does it change? Tell me? And is that change so bad when it's two people who you supposedly care about being happy together?"

"I don't know," he stumbles. "I don't know how to put it into words."

I am five seconds away from slapping him silly. "Please, Bryce. Make me understand. Because right now? Right now, I'm leaving my life that I thought I was starting to build. I'm leaving the man I love. I'm leaving my best friend. I'm leaving my pain in the ass brother who, even though I hate him right now, I still love. Want to know why? Because I won't sit back and be the reason people are miserable. I refuse to be the Yoko in this situation. So even though you can't put into words what is so wrong with this, you'll still get your way. I hope you're happy."

Bryce gives his hair a tug while letting out a frustrated breath. "You threw things for a loop! I wasn't ready."

I just shrug, because at this point I'm done. I'm tired. And this conversation isn't helping anything.

"Well, now you don't have to be. You don't have to be ready for change. You can go exactly back to how things were before. You, Lucy, and Cole will be here, and I'll be alone in Laurel Heights. You two will get to live out your childhood dreams while I go back to teach and see the same people I've seen every day for twenty-five years. One day, you'll win a championship together. Cole will find someone else to love that will meet your ridiculous notion of who he's supposed to be with, and you can build your houses next to each other like you always wanted to. Just don't invite me over for holidays. I can't be there and see the life that I thought I was going to live."

"Brenna..."

I shake my head and hold my hand up. "No, Bryce. No more. Just let me leave. I'm sorry I caused so much trouble. But I promise, I won't be trouble anymore."

And with that I grab my suitcases, the blanket, and of course, the note and flower, and walk out of Cole's apartment.

Only this time, it's forever.

"BRENNA, please call me back. I just want to make sure you're okay. And I miss you. Please, just call me."

I hang up the phone and throw it across the room. I think I hear a shatter. Ask me if I fucking care at this point.

It's been three days since the incident. Bryce and I are supposed to go back to practice tomorrow—we were suspended for two days and fined—but I'm still holding out hope that Dean can make some sort of magic work and get me traded so I can get the fuck out of here. The problem is that this isn't the peak trade window, so many teams have already filled their rosters. Or at least, that's what he's telling me.

All I know is that if I have to go back out on that field tomorrow I can't be sure what I'm going to do if provoked. My plan is to keep my head down, do my job, and get the hell out of there. I sure as hell am not going to interact with Bryce. If I do, there aren't enough team members to hold me back.

She's gone because of him. And he couldn't give a flying fuck.

I flip on a video game but I barely get five minutes in before I turn it off. I can't pay attention. I can't do anything. I've tried to draw, play video games... Hell, I even tried just getting stupid drunk. Nothing worked. Nothing took the pain away. Nothing helped me sleep.

I'm miserable. And I don't know how to make it go away.

I stand up to get my phone, suddenly realizing that if I do get traded, Dean is going to need to call me to tell me, when the door to my apartment flies open.

"You asked for a fucking trade?"

I look over to see Bryce in my doorway, looking confused and upset. I also realize that we're alone, so there will be no witnesses if I do, in fact, decide to kill him.

"None of your fucking business what I asked for," I say, picking up my phone. Cracked my screen but otherwise seems to be fine. "Get out."

"How could you ask for a trade?"

I step back and actually take a look at him, because there's no way he's this stupid. But by the look he's giving me—confusion laced in with a little panic—yup, he must be.

"Gee, let's see. The woman I love won't be with me in this city because she thinks she's ruining everyone's life around her. So I did the only thing I could to get her back, and that's to play in a city, and on a team, where she doesn't have to worry about upsetting her toddler of a brother every day."

"Cole, you can't get traded," he says, taking a few more steps inside. "You can't break us up."

Holy shit, he is that stupid.

"Are you kidding me? What on earth makes you think I want to play one more fucking second of football with you?"

"Because that's what we do."

I shake my head. "Not anymore. You ruined that. You've ruined everything. Get out of my house. Get out of my fucking life."

I stand up to go grab a beer from the kitchen, only to realize that I've drunk them all. When I come back out to the living room Bryce is sitting on my chair, head between his hands.

"How did things get this fucked up?" he mumbles as he pulls at his hair.

"That better be a rhetorical question," I say as I take a seat on the couch, leaving a good six feet between us. Probably a safe distance. For now. "Because all you have to do to find the answer is look in the fucking mirror."

He looks up at me, and for the first time in months, I see the guy who has been my best friend for twenty years. Not the angry asshole he's been passing for. "This is what I was afraid of. Since the moment you and Brenna told me about you two, this is what I was afraid of. Only in that scenario, it wasn't my fault. But now it is. Everything is fucked up."

I blink a few times because now I'm confused. "What are you talking about?"

"You and Brenna breaking up," Bryce says, falling back into the chair.

Holy shit, is he really saying now all of this has been built on a hypothetical that he has blown out of proportion?

"Let me get this straight. All of this, the whole time. All it has been is you worrying about something that might or might not happen?"

He shrugs. "Not my finest moment."

I stand up and start pacing in circles. I'm going to fucking kill him. No, I can't do that. Brenna would never forgive me.

Except maybe after I tell her why. Then she might be mad she didn't get to help.

"Okay, you better fucking explain everything. And I'm talking everything. Because I'm a miserable bastard right now and it is all your fault."

Bryce takes a breath before beginning. "Lucy for years has been hinting at you and Brenna getting together. I didn't think she was serious. For one, you never gave me any inclination that you were interested. And two, it was Brenna. I figured she was like a little sister to you."

"I thought that for a long time," I admit. "Then I held it in even longer so that those feelings were a lot deeper."

Bryce nods. "So when you told me that you two were together, and not only that, but you had been keeping it from me for years? That stung, man. And cross my heart—that was why I was so pissed at first."

That I can understand. "I get it, man. You don't do well with things being thrown at you. We knew that. But we didn't want to hide it from you, either. I don't know if there was a right move there."

"I'm not sure either," Bryce says. "And I swear to you, at first, that was the issue."

"Then what happened?" I ask. "What happened from the time you promised Brenna you would take time to process it and when you came back even more against it? And for reasons that frankly are a bunch of bullshit and you know it."

"The football bro code is sacred," he says tenuously.

I shoot him a glare. "I've punched you once this week. Don't think I won't do it again."

"Fine," he says. "I tried to come to grips with it. Every day when Lucy and I were gone, I sat back and thought about you and Brenna together. Not like in *that* way. That's gross and frankly makes me want to vomit. But I tried to think about you two together. And us together. And you know what my fucked-up brain kept going back to?"

I shake my head.

"It kept going back to the what-if."

"The what-if?" I ask, a little confused. "What what-if, exactly?"

"Everything," he says. "What if you two break up? What if

you two get married but then get divorced? If you allow your brain to go down that road, it never ends. And that's all I could think. And then what happens to us? You and me? To me and Brenna? To Lucy and Brenna? All I could think of was the absolute worst, so I thought that if you two ended it before you began, we could save ourselves the future hurt that would be ten times worse."

I feel my blood temperature rising second by second. "You motherfucker."

We both stand, because I am two seconds from punching him again when I somehow stop myself. I slowly lower my arm, but need to get out this anger. My hands land on the nearby lamp and I grip it and sling it across the room.

"I fucked up," Bryce says.

"You think?" I scream. "How dare you! And for what? On maybes? Fuck, Bryce! Maybe I could get hit by a car today. Maybe I could tear my ACL again and be done playing football forever. You can maybe yourself to fucking death! God, how could you do this?"

"I thought I was doing the right thing. That at the end of the day, this is what was best," he says. "Then I saw Brenna the day she left. The hurt in her eyes. Fuck, Cole, I hated every second of knowing that I was the reason she was doing what she was doing. But I thought that it was temporary pain that would pass."

"Who gave you the right to play God in our lives?" I ask. "What made you the keeper of our decisions? Or the verifier of feelings?"

Bryce shrugs. "I don't know. But I realized when she was leaving that I fucked up. Bad."

"What gave it away?" I deadpan.

"She said something that hit me deep. She said that one day, when everything goes back to normal, when we finally built our houses next to each other, and you were married and moved on, to not invite her to anything. Because she didn't want to see our lives without her."

"It would never happen," I say through gritted teeth. "At least not for me. You don't move on from the love of your life."

Bryce nods. "That stuck with me. Then today, when I overheard Dean and Coach McAvoy talking about a trade for you, that's when it really hit me. You really do love her."

I stare at the other lamp, my fist flexing. "No shit, you fuckhead! It took that to make you realize that I was serious about her?"

"I mean, I knew," Bryce stumbles. "But yeah. That's when it hit me."

"Listen here and listen good," I say, doing my best to stay calm. "I love your sister more than anything. More than football. More than you. More than our silly dreams and plans that we made when we were kids. More than anything. I'll do anything. I'll quit today. I'll go play in California. I don't care, if it means I get to spend the rest of my life with her. She's all that matters."

"Fuck," Bryce groans. "I'm sorry. I'm sorry for everything."

"Thank you," I say, because hell, at least he fucking said it. "I'm sorry I hit you."

He waves me off. "I deserved it. I said some pretty fucked-up things."

I shoot him a look. "You think?"

"I know," he says. "But I really need to apologize for one specific one."

"And that would be?"

"That you weren't good enough for her," he says, nothing but remorse in his eyes. "I love my sister. And I love you. And frankly, you're the only man on this earth good enough for her."

I extend my hand, and when I do, he takes it and immediately we pull each other into a bro hug. There's a lot of back slapping. There might be a tear.

Both of us will deny that until the end of time.

"I need to get her back," I say.

"Well then good thing we have another day off practice," Bryce says, holding up the keys to his truck.

"We do?"

He tosses them to me. "I worked it out with Coach. Let's go bring our girl back."

WHEN I WAS A KID, I remember watching a movie where the heroine and her children had to move back in with her mom after her husband suddenly left her. She didn't get out of bed for days. She didn't eat. She barely showered or left her room.

I always remember wondering how someone could do that. Just not care.

I get it now.

Because I don't. I don't care.

It's been four days since I showed up on my mother's doorstep, heartbroken and alone. She didn't even bat an eyelash as she opened her door and just hugged me.

It was the best hug ever. Well, not as good as Cole's hugs. But it would have to do.

I turned off my phone the second day I was here. I couldn't stand to see Cole's name pop up. I want to talk to him. I want to hear his voice. I want him to call me Trouble and tell me that everything was somehow going to be okay.

But I can't. I can't get my hopes up like that. It's easier to go no contact.

Thank goodness it's summer, and I don't have to go to work. Fuck...work. Technically I still work for the school in Nashville. Is my position in Laurel Heights even available? I never even thought about all of that.

Oh well, that's future Brenna's problem. Right now, I'm going to just lie here, under the covers, and hope that when I wake up from the nap I'm about to take, that this is all one big bad dream.

"Brenna?"

I ignore my mom and her knocking on my bedroom door. Usually when I do this, she just walks away, which is what I'm hoping she'll do. But for some reason, she decides to sit on my bed, which I only know because I feel the mattress move.

"Brenna, sweetie, you have to get up," she says, rubbing my back through the comforter.

"I really don't," I reply. No sense in pretending I'm asleep.

"Sweetie, Lucy is here."

Now that makes me pop out of my cocoon. I lower the blanket, just enough so my face is now showing. "Lucy's here?"

Mom nods. "Yeah. She wants to see you, but she didn't know if you were up for it. I told her I'd make sure you were."

I sit up slowly, knowing that I'm going to be lightheaded when I do. That's what happens when you stay horizontal for twenty hours of the day. "Why is she here?"

"I'm not sure," Mom says, pushing back one of many loose strands of hair behind my ear. "How about you talk to her?"

"Fine," I say. "She can come in."

"You act like I wasn't coming in regardless of your answer," Lucy says as she steps into view of my open door.

"Nice to see you, too."

Mom gives my leg a pat, and she nods at Lucy as she leaves, shutting the door behind her.

Lucy looks at me and pushes back yet another strand of

hair. "You're one Ben and Jerry's tub of ice cream away from being a stereotype."

"You're hilarious," I say. "What are you doing here?"

"You turned off your phone," she says with a sigh. "I was worried about you. I hated knowing that you were here alone."

"Thanks," I say. "I had to turn off the phone. Cole kept calling and texting. All I want to do is talk to him, but I know that it will only hurt more. Turning it off was my safeguard."

"I get it," she says. "I've been there."

"What did you do?" I ask. "When you thought it was over for you and Bryce?"

"Oh sweetie, your situation and mine are apples and oranges. With me and Bryce, I'd had it. I was done. I finally reached my wit's end. Was I sad? Of course. But I knew I had to wait for him to come around. It had to be him. And until then, I just had to keep pushing on. But for you? I don't know how you did what you did. You broke your own heart because you thought it was the best for everyone else. I don't know many people who would do that."

"Well, I can safely say I don't recommend it," I say. "It's literally the worst."

Lucy chuckles. "So I take it with your phone off and you living in this bed that you haven't heard the Cole news?"

I jerk upright. "No. What news? Is he okay?"

"Yes, he's fine," Lucy says as she reaches for my hand. "He asked for a trade."

Now this news is waking me up.

"A trade! Why would he do that? That's not what was supposed to happen!"

"I'm not sure," Lucy says, ducking away from me as I scramble to get out of bed. "All I know is that he called Dean after you left and said to make it happen."

"No!" I yell, grabbing a clean T-shirt and leggings from one of my suitcases. "I didn't leave just to have him go to another team. I left so he and Bryce could do what they were meant to do. They can't do that if he's not in Nashville."

I frantically look for a towel but can't seem to find one. I need to shower. I need to get my shit together. And then I need to get a hold of Cole.

When I find what I'm looking for, I catch a glimpse of Lucy, still sitting on my bed. She's wearing a smile that screams "I knew it."

"What?" I ask. "Why are you looking at me like that?"

She just laughs and shakes her head. "You and your brother. You think you're not alike at all. But that couldn't be farther from the truth."

I shake my head. "What in the hell are you talking about?"

"You'll find out soon enough," she says with a smile. "Get showered. Brush your hair. When you're ready, we're going to figure all of this out. Once and for all."

———

I can't lie, I feel like a whole new woman when I step out of the shower. Probably because I had the water temperature set to scalding and I let the hot water burn away every emotion in my body, along with the top layer of my skin.

Lucy isn't in my room when I get back there, but I don't think anything of it. Instead, I take my time to grab clothes that match and run a brush through my wet hair before making my way downstairs. I hear Lucy's voice, which means my mom probably has her wrapped up into some conversation about a visitation schedule for her and Bryce to come back to Laurel Heights. Or for when she can come to Nashville.

Mom misses us really bad.

But what I don't expect to hear are two male voices. And

even though I'm hearing them clear as day, it doesn't hit me until I turn the corner into the living room that Bryce and Cole are here.

Together.

"What's going on?" I ask, almost afraid to step into the room.

"Hey there, Trouble," Cole says soothingly, standing up and walking toward me. I'm too stunned to shy away from the kiss he presses to my cheek. Or to fully realize that Bryce isn't making some sort of obnoxious comment.

I look to Lucy, who is sitting next to Bryce with a huge smile on her face. "Lucy? What is happening? I thought you were here alone."

She nods and signals for me to have a seat. "We thought it was better if you were under the impression it was just me."

"We?" I ask, looking at everyone in the room. "When did we become a we? The last I heard there was a me, a him, and a you two."

This makes everyone laugh. Great. I'm now the resident comedian. "While I'm very glad we can find some laughter at my confusion, is anyone going to tell me what the hell is going on?"

Cole comes and sits next to me, taking my hand in both of his. I hate that it immediately relaxes me. I know it's only been a few days, but I have missed this man so much. "I think your brother is going to take it from here."

I look over to Bryce, who is currently looking at Lucy. All she does is nod at him, but I feel like that one gesture just spoke a thousand words.

"I need to start by saying how sorry I am. It might be the first time I'm saying it, but it won't be the last."

"I... I don't know what to say." It's true. I'm speechless right now.

"That's okay. Because you don't need to say anything. I, on the other hand, will need to apologize to you and Cole for many, many years."

I look over to Cole, who is smiling peacefully. And not his forced smile—his real one that I usually only see when it's the two of us.

"I've already apologized to Cole. And we had a five-hour drive here to iron out any other things that happened in what I've decided to call The Lost Months of Cole and Bryce."

"He's being very dramatic about all of this," Cole says in my ear, but loud enough for Bryce to throw a pillow at him.

"Can you blame me? I fucked up. I fucked up royally, and I almost lost not only my best friend but my sister in the process."

I'm pretty sure my jaw is on the floor. I look at Cole, then to Lucy, back to Cole before looking at Bryce. "Are you saying what I think you're saying?"

Bryce nods. "You asked me the other day what the real reason was for why I was so against you two, and I deflected. I knew it, but I was embarrassed to admit it."

Well, now I need to know. "And? What was it?"

Bryce looks at Cole. "Do I have to say it again?"

"You know the ground rules," Cole says. "You fucked this up. You unfuck it."

"I didn't completely fuck it up!"

Lucy gives him a smack against the arm. "Yes, you did. Fix it. Now."

"Fine," he says. I swear this man would jump off a bridge if she said to. "I was scared that if you two didn't work, it would drive a wedge between us. No one would talk. Everything would be a mess. I thought if it ended before it began, we could go back to the status quo."

I start to stand up, because I really want to slap my brother upside the head right now. Luckily for him, Cole brings me back to the couch. "Easy there, Trouble. Believe me, he's already got an earful from me. And his wife."

Lucy nods. "I got you, girl."

I look to Bryce, whose contrite expression speaks to his guilt. He does seem to finally understand the hell he caused. "I have so many questions," I murmur.

"I know," Bryce says. "And I'll answer every one of them. But right now, I need you to know that I'm sorry. For everything."

I stand up, and this time Cole doesn't stop me. I hold out my arms, and Bryce does the same. Now that I think about it, his reasoning is classic Bryce. I don't know why I didn't see it before. He was scared to lose Cole. His constant. The one thing and person who has never wavered from his life.

"Thank you for the apology," I say as we let go. "Does that mean...?"

I turn back to face Cole, trying not to get my hopes up. He's standing up, holding his hand out for me.

I take it. I'll always take it.

"I know you left because you thought it was the best thing for us. Hell, I requested a trade for the same reason. But there is only one right answer—only one thing that feels absolutely right—and it's you coming back to Nashville with me. With us. Like it was always supposed to be."

He doesn't need to say anything else. I jump into his arms, wrapping my legs around his waist and kiss him. God, do I kiss him. I know it has been less than a week, but I feel like it's been an eternity.

He's right, this is the only right thing. But it could be in Nashville or Laurel Heights. Hell, it could be in China or in New York; home is him. He's my home.

Forever.

"Okay, that's enough," Bryce says. "I said I was okay with this, but I'm still not okay with...*that*."

Cole and I laugh as he gives me one more kiss before putting me down. But I don't let go of him. Nope, that's not happening for a long time.

"I'D LIKE TO MAKE A TOAST."

I lift up my glass and give Brenna's leg a squeeze with my free hand, as we all raise our glasses for Bryce's upcoming words of wisdom.

Lord knows what he's about to say. But unlike a few months ago, I know it's going to be filled with love and kindness. And probably a little gloating.

"Here's to the four of us," Bryce says, looking first at Lucy then to Brenna and I. "I know I was scared of this. I know I almost made sure this didn't happen, but I'm so glad it did. And I'm so glad that everything is now working out exactly how we planned."

"Here, here!" we all say, clinking our glasses around the table at the steakhouse where we chose to celebrate.

I take my hand away from Brenna's leg and put it around her chair. Yup, this is it. This is how it's supposed to be.

We won our season opener today over Milwaukee. Bryce threw for more than three hundred yards and four touchdowns. He wasn't sacked once—a point of pride for me. The locker room has settled down since our blowup over the summer. Hell, even Dexter has backed off. Then again, rumor has it he is actually seeing someone, so that could have something to do with it.

And best of all? Earlier this week both Bryce and I renegotiated our contracts—we'll both be in Nashville for the next ten years.

"I'd also like to make a toast," Brenna says. "To making Nashville our forever home. And for Bryce and Lucy to build the bigger house so Mom eventually lives with them."

"Hell, no!" he says while the rest of us laugh. "She can have her own house. We can afford it. I'm not living with Mom."

The first thing Bryce and I did after finalizing our contracts, and making sure that we are going to be taken care of financially for a very long time, was head out to look at land to build our houses. We've talked about it forever, and the time is finally here. Somehow, we found a parcel of land about a half hour south of Nashville with plenty of space for all of us. And yes, there's even space for an in-law house.

Because that's what I will be calling it. As long as Brenna says what I think she'll say tonight.

"So do you guys want to hear the gossip that came from the wives' suite tonight?" Brenna asks.

"Brenna, we are grown men who play professional football," I begin.

"Which obviously means yes," Bryce finishes. "Now spill."

Lucy laughs. "So, we're all sitting there, fawning over Sadie's baby, when we hear a commotion outside the suite."

"Commotion?" I ask. "What kind of commotion happens on the suite level?"

Brenna wags her eyebrows. "The kind that happens when a certain someone's ex-girlfriend tries to get into the suite, claiming that she has the right to be there."

I look at Bryce, who is clearly just as confused as I am. "Ex...?" My eyes widen as I stare at Brenna. "No. She didn't!"

"Oh, but she did," Brenna says. "But that's not even the best part."

Bryce's eyes go wide. "There's a best part?"

"Yup," Lucy says. "Jessica didn't try to get in there because of Cole. Oh no, she has a new man now who apparently forgot to leave a credential for her."

I rack my brain, trying to think of anyone who... No way.

"Dexter!" I nearly yell.

Brenna and Lucy both nod. "And she didn't get in because he forgot," Lucy explains. "So my guess right now is that he's getting his ass reamed out by our favorite crazy redhead."

"Oh, this is too good," Bryce says. "Gee, Cole, now you'll get to see your ex all the time! Hey, maybe we can triple date!"

"No!" Brenna and I both yell at the same time. This gets a laugh out of the whole table.

"Do you ever wonder what might have happened if you took a different path?" Lucy asks.

Brenna tilts her head. "For anything specific or just in general?"

"I don't know," she says. "Take, for example, Cole and Jessica, which is what made me think of it. What if they would have worked out? What if her crazy was Cole's cup of tea? Or what if she was nice and normal? Then we'd be here right now with her and not you."

"Thanks for that," Brenna says dryly. "But I see what you're saying. What if I never went to Clemson that weekend to visit Bryce and Cole?"

She turns to look at me, and I bring her in, giving her a kiss on the temple. "I don't think that one counts."

She turns to look at me. "Why's that?"

I didn't know how I was going to do this tonight, but I don't see a better opening. I'll have to buy Lucy something real nice for inadvertently opening this up for me.

"Because," I say, turning in my chair to face her better. "Brenna Donald, I would have fallen in love with you at another time. I don't know when. I don't know where. But I know more than I know my own name that our love is too strong and too right to not have happened. So yes, I realized it in the back of a cop car, but I knew it long before then. And I'll know it for as long as I live."

I hear Lucy gasp as I step out of my seat and go down on one knee. Bryce knew this was going to happen sometime tonight, so he's already recording. And then there's Brenna—hands over her mouth, tears flowing down her cheeks.

I take her hand in mine and breathe in the biggest breath of my life. "Brenna, for years I was in love with the idea of you. The fantasy. But now? After being with you these last five months? I can't imagine my life without you. You are every dream come true. Every day I get to spend with you is better than the one before."

I pause for a second to open the ring box. Somehow my hands aren't shaking, even though I feel like my entire body is.

"Brenna Marie Donald, will you do me the honor of my life and be my wife?"

She doesn't say anything. Instead, she leaps out of her seat and jumps in my arms, wrapping around me like a spider monkey.

"Can I take that as a yes?"

I hear laughter in the background as Brenna looks back up at me and kisses me hard and fast. "Yes, Cole Campbell. I will marry you."

"She said yes!" Bryce yells, which in turn gets the entire restaurant in on the celebration.

I stand up, Brenna still in my arms, as we embrace in the moment. When I finally put her down so I can put the ring on her finger, she doesn't let me go.

Good. I'm never letting her go either.

"Holy shit!" Bryce yells, putting down his cell phone. "We're going to be actual brothers!"

Lucy gives him a confused look. "Did you never think of that?"

"I mean, I did, but it really just hit me! This is the best day ever!"

Brenna and I laugh at Bryce's antics, while Lucy just shakes her head.

When the commotion settles down, Brenna signals for me to come down a bit so she can whisper something to me.

"Did you pay the check?" she asks.

I raise an eyebrow. "Why do you ask?"

Her eyes all of a sudden become heated. "Because as a now-engaged woman, I would like to have sex with my fiancé *very soon* while wearing only this ring. So, if we're not out of here in ten minutes, we're going into the bathroom, and I don't care who hears."

I take her chin in my fingers and kiss her again. I know she's serious as a heart attack right now, and it wouldn't be the first time we hit up a restaurant bathroom.

But tonight? Tonight is for her and me only.

EPILOGUE

BRENNA

TWO YEARS LATER

AFTER EVERY GAME in high school, I'd always make sure to find Cole in the crowd and give him a thumbs up.

Tonight he is getting so much more than that.

That's what happens when you win the league championship for the first time in your career.

"Oh my God! They did it!" I yell as I run and jump on Lucy, giving her a huge hug. Then I remember that I probably shouldn't have done that. "Oh, shit. Sorry! I'm just so excited I forgot that my favorite nephew was in there."

Lucy rests her hands on her stomach as what I'm guessing are happy tears pour from her eyes. "How could you forget? You already have three best-aunt-in-the-world shirts despite being his only aunt. You also organized the baby shower. How could you possibly forget that I'm about to have a baby?"

"I mean, can you blame me?" I say, holding our hands together in the air as the confetti still pours down from the rafters of the stadium. "I'm just... I'm just so proud of them, you know?"

Lucy nods, fighting back another round of tears. "They really did it."

We link arms as we watch Bryce and Cole on stage together, embracing the way only best friends can. The sight brings tears to my eyes, though there could be several reasons for that tonight.

The two of them have dreamed about this for so long. I remember growing up hearing them in Bryce's room, practicing in the mirror how each of them would say that since they just won the championship, they were going to Disney World. And tonight, Bryce will get to say it as he's been named the game's MVP.

Though, if I had a vote, the MVP would obviously go to Cole. I've learned a lot about football over the past few years, and I know Bryce can't do what he does without a good offensive line. And considering that Bryce wasn't sacked once tonight and threw for nearly four-hundred yards, I'd say my man and his line were of the utmost value.

"I'm going to sneak on stage," I say. "It's about time I show my man exactly how proud of him I am."

Lucy laughs at me. "You go do that."

I give her one more quick hug before making my way to the stage where all of the Fury players are currently gathered in celebration. Most of the guys have their phones out, recording every second of this amazing win. Everyone already has on their league championship hats. I laugh as I watch Dexter dance around the stage, spraying everyone with a bottle of champagne.

Champagne and Dexter... I can laugh about it now. That fateful date seems like so long ago, but it was really only two years. Amazing how much can happen in that time.

Dexter and Jessica dated and got married. And got divorced. I actually think they got divorced before our gift arrived at their home. Then again, I never got a thank you note. I don't know why. I figured she'd love the sheet and blanket set made from sweatpants material.

Bryce and Lucy are doing as well as ever and are weeks away from welcoming their first son. They are all moved into the new home that they built in Franklin, complete with a practice football field in the backyard.

And yes, our house is right next to theirs. They have the practice field. We have the custom gym and game room, which is actually like a mini movie theater. Lucy and I didn't even try and talk them out of it. We knew it was a lost cause. But at least they built us a she-shed that is big enough to fit every Fury wife and girlfriend for book club.

Smart men.

I say hi to Sadie, Bethany, and a few of the other wives and girlfriends as I make my way to the stage. I hear the announcer ask Bryce to come to the microphone to give his MVP speech, so I hurry and pull out my phone, needing to get this on video.

"There was a day I never thought this would happen," he begins. "Hell, there were more than a few days. But here we are, Nashville! At the top of the football world!"

I join the fans who made their way to Miami in screaming and applause. Bryce actually has to signal for them to quiet down so he can continue.

"I might be holding this MVP trophy, but one player isn't the team. I need to thank every single man who puts on the uniform with me every day. I'm not here without each one of you. I'd be remiss if I didn't give a special nod to Cole Campbell. My brother. My best friend. Who knew that what we dreamed of as kids would actually come true? And to my coaches...."

Bryce's speech continues, but I'm interrupted by a pair of hands snaking around my waist.

"We fucking did it, Trouble."

I turn around and leap into Cole's arms. Before I can make sure he doesn't drop me, my mouth is on his, kissing the living crap out of him.

"I must say," he says as I come up for air, "this is much better than two thumbs up."

"I thought so," I say as he gently puts me down. "Though I must say that I miss painting your number on my face."

"I don't know," he says, holding up my left hand. "I like this a lot better."

I smile as I look at my wedding ring. It's nearly been a year since we said "I do." In classic Cole and Brenna fashion, the wedding was filled with love, laughter, and chaos. I thought then that it was the best day of my life.

Though today might give it a run for its money.

"I'm so proud of you," I say. "I always knew you could do this."

"It doesn't feel real yet," he says, catching a glimpse at Bryce, who is waving to the crowd as he wraps up his speech.

"What does it feel like?"

"I can't describe it," he says. "Like I'm floating. Like nothing can go wrong. Like I'm at the top of the mountain, and somehow, if I jump, I'll be okay. I don't know how this night can get any better."

This is it. Not that I'm worried that he'll take this news badly, but why not keep pouring the good, even if unexpected, news coming?

"I bet you it can," I say.

He quirks a brow. "How so? And don't suggest locker room sex. I'm not going to get fined again for that one."

I shake my head and laugh. Yeah, we might have got caught, but the orgasm was worth it. "No. Though we could check another city off the list?"

Now I get both eyebrows raised. "I'll bring you back here for vacation. Now, what's the news?"

I reach into my purse and bring out a little treat bag. It's reminiscent of the ones I used to give him in high school before any big game.

"A treat bag?" he asks, clearly confused. "Aren't I supposed to get this before the game?"

I shake my head. "Not this treat."

He opens the bag and it takes him a second to realize what I put in there.

A baby Fury jersey with his number on it and a positive pregnancy test.

"Brenna..." he says through a breath, though nothing follows.

"You're going to be a daddy, Cole Campbell."

He doesn't say another word. He just drops the shirt and test and picks me up, swinging me around while peppering kisses on my face. I laugh as he puts me down. I don't think I've ever seen him this excited over anything.

"I'm going to be a dad," he says, almost in a whisper.

I nod. "You're going to be the best dad."

He cups my face in his hands, bringing me in for another kiss. "I love you so much."

"I love you, too."

Both of us just stand there for a few minutes, soaking everything in. And for me? I'm not just soaking in tonight, or when I found out I was pregnant last week. No, for me? I'm soaking in all the years and everything it took to get here.

All the little league and high school football games.

The trip to Clemson, when I just wanted to party and instead started on a path I didn't even know about.

The perfect storm of Cole and Bryce getting drafted to the

same team, allowing them to live young dreams that some might have thought impossible.

The actual storm that led to my apartment building being flooded, which forced me to eventually move in with Cole.

Bryce and Lucy's wedding.

The fallout.

The love.

The almost never.

And now...the happily ever after.

Bryce and Cole have talked about it forever and the time is finally here: Move in day to the new houses. Now the question begs to be asked: which room will Cole and Brenna christen first? Click here to find out in the extended epilogue!

ACKNOWLEDGMENTS

I have waited two-plus years to write this book. And now that it's here, I can't believe the Nashville Fury series has come to a close.

When I was first dreaming up the world, Cole and Brenna were the second story I thought of, behind Sadie and Hunter. But I knew they were last. I don't know why, but I knew they were my ending.

I'm glad I did, because they were my perfect ending. I loved writing these two so much. I laughed. I cried. I put off writing the epilogue for days because I didn't want to say goodbye.

But here they are, and all good things must come to an end.

So goodbye Nashville Fury. I love you so much.

At least for now...

Now to the thank yous.

First and foremost, my parents. As always, you are my biggest cheerleaders even if you still have no idea what I'm doing. You've allowed me to follow my dreams and my path, and for that I am forever grateful.

To my family and friends: Your support has been amazing. Many of you have no clue how I ended up here, but that doesn't mean the support hasn't been there. I love you all.

Kelly, you've been with me on this book journey since day one. Not only are you an amazing alpha reader, but you are an amazing friend.

Julia, Georgia, Mae and Claire: How did I write a book

before I met you ladies? All I know is I don't ever want to write one without y'all again. A special shout out to Julia who not only is my emotional support Canadian, but the best author critique buddy to ever have.

Amy, my knight in shining armor. Thank you for answering my desperate cry for help and making this book the best it could be. Kiezha, thank you for correcting my bad grammar habits and the not making fun of me when I thought I sent you the wrong email. Michele, your watchful eye is always appreciated.

Amanda, who would have thought when we met seven years ago that one day we'd be here together? Thank you for keeping my life in order. Thank you for reminding me to drink water. And thank you for being my best friend.

Corinne, I'm here because of you. If you wouldn't have given me a chance I wouldn't have started writing. You forever changed my life.

Adriana, thanks for always picking up the phone.

Last but not least: Readers. I love you all. Whether this was your first book by me, or you've been here since Reformation, I'm truly thankful for all of you. There are so many amazing authors you could be reading. I'm humbled that you chose me.

ABOUT THE AUTHOR

Known for her witty sense of humor, Chelle Sloan is a former sports editor who after years in the newspaper business, decided to become a romance author. You know, because that's the normal path to writing happily ever afters.

An Ohio native, she's fiercely loyal to Cleveland sports, is the owner of way too many tumblers and will be a New Kids on the Block fan for life. She does her best writing at Panera, or anywhere that's not her office.

When she's not writing, you can find her in the kitchen attempting to become a baker, fixing up her condo (badly and by watching YouTube videos), or falling in love with a book.

As for her own happily ever after? Maybe one day...

Stay up to date with all things Chelle & join the VIP Squad!

ALSO BY CHELLE SLOAN

THE NASHVILLE FURY, PRO FOOTBALL SERIES

Off the Record: A secret office romance

Off Track: A surprise pregnancy romance

Off Season: A second chance romance

Off Limits: A sibling's best friend romance

NASHVILLE FURY WORLD

Off the Market at Christmas: A childhood friends-to-lovers romance

LOVE ONLINE SERIES

Thirst Trap: A social media romance

Match Maker: A fake dating romance

Run Run Rudolph: A celebrity, holiday romance

ROLLING HILLS

The One I Want: A single dad/nanny romance

The One I Need: An accidental marriage romance

The One I Love: A friends to lovers romance

The One I Hate: An enemies to lovers romance

GUIDE TO LOVE SERIES

Runaway Bride's Guide to Love: A brother's best friend romance

Single Mom's Guide to Love: A marriage of convenience romance

Roommate's Guide to Love: A fling to forever, single dad, romance

Good Girl's Guide to Love: A fake dating, football romance

www.ingramcontent.com/pod-product-compliance
Lightning Source LLC
Chambersburg PA
CBHW071359300726
48976CB00006B/1933